DEPTH

inter-
uthor of the Inspector
ries, now dominating bestseller
lists throughout Europe. He devotes much of his free time to working with Aids charities in Africa, where he is director of the Teatro Avenida in Maputo.

Laurie Thompson is the translator into English of several other books by Henning Mankell, as well as novels by Åke Edwardson, Hakan Nesser and Mikael Niemi.

ALSO BY HENNING MANKELL

Kurt Wallander Series

Faceless Killers
The Dogs of Riga
The White Lioness
The Man Who Smiled
Sidetracked
The Fifth Woman
One Step Behind
Firewall
Before the Frost
The Pyramid

Fiction

The Return of the Dancing Master
Chronicler of the Winds
Kennedy's Brain
The Eye of the Leopard
Italian Shoes
The Man from Beijing

Non-Fiction

I Die, But The Memory Lives On

Young Adult Fiction

A Bridge to the Stars
Shadows in the Twilight
When the Snow Fell
The Journey to the End of the World

Children's Fiction

The Cat Who Liked Rain

HENNING MANKELL

Depths

TRANSLATED FROM THE SWEDISH BY
Laurie Thompson

Published by Vintage 2010

2 4 6 8 10 9 7 5 3 1

First published with the title *Djup* by Leopard Förlag, Stockholm

First published in Great Britain in 2006 by
Harvill Secker

First published in paperback in 2007 by
Vintage
Random House, 20 Vauxhall Bridge Road,
London SW1V 2SA

www.vintage-books.co.uk

Addresses for companies within The Random House Group Limited can be found at: www.randomhouse.co.uk/offices.htm

The Random House Group Limited Reg. No. 954009

A CIP catalogue record for this book
is available from the British Library

ISBN 9780099542193

The Random House Group Limited supports The Forest Stewardship Council (FSC), the leading international forest certification organisation. All our titles that are printed on Greenpeace approved FSC certified paper carry the FSC logo. Our paper procurement policy can be found at:

CONTENTS

PART I

The Secret Affinity with Leads

CHAPTER 1

They used to say that when there was no wind the cries of the lunatics could be heard on the other side of the lake.

Especially in autumn. The cries belonged to autumn.

Autumn is when this story begins. In a damp fog, with the temperature hovering just above freezing, and a woman who suddenly realises that freedom is at hand. She has found a hole in a fence.

It is the autumn of 1937. The woman is called Kristina Tacker and for many years she has been locked away in the big asylum near Säter. All thoughts of time have lost their meaning for her.

She stares at the hole for ages, as if she does not grasp its significance. The fence has always been a barrier she should not get too close to. It is a boundary with a quite specific significance.

But this sudden change? This gap that has appeared in the fence? A door has been opened by an unknown hand, leading to what was until now forbidden territory. It takes a long time for it to sink in. Then, cautiously, she crawls through the hole and finds herself on the other side. She stands, motionless, listening, her head hunched down between her tense shoulders, waiting for somebody to come and take hold of her.

For all the twenty-two years she has been shut away in the asylum she has never felt surrounded by people, only by puffs of breath. Puffs of breath are her invisible warders.

The big, heavy buildings are behind her, like sleeping beasts, ready to pounce. She waits. Time has stood still. Nobody comes to take her back.

Only after prolonged hesitation does she take a first step, then another, until she disappears into the trees.

She is in a coniferous forest. There is an acrid smell, reminiscent of rutting horses. She thinks she can make out a path. She makes slow progress, and only when she notices that the heavy breathing which surrounded her in the asylum is no longer there can she bring herself to turn round.

Nothing but trees on every side. She does not worry about the path having been a figment of her imagination and no longer discernible, as she is not going anywhere in particular. She is like scaffolding surrounding an empty space. She does not exist. Within the scaffolding there has never been a building, or a person.

Now she is moving very quickly through the forest, as if she did have an objective beyond the pine trees after all. From time to time she stands, stock-still, as if by degrees turning into a tree herself.

Time does not exist in the forest. Only trunks of trees, mostly pine, the occasional spruce, and sunbeams tumbling noiselessly to the damp earth.

She starts trembling. A pain comes creeping under her skin. At first she thinks it is that awful itchy feeling that affects her sometimes and forces the warders to strap her down to prevent her from scratching herself raw. Then it comes to her that there is another reason for her trembling.

She remembers that, once upon a time, she had a husband.

She has no idea what has prompted that memory. But she recalls very clearly having been married. His name was Lars, she remembers that. He had a scar over his left eye and was twenty-three centimetres taller than she was. That is all she can remember for the moment. Everything else has been repressed and banished into the darkness that fills her being.

But her memory is reviving. She stares round at the tree trunks in confusion. Why should she start thinking about her husband just here? A man who hated forests and was always drawn to the sea? A midshipman, and eventually a hydrographic survey engineer with the rank of Commander, employed on secret military missions?

The fog starts to disperse, melting away.

She stands rooted to the spot. A bird takes off, clattering somewhere out of sight. Then all is silent again.

My husband, Kristina Tacker thinks. I once had a husband, our lives were intertwined. Why do I remember him now, when I have found a hole in the fence and left all those watchful predators behind?

She searches her mind and among the trees for an answer.

There is none. There is nothing.

CHAPTER 2

Late in the night the warders find Kristina Tacker.

It is frosty, the ground creaks under their feet. She is standing in the darkness, not moving, staring at a tree trunk. What she sees is not a pine tree but a remote lighthouse in a barren and deserted archipelago at the edge of the open sea. She scarcely notices that she is no longer alone with the silent tree trunks.

That day in the autumn of 1937 Kristina Tacker is fifty-seven years old. There is a trace of her former beauty lingering in her face. It is twelve years since she last uttered a word. Her hospital records repeat the phrase, day after day, year after year:

The patient is still beyond reach.

That same night: it is dark in her room in the rambling mental hospital. She is awake. A lighthouse beam sweeps past, time after time, like a silent tolling of light inside her head.

CHAPTER 3

Twenty-three years earlier, also on an autumn day, her husband was contemplating the destroyer *Svea*, moored at the Galärvarv Quay in Stockholm. Lars Tobiasson-Svartman was a naval officer and cast a critical eye over the vessel. Beyond her soot-stained funnels he could make out Kastellet and Skeppsholm Church. The light was grey, forcing him to screw up his eyes.

It was the middle of October 1914, the Great War had been raging for exactly two months and nineteen days. Lars Tobiasson-Svartman did not have unqualified faith in these new armoured warships. The older wooden ships always gave him the feeling of entering a warm room. The new ones, with hulls comprising sheets of armour-plating welded together, were cold rooms, unpredictable rooms. He felt deep down that these vessels would not allow themselves to be tamed. Beyond the coal-fired steam engines or the new oil-driven ones were other forces that could not be controlled.

Now and then came a gust of wind from Saltsjön.

* * *

He stood by the steep gangplank, hesitating. It made him feel confused. Where did this insecurity come from? Ought he to abandon his voyage before it had even begun? He searched for an explanation, but all his thoughts had vanished, swallowed up by a bank of mist sweeping along inside him.

A sailor hurried down the gangplank. That brought Tobiasson-Svartman down to earth. Not being in control of himself was a weakness it was essential to conceal. The rating took his suitcases, his rolled-up sea charts and the brown, specially made bag containing his most treasured measuring instrument. He was surprised to find that the rating could manage all the cumbersome luggage without assistance.

The gangplank swayed under his feet. He could just make out the water between the quay and the hull of the ship, dark, distant.

He thought about what his wife had said when they said goodbye in their flat in Wallingatan.

'Now you're embarking on something you've been aching to do for so long.'

They were standing in their dimly lit hall. She had intended to accompany him to his ship before saying goodbye, but as she started to put on her gloves she hesitated, just as he had done at the foot of the gangplank.

She did not explain why the leave-taking had suddenly become too much for her. That was not necessary. She did not want to start crying. After nine years of marriage he knew it was harder for her to let him see her crying than to be naked before him.

They said goodbye hurriedly. He tried to reassure her that he was not disappointed.

In fact, he felt relieved.

He paused halfway along the gangplank, savouring the almost imperceptible motion of the ship. She was right. He had been longing to get away. But he was not at all sure what he was longing for.

Was there a secret inside him of which he was not aware?

He was very much in love with his wife. Every time he had to leave for a tour of duty and said goodbye to her, he unobtrusively breathed in the scent of her skin, kissing her hastily. It was as if he were laying down that perfume, as you do a fine wine, or perhaps an opiate, to take out whenever he felt so forlorn that he risked losing his self-possession.

His wife still used her maiden name. He had no idea why, and did not want to ask.

A tug boomed from the direction of Kastellholmen. A seagull hovered in the updraught over the ship.

He was a solitary man. His solitary nature was like an abyss that he was afraid he might one day fall into. He had worked out that the abyss must be at least forty metres deep, and that he would leap into it head first, so as to be certain of dying.

He was at the exact middle of the gangplank. He had estimated its total length by eye at seven metres. So now he was precisely three and a half metres from the quay and just as far from the ship's rail.

* * *

His earliest memories were to do with measurements. Between himself and his mother, between his mother and his father, between the floor and the ceiling, between sorrow and joy. His whole life was made up of distances, measuring, abbreviating or extending them. He was a solitary person constantly seeking new distances to estimate or measure.

Measuring distances was a sort of ritual, his personal means of reining in the movements of time and space.

From the start, from as far back as he could remember, solitude had been like his own skin.

Kristina Tacker was not only his wife. She was also the invisible lid he used to cover the abyss.

CHAPTER 4

On that October day in 1914, Stockholm was enveloped by barely noticeable drizzle. His luggage had been brought by handcart from Wallingatan, over the bridge to Djurgården and the Galärvarv Quay. Although there were just the two of them, the porter and himself, he felt as if he were taking part in a procession.

His suitcases were of brown leather. The specially made, calf-leather bag contained his most precious possession. It was a sounding lead for the advanced measuring of the ocean depths.

The lead was made of brass, manufactured in Manchester in 1701 by Maxwell & Swanson. Their skilled craftsmen made optical and navigational instruments and exported them all over the world. The company had acquired renown and respect when they made the sextants used by Captain Cook on what was to be his final voyage to the Pacific Ocean. Their advertisements claimed that their products were used even by Japanese and Chinese seafarers.

Sometimes when he woke up during the night, filled with a mysterious feeling of unrest, he would get up and fetch his lead. Take it back to bed with him and hold it, pressed tightly to his chest. That usually enabled him to go back to sleep.

The lead breathed. Its breath was white.

CHAPTER 5

The destroyer *Svea* was built at the Lindholmen shipyard in Gothenburg, and had left the slipway in December 1885. She was due to be taken out of active service in 1914 as she was already out of date, but that sentence had been suspended because the Swedish Navy had not prepared for the Great War. Her life had been saved at the very last second. She was like a working horse that had been spared at the moment of slaughter, and allowed back into the streets again.

Lars Tobiasson-Svartman reminded himself of the most important measurements relevant to the ship. *Svea* was seventy-five metres long and at the broadest point just aft of amidships she was slightly more than fourteen metres. The heavy artillery comprised two long-range 254-millimetre guns of the M/85 type, made by Maxim-Nordenfelt in London. The medium-range artillery was made up of four 150-millimetre guns, also made in London. In addition there was some light artillery and an unknown number of machine guns.

He continued thinking over what he knew about the vessel he was about to board. The crew comprised 250 regular and conscripted ratings, and twenty-two regular officers. The driving power, currently making the ship throb, came from two horizontal compound engines whose horsepower was generated by six boilers. In trials she had attained a speed of 14.68 knots.

There was one further measurement that interested him. The gap between the bottom of *Svea*'s keel and the bottom of the Galärvarv Quay was just over two metres.

He turned round and looked down at the quay, as if hoping that his wife might have turned up after all. But there was nothing to be seen apart from a few boys fishing and a drunken man who slumped on to his knees then slowly toppled over.

The gusts from Saltsjön were growing stronger. They were very noticeable on deck next to the gangplank.

CHAPTER 6

He was jolted from his reverie by a first mate who clicked his heels and introduced himself as Anders Höckert. Tobiasson-Svartman responded with a salute, but felt uncomfortable doing so. He shuddered every time he was forced to raise his hand to the peak of his cap. He felt silly, as if he were playing a game he hated.

Höckert showed him to his cabin, which was situated below the port companionway leading up to the bridge and the artillery firing base.

Anders Höckert had a birthmark on the back of his neck, just above his collar.

Tobiasson-Svartman frowned and fixed his eyes on the birthmark. Whenever he saw a mole on somebody's body he always tried to work out what it resembled. His father, Hugo Svartman, had a group of moles high up on his left arm. He imagined them to be an archipelago of small, anonymous islands, rocks and skerries. His white skin formed the navigable channels that combined and criss-crossed one another. Where were the deepest channels on his father's left arm? Which would be the safest route for a vessel to take?

The secret affinity with leads, measurements and

distances characteristic of his life was based on that image and the memory of his father's birthmarks.

Lars Tobiasson-Svartman thought to himself: Deep down inside me I am still searching for unknown shallows, another unsounded depth, unexpected troughs. Even inside myself I need to chart and mark out a safely navigable channel.

Anders Höckert's birthmark on the back of his neck, he decided, resembled a wild beast, ready to charge, horns lowered.

Höckert opened the door to the cabin Tobiasson-Svartman had been allocated. He was on a secret mission and hence could not share a cabin with another of the ship's officers.

His luggage, the rolled-up charts and the brown bag containing his depth-sounding instrument were already stacked on the floor. Höckert saluted and left the cabin.

Tobiasson-Svartman sat down on his bunk and let the solitude envelop him. The engines were throbbing as the boilers were never shut down completely even when the vessel was in dock. He looked out of the porthole. The sky had turned blue, the drizzle had lifted. That cheered him up, or perhaps made him feel relieved. Rain tended to depress him, like small, almost invisible weights beating against his body.

For a moment he felt an urge to abandon ship.

But he did not move.

Then slowly he began to unpack his bags. His wife had carefully chosen every item of clothing for him. She knew what he liked best and would want to have with him. Each one was lovingly folded.

Even so, it seemed to him that he had never seen them before, never mind held them in his hands.

CHAPTER 7

The destroyer *Svea* left Galärvarv Quay at 18.15 that same evening. At midnight, they emerged from the Stockholm archipelago and headed south-south-east and raised their speed to twelve knots. The north wind was squally, eight to twelve metres per second.

That night Lars Tobiasson-Svartman clung tightly to his lead. He lay awake for hours, thinking about his wife and her fragrant skin. Occasionally he also thought about the mission that lay ahead.

CHAPTER 8

At dawn, after a night's fitful sleep riddled with vague and elusive dreams, he left his cabin and went on deck. He found a place on the lee side, where he knew he could not be seen from the bridge.

One of his secrets was hidden in a rolled-up chart in his cabin. That is where he kept the designs for the destroyer *Svea*. The vessel had been constructed by master shipbuilder Göthe Wilhelm Svenson at the Lindholmen yard. After his time as an engineer at the Royal Naval Engineering Establishment in 1868, Svenson carved out an astonishing career for himself as a shipbuilder. In 1881, at the age of fifty-three, he had been appointed Director-in-Chief of the Royal Naval Engineering Establishment.

The very day Tobiasson-Svartman had been told that *Svea* would be the base for his secret mission, he wrote to Svenson and asked for a copy of the construction designs. He gave as justification his 'inveterate and perhaps somewhat ridiculous interest in collecting designs of naval vessels'. He was prepared to pay one thousand kronor for the drawings.

Three days later a courier arrived from Gothenburg. The man who handed over the plans was a clerk by the name of Tånge. He had put on his best suit. Tobiasson-Svartman assumed it was Svenson who had instructed him to be elegantly dressed.

Tobiasson-Svartman had not doubted for a second that the drawings would be for sale. A thousand kronor was a lot of money, even for a successful engineer like Göthe Wilhelm Svenson.

CHAPTER 9

He clung to the ladder, trying to follow the rolling of the ship with his body. He recalled the evening he had spent in his living room in Wallingatan, poring over the drawings. That was when his journey had effectively begun.

It was the end of July, the heat was oppressive and everybody was waiting for the outbreak of the war, which now seemed inevitable. The only question was when the first shots would be fired and by whom, at whom. Newspaper offices filled their windows with highly charged reports. Rumours were started and spread, only to be denied immediately; nobody knew anything for certain, but everyone was convinced that they alone had drawn the correct conclusions.

A succession of invisible telegrams flew back and forth across Europe, between kaisers, generals and ministers. The messages were like a stray but deadly flock of birds.

On his desk was a newspaper cutting with a photograph of the German strike-cruiser *Goeben*. The 23,000-tonne vessel was the most handsome yet most frightening ship he had ever set eyes on.

His wife came into the room and stroked him gently on the shoulder.

'It's getting late. What are you doing that's so important?'

'I'm studying the ship I shall have to join soon. When it's time for my mystery voyage.'

She was still stroking his shoulder.

'Mystery voyage? Surely you can tell me where you're going?'

'No. I can't tell even you.'

Her fingers caressed his shoulder. Her hand barely touched his shirt, yet he could feel her movements deep down inside him.

'What do all those lines and figures mean? I can't even see that they represent a ship.'

'I like being able to see what is not seeable.'

'Meaning what?'

'The idea. What lies behind it all. The will, perhaps? The intention? I'm not sure. But there's always something there that you cannot see at first.'

She sighed impatiently. She stopped stroking his shoulder and instead started tapping anxiously at his collarbone. He tried to work out if she were sending him a message.

In the end she took her hand away. He imagined it was a bird taking flight.

I am not telling her the truth, he thought. I am keeping from her what I am really doing. Not admitting that I am studying the plans in order to find a point on deck where nobody could see me from the bridge.

What I am really doing is searching for a hiding place.

CHAPTER 10

He gazed out to sea.

Ragged shreds of mist, a solitary line of seabirds.

Recalling memories involved meticulous care and patience. What happened afterwards, that evening in July, just before war was declared? Those oppressively hot days and the millions of young men all over Europe hastily called up?

After studying the drawings for nearly an hour he had found the spot where his hiding place would be.

He pushed the plans aside. From the street outside he could hear the neighing of a restless dray horse. In another room of their large flat Kristina was rearranging the china figurines she had inherited from her mother. There was a clinking noise, as if from muffled bells. Although they had been married for ten years and scarcely an evening went by without her rearranging the figurines on the shelves, not a single one had ever fallen and shattered.

But afterwards? What happened then? He could not remember. It was as if a leak had sprung in the flow of memories. Something had seeped away.

It had been a windless July evening, the temperature twenty-seven degrees. Occasional rumbles of thunder had drifted in from the Lidingö direction, where dark clouds were gathering from the sea.

He thought about those clouds. He was troubled by the fact that he found it easier to recall the shape of clouds than his wife's face.

He brushed such thoughts aside and gazed into the dawn. What exactly can I see? he thought. Dark rocky outlines early on a Swedish autumn morning. At some point during the night the duty officer had ordered a change of course to a more southerly direction. Their speed was about seven, possibly eight knots.

Five knots is peace, he thought. Seven knots is a suitable speed when you are being sent out on a secret and urgent mission. And 27.8 knots means war. That is the highest speed achieved by the *Goeben*, although her steam engines were rumoured to have a construction fault causing severe leakages.

It struck him that you can predetermine the moment when a war starts, but never when it will finish.

CHAPTER 11

On the starboard side, where he stood concealed by the companionway, the shoreline could just be made out in the dawn light. Rocks and skerries rose and fell in the choppy sea.

This is where a land starts and ends, Tobiasson-Svartman thought. But the boundary keeps shifting, there is no precise point where the sea comes to an end and land begins. The rocks are barely visible above the water. In olden days seafarers used to regard these rocks and reefs and outcrops as peculiar and terrifying sea monsters. I can also imagine the rocks slowly climbing up out of the sea becoming animals, but they do not terrify me. For me, they are no more than thought-provoking but perfectly harmless hippos rearing up among the waves, of a kind found only in the Baltic Sea.

This is where a land starts and ends, he thought once more. A rock leisurely straightening its back. A rock by the name of Sweden.

He walked to the rail and peered into the blue-grey water rushing along the hull of the destroyer. The sea never gives way, he thought. The sea never sells its skin. In the winter this sea is like frozen skin. Autumn is all calm, waiting. With sudden gusts of howling gales. Summer is no more than a brief glint in the mirror-calm water.

The sea, the elevation of the land, all these incomprehensible phenomena, they are like the slow progress from childhood to adulthood and death. An elevation of the land takes place inside every human being. All our memories come from the sea.

The sea is a dream that never sells its skin.

He smiled. My wife does not want me to see her crying. Perhaps that is for the same reasons, whatever they are, that I do not want her to see who I am when I am alone with the sea?

He returned to his sheltered spot. A freezing cold sailor emptied a bucket of waste food over the stern. Seagulls were following in the wake of the ship like a watchful rearguard. The deck was deserted again. He continued to contemplate the rocks. It was getting lighter.

These reefs and rocks are not only animals, he thought. They are also stones that are breaking free from the sea. There is no such thing as freedom without effort. But these stones are also time. Stones rising slowly out of the sea, which never lets go of them.

He tried to work out where they were. It was eleven hours since they had left Stockholm. He estimated the speed again and adjusted his previous conclusion to nine knots. They must be somewhere in the northern Östergötland archipelago, south of Landsort, north of the Häradskär lighthouse, to the south or east of Fällbådarna.

He went back to his cabin. Apart from the rating on deck he had not set eyes on a single member of the ship's large crew. Nobody could very well have seen him either, nor his hiding place.

He closed his cabin door and sat down on his bunk. In half an hour he would take breakfast in the officers' mess. At half past nine he was due to meet the ship's captain in his quarters. Captain Hans Rake would hand over the secret instructions presently locked in the ship's safe.

CHAPTER 12

He wondered why he so seldom laughed.

What was he missing? Why did he so often think he must be fashioned out of faulty clay?

CHAPTER 13

He sat on the edge of his bunk and let his eyes wander slowly around the cabin.

It was three metres square, like a prison cell with a round, brass-framed porthole. On the deck immediately below it was a corridor linking the various sections of the vessel. According to the plans, which he had memorised in minute detail, there were also two watertight, vertical bulkheads to the left of his cabin but two metres lower down in the ship. Above his head was the companionway leading to the starboard midships gun.

He thought: The cabin is a point. I am in the middle of that point at this very moment. One of these days there will be measuring instruments so precise that it will be possible to establish the exact location of this cabin in terms of latitude and longitude at any given moment. Its position will be capable of being fixed on a map of the world down to a fraction of a second. When that happens there will no longer be a place for gods. Who needs a god when the precise location of every human being can be established, when a person's inner location will coincide exactly with his external location? People making a living out of speculating about superstition and religion will have to find something else to live off. Charlatans and hydrographic engineers stand irrevocably on different sides of the crucial dividing line. Not the date line or the prime meridian line, but the line that separates the measurable from what cannot be measured and hence doesn't exist.

He gave a start. Something in that thought confused him. But he could not put his finger on what it was.

He took his shaving mirror from the sponge bag Kristina Tacker had embroidered with his initials and a childishly formed rose.

Each time he looked at his reflection he took a deep breath. As if he were preparing himself for descending into a chasm. He imagined being confronted by a face he did not recognise in the mirror.

CHAPTER 14

He always felt a strong sense of relief to encounter those eyes, his furrowed brow and the scar over his left eye.

He examined his face and thought about who he was. A man who had made his career in the Swedish Navy, whose ambition was one day to become chiefly responsible for mapping the secret naval channels that were a key part of the Swedish defences.

Was he anything more?

A person who constantly measured distances and depths, both in external reality and in the oceans inside him that were as yet uncharted.

CHAPTER 15

He stroked his cheeks and replaced the mirror in his sponge bag. He was also a man who had changed his surname. His father had died at the beginning of March 1912. A few weeks before the Olympic Games were due to be opened in the newly built stadium in Stockholm, he applied to the Royal Patents and Registrations Office with a request to change his name. To distance himself from his dead father, he had decided to insert his mother's maiden name between his Christian name and his surname, Svartman. His mother had always tried to protect him from his moody and perpetually irascible father. His father was dead now, but dead people can also be a threat. The protective wall his mother had thrown up would be extended into his name.

He put away his sponge bag and opened the lid of a wooden box he had placed on the low table with raised edges to stop items falling off in stormy seas. It contained four watches. Three of them showed exactly the same time. They were a check on one another. The hands on the fourth, which he had inherited from his father, were still. In that one, time had stopped.

He closed the lid again. Three of the watches told him the time, the fourth represented death.

CHAPTER 16

Three officers got to their feet and eyed him with interest as he entered the mess. He recognised one of them, the short-sighted first mate who had welcomed him by the gangplank the previous evening. Höckert introduced his two colleagues.

'May I introduce you to Lieutenant Sundfeldt and Artillery Captain von Sidenbahn?'

The latter was tall and slim, and smelled strongly of either aftershave or gin.

'No doubt you are wondering what an artillery captain is doing on board a ship,' he said. 'We are usually more at home and more effective on dry land, but sometimes an artillery captain can be of use on board a warship. Especially when guns have to be broken in and adjusted and there is a shortage of officers.'

They sat down. A waiter served coffee. Nobody asked any questions. Captain Rake had naturally informed his officers that they would be accompanied on their voyage to the outer edge of the Östergötland archipelago by an officer on a secret mission.

Sundfeldt and von Sidenbahn left the mess.

'Have you met the ship's captain yet?' said Höckert.

He spoke with a pronounced accent, possibly a Småland dialect, or perhaps he came from Halland or Bohuslän.

'No,' said Tobiasson-Svartman. 'I know Captain Rake only by reputation so far.'

'Reputations are generally misleading or exaggerated. But there is always a grain of truth in what is said. The truth about Rake is that he's very competent. Possibly a bit on the lazy side, but aren't we all?'

Höckert stood up, clicked his heels and gave an apology of a salute. Tobiasson-Svartman finished his breakfast alone. He could hear Lieutenant Sundfeldt's angry tones from the deck, but could not make out what had upset him.

It was broad daylight by now. Captain Rake would be waiting for him, preparing to produce the secret orders from the ship's safe.

The *Svea* was heading south. The wind was still squalling and appeared to be veering in different directions. Towards the shore it had started raining again.

CHAPTER 17

The meeting between Captain Rake and Lars Tobiasson-Svartman was interrupted by an unexpected incident. They had just shaken hands and sat down in the leather chairs fixed to the floor of Rake's suite when Lieutenant Sundfeldt marched in and announced that one of the crew had fallen ill. He could not judge if the man's state was life-threatening, but he was in a lot of pain.

'Nobody can simulate such fearful pain,' said Lieutenant Sundfeldt.

Rake said nothing for a moment, staring at his hands. He was known to be a man who backed his crew to the hilt, and so Tobiasson-Svartman was not surprised when Rake rose to his feet.

'The unfortunate fact is that our ship's doctor, Hallman, has been given leave to attend his daughter's wedding. I'm afraid we shall have to postpone our meeting.'

'Of course.'

Rake was about to leave when he paused and turned.

'Why not come along as well?' he said. 'Taking a look at a sick crewman is an excellent way of having a look round the ship. Who is he?'

The question was directed at Lieutenant Sundfeldt.

'Johan Jakob Rudin. Bosun. Permanent crew member.'

Rake racked his brain.

'The Rudin who signed on in August, in Kalmar?'

'That's the one.'

'What is he suffering from?'

'Stomach pains.'

Rake nodded.

'My bosuns don't complain without good cause.'

They walked down a narrow corridor then up a companionway and on to the deck. The cold, squally wind made them crouch down. Lieutenant Sundfeldt took the lead, followed by Captain Rake, with Tobiasson-Svartman bringing up the rear.

Once more he had the feeling he was taking part in a procession.

'I have been in command of naval ships for nineteen years,' said Rake. He was shouting, to make himself heard above the wind. 'So far I've only lost four crew members,' he went on. 'Two died of a raging fever before we could get them to land, an engineer fell backwards off a companionway and broke his neck. I still believe the man was drunk, although it couldn't be proved. Then I once had a mentally ill petty officer who threw himself overboard just off the Grundkallen lighthouse. There was something shameful behind the catastrophe, debts and forged bonds. I suppose I ought to have seen it coming, but it's generally hard to stop a sailor who has really made up his mind to jump. Of course, we always carry a ship's doctor – but this trip is an exception. It also has to be said that naval doctors are seldom the most competent ones around.'

Rake paused and was clearly annoyed as he pointed

at a bucket standing next to a companionway. Lieutenant Sundfeldt ordered a rating to remove it immediately.

'I learned a bit about medical diagnosis quite early in my career,' Rake continued. 'And I can pull teeth, of course. There are a few very simple ways of keeping folk alive for a bit longer. I console myself, and possibly also flatter myself, that I have significantly fewer deaths on my ships than any of my colleagues.'

They went on down various companionways until they came to the very bottom of the ship. Tobiasson-Svartman could feel that they were down by the waterline. The air was oppressive and the smell of oil stifling.

They continued their way downwards.

CHAPTER 18

The bosun was in his hammock. It smelled stuffy, with a stench of sweat and fear.

It was dark, and Tobiasson-Svartman had difficulty making out details. It was a considerable time before his eyes got used to the transition from light space to darkness.

Rake took off his gloves and leaned over the hammock. Rudin's face was glistening, his eyes flickering restlessly. He looked like a terrified, cornered animal.

'Where does it hurt?' Rake said.

Rudin folded back the blanket to reveal his nightshirt. He pulled it up over his chest. All three men leaned over the hammock. Rudin pointed to a spot to the right of his navel. Moving his hand made him grimace in pain.

'Has it been hurting for long?' Rake said.

'Since yesterday evening. We'd just left Stockholm when it started.'

'Constant or on and off?'

'On and off at first, but now all the time.'

'Have you had anything like this before?'

'I don't know.'

'Think. Think hard.'

Rudin lay still, thinking.

'No,' he said eventually. 'This is something new. I've never felt anything like it before.'

Rake lay his slender hand on the area Rudin had indicated. He pressed down, gently at first, then harder. Rudin pulled a face and groaned. Rake took his hand away.

'I think it's appendicitis.'

He straightened his back.

'You need an operation. It'll be OK.'

Rudin eyed his captain gratefully as he pulled the blanket up to his chin again. Despite lying down and being in pain, he saluted.

They returned to the upper deck. On the way Rake instructed Sundfeldt to tell the wireless operator to contact the *Thule*, one of the class 1 gunboats the *Svea* was due to meet east of the Sandsänkan lighthouse.

'They ought to be heading north, somewhere between Västervik and Häradskär,' Rake said. 'The gunboat must come and meet us as quickly as possible, take Rudin on board and transport him to Bråviken. There's a good hospital in Norrköping. I've no intention of losing one of my best bosuns unnecessarily.'

Lieutenant Sundfeldt saluted and made off. They returned to the captain's quarters without speaking. Rake offered him a cigarette. Tobiasson-Svartman declined. He had tried to start smoking when he embarked on his naval officer training. He was one of only three on the course who did not smoke. But he never managed it. Inhaling the smoke from a cigarette or cigar made him feel as if he were choking, and he was in danger of panicking.

Rake lit his cigar with great attention to detail. All the time he was listening to the vibrations in the ship's hull. Tobiasson-Svartman had noticed how older, more experienced sea dogs used to do this. They were always on the bridge in spirit, even when they were in their own quarters smoking a cigar. The vibrations were evidently transformed into images so that your experienced sailor always knew exactly what was what.

Then they talked about the war.

CHAPTER 19

Rake told how the British Fleet had left Scapa Flow as early as 27 July, in great haste and a certain degree of disarray, even though war had not yet been declared. The Admiralty had made it clear they had no intention of allowing the German blue-water fleet the least opportunity to attack British warships trapped in their bases. The periscopes of German submarines had been spotted by the crews of British fishing boats at dawn on 27 July. Trawlers on the way through the Pentland Firth to Dogger Bank further out in the North Sea had sighted at least three submarines.

Tobiasson-Svartman could see the charts in his mind's eye. He had an almost photographic memory where sea charts were concerned. Scapa Flow, Pentland Firth, the British naval bases in the Orkney Islands: he could even recall the crucial details of depth soundings in the entry channels to the natural harbours.

'It's possible that the British Fleet is in for a surprise,' Rake said thoughtfully.

Tobiasson-Svartman waited for more, but nothing more came.

'What kind of a surprise?' he asked after measuring out an appropriate silence.

‘That the German Navy is much better equipped than the arrogant English imagine.’

Rake’s words carried a clear implication. Sweden was not yet involved in the war. The Swedish Navy was preparing itself for circumstances in which that would no longer be the case. If that did happen, there should be no doubt as to where the sympathy of the Swedish military lay. Even if the government and parliament had declared their country’s neutrality.

The conversation died out.

Rake put down his cigar on a heavy green porphyry ashtray, stood up, produced a key attached to his watch chain, then knelt down in front of the large black safe screwed to the floor.

The secret instructions were in a plain, cloth-bound folder, tied with a thick blue-and-yellow silk ribbon. Rake handed over the folder, then returned to his cigar.

Tobiasson-Svartman opened the folder. Although he knew the general objective of his mission, he was not aware of the more detailed plans that had been drawn up by Naval Headquarters. He sat back comfortably in his chair, balanced the folder on his knee and started reading.

In the corner of his eye he could see Rake studying the course of the smoke from his cigar.

CHAPTER 20

The ship was throbbing like a panting beast.

Tobiasson-Svartman often compared various types of ship with animals to be found in Sweden. Torpedo boats were like weasels or polecats, destroyers were falcons eager to pounce on their prey, cruisers hunted like packs of hungry wolves, the big battleships were solitary bears that did not like to be disturbed. Animals that were normally enemies could be persuaded, in their symbolic roles as warships, to cooperate and even to sacrifice themselves for one another.

He saw from the folder that the instructions were *Confidential and for the Eyes of Commander Lars Svartman Only*. Certain sections could be copied, but the original was to be handed back to Rake without ever having left his cabin.

As far as the Swedish Navy was concerned, his name had not been changed, despite the fact that he had informed his superiors the moment he heard from the Royal Patents and Registrations Office.

On board this vessel and as far as the Joint Staff of the Swedish Armed Forces was concerned, he was still Lars Svartman, that was all.

* * *

He read:

> Your mission is to make depth soundings, without delay, of the dedicated and secret naval channels linking Kalmar Sound, southern section, with the northern, central and southern approaches to Stockholm. It is especially important to check the readings of the sounds, passages and other approaches made in 1898 and 1902 in relation to the deepest possible draught claimed for each type of vessel at Sandsänkan Lighthouse. Your base for these soundings will be the destroyer *Svea*. The vessel you will use for making the soundings will be the gunboat *Blenda*, which will supply the necessary launches and picket boats.

This introductory statement was followed by all the associated specific orders that were to be complied with.

He closed the file and retied the silk ribbon. Rake eyed him up and down.

'No notes?'

'I don't think I need any.'

'You are still young,' said Rake with a smile. 'Old men never rely on their memories. Young men sometimes rely on theirs too much.'

Tobiasson-Svartman stood up and clicked his heels. It felt as if he were giving himself a kick. Rake pointed to the table, indicating where the file should go.

'It's going to be a long war,' Rake said. 'Lord Kitchener in the British high command has realised that. I'm afraid his German equivalent hasn't yet grasped that this war is going to be on a bigger scale than any previous one throughout the awful history of mankind.'

Rake paused, as if his thoughts had become too overwhelming for him to bear. Then he went on.

'Thousands of men are going to die. Hundreds of thousands, perhaps millions. In that respect this war is going to be bigger than any previous one. And it's going to be long and drawn-out. There are some who say it will be all over by Christmas. Personally, I'm convinced it will last for years. More ships are going to be sunk than in any other. The tonnage that's going to be blown up and sunk will have to be totted up in millions.'

Rake paused again. He fiddled absent-mindedly with the blue-and-yellow silk ribbon.

More people are going to be drowned than ever before, thought Tobiasson-Svartman. Officers and men will be burned to death in blazing infernos. The Baltic Sea and the North Sea, the Atlantic and perhaps other oceans as well will be filled with screams that slowly grow fainter and then cease altogether.

A thousand sailors weigh about sixty tonnes. War is not only about how many sailors die. It is also about how many living tonnes are transformed into dead tonnes. You talk about the deadweight of a vessel. Human beings can be reckoned in terms of deadweight as well.

CHAPTER 21

He left the captain's cabin.

Jagged clouds were scudding across the October sky. He thought about the task ahead of him. He also wondered whether Rake was right. Would the war really be as terrible and long-drawn-out as he had predicted?

The ship suddenly lost speed and turned slowly so as to head into the wind. He realised this must be a heave-to manoeuvre in preparation for transferring Rudin on to the gunboat that would take him to Norrköping.

He went back to his cabin. He hung up his tunic, removed his shoes and stretched out on his bunk. Somebody had made up the bed while he had been with Rake.

He lay with his hands behind his head, feeling the vibrations that were throbbing through the ship, and thought about what was in store.

CHAPTER 22

It was a sort of ritual.

A new mission did not necessarily have to be frightening just because it was secret. What he was going to do would be characterised by routines, not by sudden dramatic incidents.

He hated disorder and chaos. Charting the depths of the sea demanded total serenity, a virtually meditative calm.

Times of peace are used to prepare for new wars, he thought. Since the middle of the nineteenth century the Swedish Navy has sent out lots of expeditions to seek out alternative shipping routes along the Swedish coasts. Some of those expeditions have been badly organised and inadequately led, others have been successful.

The starting point was simple. An aggressor might set up blockades, often in the last ten years or so by laying mines, preventing use of the usual shipping lanes marked on the charts available to the public and used by various merchant navies. To counter this, there is a network of secret routes and channels used for military purposes. The fear that spies might get hold of information about these routes was both considerable and justified. An aggressor who had succeeded in uncovering these secret channels could cause a lot of damage. As the draught of modern ships was increasing all the time, the routes had to be constantly checked. Were there alternative routes that could accommodate ships with bigger draughts? Could shallows that restricted access be dredged in secret, without the changes being marked on publicly available navigational charts?

These were the questions he would have to answer. In addition, he would also have to consider the possible threat from submarines. There was no doubt that submarines presented a completely new danger with potentially limitless consequences. But how could they be stopped? If the channels were deep enough, a submarine could penetrate to the very centre of Stockholm.

He thought back to the years between 1909 and 1912 when he had been involved in redrawing secret naval routes through the archipelago between Landsort and Västervik. In the early days he had played a junior role, but later, from the spring of 1910 onwards, he had been promoted rapidly and placed in charge of the whole operation.

Those had been happy days. In just a few years a large number of his dreams had come true.

But he then realised that he had a quite different dream. It had been unexpected, but it was that dream he now hoped to be able to turn into reality.

The dream of discovering the greatest depth of all.

CHAPTER 23

The vibrations faded away.

The ship was still.

The beast was holding its breath.

He put on his tunic again, went on deck and stood in the spot where he knew he was invisible. The gunboat *Thule*, with her three funnels, was drawing alongside to leeward. The sick rating had already been carried out on deck. When the *Thule* had completed the manoeuvre Rudin was lowered carefully down in a skilfully made sling. The smoke from the *Thule*'s funnels swallowed him up. There was no sign of Captain Rake: the operation was being directed by Lieutenant Sundfeldt. As soon as Rudin was safely on board the gunboat, the empty sling was retrieved, the *Thule* backed away and then set off in a north-westerly direction towards Bråviken.

He stayed on deck and watched the *Thule* until she was out of sight. The smoke from her funnels blended into the scudding clouds.

Rudin was one sailor who had escaped from a terrifying trap, he thought. Swedish ships would be sunk even if Sweden managed to stay out of the war. The sailors most at risk would be in the merchant navy, but even the crews of warships would be torpedoed or blown up by mines. If Rudin did not return to his ship, he would not need to run the risk of being killed by an exploding boiler. Thanks to his inflamed appendix he might be one of the lucky sailors who would escape death.

Tobiasson-Svartman screwed up his eyes and searched for traces of the *Thule.* There was no sign of her now; she had disappeared into the grey coastline.

He went back to his cabin. The ship was turning back into the wind again.

CHAPTER 24

He paused in the doorway and tried to imagine what his wife was doing at this particular moment. But he could not envisage her. He had no idea what she did when she was alone in the flat. He did not like that notion. It was like holding a chart in your hand and suddenly finding that all the writing, the outlines of the islands, the areas covered by the lighthouses, the buoyage, the depth contours had all been erased.

He wanted to know what routes his wife used when he was away.

I love her, he thought. But I do not really know what love is.

He sat down at the little table and unpacked his lead. The brass gleamed. For one brief moment he had the feeling that Kristina Tacker was standing behind him, leaning over his shoulder.

'Something is going to happen,' she whispered. 'There is a point where your lead will never reach the bottom. There comes a point where everything is found wanting, my darling husband.'

PART II

The Navigable Channel

CHAPTER 25

The evening before Lars Tobiasson-Svartman started on his mission, a petty officer came to his cabin to tell him that Captain Rake wanted to give him the final instructions.

He put on his naval jacket and hurried up the slippery companionway. The crescent moon kept appearing through the clouds. The *Svea* was anchored to the north-east of the Häradskär lighthouse.

He paused halfway up the stairs and gazed out over the dark sea to where the lights of gunboats could be seen. The Häradskär light had been turned off. He thought about all the shells, all the torpedoes out there. Every vessel was laden with the man-made fury known as dynamite or gunpowder.

The hardest place to estimate distances was over open water, but not when it was dark. He judged the nearest gunboat to be 140 metres distant, with a margin of error no greater than ten metres either way.

Before entering the captain's quarters, he removed his dark blue naval cap.

Rake offered him a brandy. Normally, Tobiasson-Svartman never touched alcohol when he was working, but he could not bring himself to refuse it.

Rake emptied his glass and said: 'They are very much

concerned in Stockholm, and rightly so. They say on the wireless that Russian and German naval vessels have been sighted to the east of Gotland. But there haven't been any reports of action. The whole of the Gotland coastline is crammed full of people with good hearing, straining to detect the sound of guns or torpedoes.'

'There's no concern worse than the sort you feel when you don't know what's going on,' said Tobiasson-Svartman. 'Concern based on knowledge is always easier to handle.'

Rake handed him the sheet of paper he was holding.

'Nobody knows if any of these nations intend attacking Sweden. We are going to switch off all our lighthouses and creep down into our burrows.'

'Are people worried more about the Russians or the Germans?'

'Both. You don't need to be one of the navy's most experienced officers or even the Minister of Defence to know that. On the one hand both Germany and Russia have an interest in Sweden being kept out of the war. On the other hand both of them probably suspect that Sweden won't be able to hang on to its neutrality in the long run. That could lead to either or both of them launching a pre-emptive strike. The other possibility, of course, is that they decide to leave us alone. Being an insignificant country can be both an advantage and a drawback.'

Tobiasson-Svartman read through the list of lighthouses that had been switched off, and which other navigation marks had been covered up or hastily dismantled. He could picture the sea charts. At night in total darkness it would be very difficult for a foreign warship to sail through the archipelago.

Rake had rolled out a chart on his table and placed an ashtray on each corner. It covered the area between Gotska Sandön and the southern tip of Gotland. He pointed at a spot out to sea.

'A German convoy – comprising a couple of cruisers, a few small destroyers, torpedo boats, minesweepers and probably some submarines – has been seen here, travelling north. They are said to be travelling at speed, around twenty knots. They were on a level with Slite when they were spotted by a fishing boat from Fårösund. At four o'clock this afternoon they vanished into a belt of fog north-east of Gotska Sandön. At about the same time another fishing boat discovered a number of Russian ships also on their way north, but a bit further to the east. The skipper of the fishing boat was not sure of their exact course. He wasn't sure about anything, in fact. He might well have been drunk. Even so, he can't very well have imagined it all. In my view – and the Naval HQ in Stockholm agrees – the two convoys can hardly have been in contact with each other. We can assume that they are not cooperating and have different intentions. But what? Who are they aiming at? We don't know. They could be diversionary moves, intended to create confusion. Uncertainty is always more difficult to cope with at sea than on land. But the lighthouses have been switched off anyway. Those in charge in Stockholm evidently don't dare to take any risks.'

Rake picked up the bottle and looked questioningly

at Tobiasson-Svartman, who shook his head and then regretted it immediately. Rake filled his own glass, but not to the brim this time.

'Does this affect my mission?'

'Only in that from now on, everything has to proceed at great speed. In wartime you can never assume that there will be plenty of time available. And that's the situation we're in now.'

The conversation with Rake was at an end. The captain seemed uneasy. He scratched at his forehead, which showed traces of red spots.

Tobiasson-Svartman left the captain's quarters. The October evening was chilly. He paused on the companionway and listened. The sea was booming away in the distance. He could hear somebody laughing in the gun room. He thought he recognised Anders Höckert's voice.

He closed the door of his cabin and thought about his wife. She always used to go to bed early when he was away, she'd told him that in a letter the same year they were married.

He closed his eyes. After a few minutes of trying, he managed to conjure up her smell. It was soon so strong that it filled the whole cabin.

CHAPTER 26

It rained during the night.

He slept with his lead clutched tightly to his chest. When he got up, shortly before six, he had a nagging headache.

He wanted to run away, escape. But it was only that he was impatient at still not having embarked on his mission.

CHAPTER 27

At dawn on 22 October, Lars Tobiasson-Svartman transferred to the gunboat *Blenda*.

The waiting was over.

He was welcomed at the end of the gangway by the commanding officer, Lieutenant Jakobsson, who had a squint in his left eye and a deformed hand. He spoke with a pronounced Gothenburg accent, and despite his squint his expression seemed friendly and sincere. Tobiasson-Svartman could not help thinking that Jakobsson reminded him of some character he had seen in one of those newfangled films, or whatever they were called. One of the police officers, perhaps, who were forever chasing the star but never managed to catch him?

Lieutenant Jakobsson inspired him with confidence. To his surprise, he was allocated the captain's cabin.

'This isn't necessary,' he insisted.

'I'll bunk with my second in command,' said Lieutenant Jakobsson. 'It's a bit cramped and crappy on these gunboats, the more so as we've had to take on extra crew because of the particular nature of the mission. And my orders include that you have the best possible conditions in which to carry out your task. As I see it, a good night's sleep is one of the cornerstones of human existence. And so I'm prepared to put up with my cabin-mate grinding his teeth in his sleep. It's like sharing a cabin with a walrus. Assuming walruses grind their teeth, that is.'

He asked Jakobsson to tell him the history of the ship.

'Parliament voted for it in 1873. She was the first of a series of gunboats, and none of the farmers who dominated parliament in those days had any idea about how many there should be. We have room for eighty tonnes of coal in the bunkers, and that's enough to see us through 1,500 nautical miles. The engines are horizontal compounders, in accordance with the Wolf system. I'm not at all sure what's special about the Wolf system, but it seems to work. She's a good ship, but getting on in years. I suspect they'll soon retire her.'

Tobiasson-Svartman went to his cabin. It was bigger than the one he'd had on the *Svea*. But it had a different smell to it. Like an anthill, he thought. As if there had been an anthill in the cabin, but it had been removed during the night.

He smiled at the thought. He imagined explaining to his wife about his first impressions of his cabin, and the smell of formic acid.

He went up on deck and asked Lieutenant Jakobsson to assemble the crew. It was a fine day, with a southerly breeze.

The crew consisted of seventy-one men. Eight of the ratings and a naval engineer had joined the ship to help with the expedition. What they knew about the work in store was little enough.

The crew assembled following a whistle from the second in command, whose name was Fredén.

Tobiasson-Svartman was always nervous when required to address a crew. To conceal his unease, he came across as strict and liable to lose his temper.

'I will not stand for any slapdash work,' he began. 'Our mission is important. These are unsettled times and battle fleets are sailing round our coasts. We shall be remeasuring the depths of parts of the shipping route used by the navy, to the north and south of where we are now. There is no margin for error. A sounding that is out by even one metre could result in disaster for a ship. Shallows that are overlooked or wrongly positioned on a chart could wreak devastation.'

He paused and surveyed the crew, standing in a semicircle before him. Many of them were young, barely twenty. They eyed him expectantly.

'We'll be looking for what cannot be seen,' he went on. 'But because it cannot be seen, that doesn't mean it isn't there. There could be sandbanks just below the surface that have not previously been discovered or charted. There might also be unexpected depths. We shall be looking for both of these features. We'll be mapping out a route along which our warships can proceed in safety. Any questions?'

Nobody had a question. The gunboat rocked up and down in the swell.

The rest of the day was spent establishing the necessary

routines and organising reliable procedures. Lieutenant Jakobsson plainly had the confidence of his crew. Tobiasson-Svartman could see that he had been lucky. A naval officer forced to hand over his cabin to a colleague on a temporary, confidential mission could easily have reacted sourly, but Lieutenant Jakobsson did not seem put out. He gave the impression of being one of those rare people who do not conceal their true character behind a false front. In that respect Lieutenant Jakobsson was the opposite of himself.

The routines were duly established. Every fourth day he would report to Captain Rake. It was estimated that in ideal weather conditions the destroyer would pass their position every ninety-sixth hour. Rake had at his disposal cryptographers who would encode Tobiasson-Svartman's reports and transmit them to Naval Headquarters. Within a few days the changes that needed to be made to the charts would be with the cartographers in Stockholm. The work would proceed at tremendous speed.

Late that afternoon Lieutenant Jakobsson fixed an exact bearing. They were three degrees north-north-east of the Sandsänkan lighthouse. According to the latest charts the depths around the Juliabåden buoy were twelve, twenty-three and fourteen metres.

Tobiasson-Svartman gave the order that the *Blenda* should stay where it was until the following day. This was where the measuring work would begin.

He studied the sea through his telescope, scrutinising the distant horizon, and the lighthouses within view. Then he closed his eyes, but without taking away the telescope.

He dreamed of the day when only in exceptional circumstances would he need the help of various instruments. He dreamed of the day when he himself had become the only instrument he needed.

CHAPTER 28

The following day. Three minutes past seven. Lars Tobiasson-Svartman was on deck. The sun was hidden behind low clouds. He was dressed in uniform. It was plus four degrees, and almost dead calm. A musty smell of seaweed was coming from the sea. He was tense, nervous about the work that was about to begin, afraid of all the mistakes waiting in store for him, mistakes he hoped not to make.

A submerged sandbank long used by herring fishermen, marked on the charts as Olsklabben, was 150 metres to the west of the ship. He had in one of his suitcases an archive that he always carried around with him. He had read in an old tax roll that this sandbank had been 'used by fishermen and seal hunters since the sixteenth century and belonged to the Crown'.

The sun broke through the clouds. He noticed a drift net, gliding through the water. He did not realise what it was at first. Perhaps some tufts of seaweed had been disturbed by the anchor? Then he realised it was a net that had broken loose. There were dead fish caught in the mesh, and the carcass of a duck.

It occurred to him that he was looking at an image of freedom. The drift net stood for freedom. A prison that had broken loose, with some of its dead prisoners still clinging to their bars that were the mesh.

Freedom is always taking flight, he thought. He watched the net until it had drifted out of sight. Then he turned to Lieutenant Jakobsson, who had come to stand beside him.

'Freedom is always taking flight,' he said.

Jakobsson looked at him in surprise.

'I beg your pardon?'

'Oh, nothing. Just a line from a poem, I think. Maybe something of Rydberg's? Or Fröding?'

There was a long pause. Then Lieutenant Jakobsson clicked his heels and saluted.

'Breakfast is served in the wardroom. Somebody who is used to the space available on a destroyer will find that everything is much more cramped on a gunboat. Here we cannot have crew members who make sweeping gestures. You can speak loudly, but not wave your arms about.'

'I don't expect special privileges, and very seldom do I wave my arms about.'

When he had finished breakfast, which consisted mainly of an over-salty omelette, it was a quarter past eight. Two grey-painted launches, each seven metres long, were lowered into the water. Sub-Lieutenant Welander, the naval engineer, took command of one of the launches, and Tobiasson-Svartman the other. Each of the boats carried three oarsmen and a rating selected to take charge of the sounding lines.

* * *

They started sounding along a line leading south-west from Sandsänkan lighthouse. Tobiasson-Svartman's aim was to find out if it were possible for ships with a bigger draught than the ones given on the present chart to pass this far into the archipelago, shielded by the surrounding skerries and rocks.

Sounding lines were lowered and raised, depths established and compared with the figures on the charts. Tobiasson-Svartman was in overall charge, giving instructions when necessary. He took some measurements himself as well, the brass of his instrument gleaming as it glided up and down through the water. Readings were noted down in a diary.

The sea was calm. There was a strange atmosphere of peace around the boats, the sounding leads sinking and rising, the figures being called out, repeated then noted down. The oarsmen rowed as noiselessly as they could. Every sound bounced back and forth over the water.

On board the *Blenda* Lieutenant Jakobsson smoked his pipe and talked non-stop to one of the stokers about a leaking cooling tube. It was a friendly chat, like good-natured conversation outside church after a service.

Tobiasson-Svartman squinted into the sun and estimated the distance to the *Blenda* as sixty-five metres.

They progressed gradually westwards. The two launches proceeded with slow, steady strokes of the oars, on a parallel course, five metres apart.

CHAPTER 29

Shortly after eleven in the morning they found a depth that did not correspond to the depth recorded on the chart. The disparity was considerable, all of three metres. The correct depth was fourteen metres, not seventeen. They checked the surrounding depths, but found no deviations from the figures on the chart. They had stumbled upon an unexpected projection deep below the surface. Some sort of narrow and pointed rock formation in the middle of an area where the rest of the bottom was flat.

Tobiasson-Svartman had found the first of the points he was looking for. A wrong measurement that he could correct. A depth had become less deep.

But in his heart of hearts he was looking for something quite different. A place where the sounding lead never reached the bottom: a point where the sounding line ceased to be a technical instrument and was transformed into a poetic tool.

CHAPTER 30

The stretch where they were measuring at present curved round a series of small rocks and shallows to the south of the skerry known as Halsskär at the edge of the open sea. The west side had never been charted. There was a possibility that they might find a channel sufficiently deep and wide to take a vessel with a draught as big as the destroyer *Svea*.

In his travelling archive he found a note to the effect that until the eighteenth century the skerry had been called Vratholmen. He tried to discover why this barren little island no more than one thousand metres in diameter would have had its name changed. A person can change his name for any number of reasons. He had done so himself. But why a skerry at the edge of the open sea?

Could the original name have something to do with wrath, with anger? Records showed that it had been called Vratholmen for at least 250 years. Then, at some time between 1712 and 1740, its name had changed. From then on, there was no Vratholmen, only Halsskär.

He thought about the riddle for some time, but he could find no plausible answer.

In the evening, after copying his own and Sub-Lieutenant Welander's notes into the main expedition record book, he went on deck. The sea was still calm. Some ratings were busy repairing the gangway. He paused and gazed out at Halsskär.

Suddenly, there was a flash of light. He screwed up his eyes. It did not happen again. He went to his cabin and fetched his telescope. There was nothing to be seen on the smooth rocks apart from darkness.

Later that night he wrote a letter to his wife. It was a scrappy description of days that could hardly be distinguished from one another.

He did not write anything about Rudin. Nor did he mention the drift net he had seen that morning.

CHAPTER 31

The following day, as dawn broke, he clambered into one of the tenders tied to the *Blenda*'s stern. He unfastened the painter and rowed towards Halsskär. It was dead calm, and the sea smelled of salt and mud. He rowed through the gentle swell with powerful strokes and found a tiny cove on the west side of the skerry where he could land without getting his feet wet. He beached the tender, tied the painter round a large stone then leaned back against the sloping cliff.

The *Blenda* was anchored off the east side of Halsskär. He was alone. No sound reached him from the ship.

The skerry was resting in the sea. It was like being in a cradle, or on a deathbed, he thought. All the voices hidden in the cliff were whispering. Even rocks have memories, as do waves and breakers. And down below, in the darkness where fish swam along invisible and silent channels, there were also memories.

The barren skerry was a poor and destitute being, devoid of desires. The only vegetation on the rocky islet was patches of lichens, clumps of heather, occasional tufts of grass, short, windswept juniper bushes and some strips of seaweed at the edge of the water.

The skerry was a mendicant friar who had renounced all earthly possessions and wandered alone through the world.

He was all of a sudden overcome by a powerful longing for his wife. The next time he saw Captain Rake he would ask him to post the letter he had written to her.

Only then could he count on receiving a letter from her. He was married to a woman who answered letters, but was never the first to write.

He climbed to the top of the cliff. The rocks were slippery and he kept stumbling. From the summit he could see the *Blenda*, riding at anchor in the distance. He had his telescope with him and aimed it at the ship. Watching people and things through a telescope always gave him a feeling of power.

Lieutenant Jakobsson was standing by the rail, peeing out over the water. He was holding his penis in his deformed hand.

Tobiasson-Svartman put the telescope down. What he had seen disgusted him. He took a deep breath.

From now on he would feel repugnance towards Jakobsson. Every time they sat down at table together he would have to fight back the image of the man peeing through the rail, using his deformed hand.

He wondered what would happen if he wrote in the

letter to his wife: 'This morning I surprised the ship's master with his trousers down.'

He sat down in a rocky hollow where the ground was dry and closed his eyes. After a few seconds he had conjured up the smell of his wife. It was so strong that when he opened his eyes he half expected to see her there on the skerry, standing close to him.

Shortly afterwards he climbed down to the tender and rowed back to the gunboat.

That same afternoon they progressed as far as Halsskär and began a methodical search for a sufficiently deep channel along the west side of the skerry.

CHAPTER 32

It took them seven days of hard, relentless work to confirm that it was possible to route the navigable channel on the west side of Halsskär. All the ships in the Swedish Navy, apart from the largest of the battleships, would be able to pass with a satisfactory safety margin.

At dinner, consisting of poached cod with potatoes and egg sauce, he told Lieutenant Jakobsson what they had established. He was not absolutely certain that he was allowed to pass on such details, but on the other hand it seemed odd not to be able to speak openly with a man who could observe what was going on with his own eyes.

'I'm impressed,' said Jakobsson. 'But I have a question: Did you know in advance?'

'Know what?'

'That it was deep just there? That it was deep enough for the big naval vessels?'

'Hydrographic surveyors who guess their way forward are seldom successful. The only thing I know for sure is that it's impossible to predict what is hidden under the surface of the sea. We can pull up mud and fish and rotten seaweed from the sea, but we can also bring up some significant surprises.'

'It must be a remarkable feeling, to look at a sea chart and tell yourself that you were responsible for its accuracy.'

The conversation was interrupted by Jakobsson's second in command, Fredén, appearing to announce that the *Svea* had been sighted, heading northwards.

Tobiasson-Svartman quickly finished his meal and hurried to write up the latest of his data. He checked through the notes briefly, then signed the record book.

Before leaving his cabin he wrote another short letter to his wife.

The destroyer towered over the *Blenda*. As it was almost perfectly calm, a gangplank was laid out to act as a bridge between the two vessels.

Captain Rake had a bad cold. He asked no questions, merely accepted the record book and passed it on to one of the cryptographers. Then he offered Tobiasson-Svartman a brandy.

'Bosun Rudin?' Tobiasson-Svartman asked. 'How is he?'

'I'm afraid he died during the operation,' Rake said. 'It's very sad. He was a good bosun. Besides, with his death my personal statistics look less good.'

Tobiasson-Svartman suddenly felt sick. He hadn't expected Rudin to be dead, and for a moment he lost his self-possession.

Rake was watching him intently. He had noticed the reaction.

'Are you not well?'

'I'm fine, thank you. It's just that my stomach has been a bit upset these last few days.'

Neither of them spoke. The shadow of Bosun Rudin passed through the cabin.

They took another glass of brandy before Tobiasson-Svartman left.

CHAPTER 33

On 31 October, early in the afternoon, the central east coast of Sweden was struck by a storm that forced the hydrographers to stop work. It was not without a degree of satisfaction that Tobiasson-Svartman ordered the launches back to the mother ship. Early that morning, when he had checked the weather, all the indications were that a storm was approaching. At breakfast he had asked Jakobsson what he thought about the weather prospects.

'The barometer is falling,' Jakobsson said. 'We might get a strong southerly wind approaching gale force, but probably not until after nightfall.'

More probably by this afternoon, Tobiasson-Svartman had thought. And the wind is going to be more of an easterly. And it will be storm force. But he said nothing. Neither at breakfast, nor when the storm hit them.

The *Blenda* tossed and turned in the rough seas. The engines were at full throttle, to keep the ship heading into the wind. He was alone at the meal table for two days. Lieutenant Jakobsson suffered badly from seasickness and did not appear. Tobiasson-Svartman had never had that problem, not even during his early days as a cadet.

For some reason, that gave him a bad conscience.

CHAPTER 34

The storm blew itself out during the night of 2 November.

When Tobiasson-Svartman came out on deck at dawn ragged clouds were scudding across the sky. The temperature was climbing. They could restart their depth sounding. His overall plan had incorporated time to make up for delays and he was confident that they would still finish on time. He had allowed for three severe storms.

He checked his watch and saw that it was time for breakfast.

Then he heard a shout. It sounded like a lamentation. When he turned round he saw a rating leaning over the rail, gesticulating wildly with his hand. Something in the water had attracted the sailor's attention.

Lieutenant Jakobsson and Tobiasson-Svartman hurried to where the sailor was standing. Half of Jakobsson's face was covered in shaving foam.

There was a dead body bobbing up and down in the water by the side of the ship. It was a man lying face downwards. His uniform was not Swedish. But was it German or was it Russian?

Ropes and grappling irons were used to hoist the body on board. The ratings turned him on his back.

The face was that of a young man. He had blond hair. But he had no eyes. They had been eaten by fish, eels or perhaps birds. Lieutenant Jakobsson groaned out loud.

Tobiasson-Svartman tried to grab hold of the rail, but fainted before he could reach it. When he came round, Jakobsson was bent over him. Some drops of the white lather dripped on to Tobiasson-Svartman's forehead. He sat up slowly, waving away the crew members who were trying to help him.

Feelings of humiliation were swelling up inside him. Not only had he lost control of himself, he had shown weakness in full view of the crew.

First Rudin had died, and now this body had been pulled up from the sea. That was too much, more than he could bear.

Before today Tobiasson-Svartman had only ever seen one dead body in all his life. That was his father, who had suffered a massive heart attack one evening when he was getting changed. He had died on the floor beside his bed, just as Tobiasson-Svartman had put his head round the door to tell him that dinner was ready.

At the moment of death Hugo Svartman had pissed himself. He lay there with his stomach uncovered and his eyes wide open. He was holding a shoe in one hand, as if to defend himself.

Tobiasson-Svartman had never managed to forget the sight of that fat, half-naked body. He often thought that his father had decided to punish him one last time by dying before his very eyes.

The dead man was very young. Lieutenant Jakobsson bent down and placed a handkerchief over the empty eye sockets.

'The uniform is German,' he said. 'He belonged to the German Navy.'

Jakobsson unbuttoned the dead man's tunic. He produced some soaking wet documents and photographs from the inside pockets.

'I don't have much experience of dead sailors,' he said. 'That doesn't mean of course that I've never fished dead men out of the sea. I don't think this man has been in the water all that long. He doesn't appear to have any wounds to suggest that he died in battle. Presumably he fell overboard by accident.'

Jakobsson stood up and ordered the body to be covered. Tobiasson-Svartman accompanied him into the mess. When they had sat down, and the papers and photographs were laid out on the table, Jakobsson realised that half of his face still had shaving foam on it. He shouted for the steward to bring him a towel and wiped his face clean. When Tobiasson-Svartman saw the half-shaved face, he could not help but burst into insuppressible laughter. Lieutenant Jakobsson raised an eyebrow in surprise. It occurred to Tobiasson-Svartman that this was the first time he had laughed out loud since coming on board the *Blenda*.

The idea of Lieutenant Jakobsson as a comic figure in a cinematographic farce came to him for the second time.

CHAPTER 35

Lieutenant Jakobsson started going through the dead sailor's papers. Carefully he separated the pages of a military pay book.

'Karl-Heinz Richter, born Kiel 1895,' he read. 'A very young man, not twenty. Short life, violent death.'

He was, with difficulty, deciphering the water-damaged writing.

'He was a crew member of the battleship *Niederburg*,' he said. 'I think the Naval Headquarters in Stockholm will be surprised to hear that the *Niederburg* is operating in the Baltic.'

Tobiasson-Svartman thought to himself: One of the smaller battleships in the German Navy, but even so it has a crew of more than eight hundred men. One of the heavy German naval vessels that could travel at impressively high speeds.

Jakobsson was poring over the photographs. One was a miniature in a glazed frame.

'Frau Richter presumably,' he said. 'A woman with a friendly smile sitting in a photographer's studio, never dreaming that her son will drown and have this photograph with him. A pretty face, but a bit on the plump side.'

He scrutinised the miniature more closely.

'There's a little blue butterfly behind the photograph,' he said. 'Why, we shall never know.'

The other photograph was blurred. He studied it for a long time before putting it down.

'It could just possibly be a dog. A Swedish foxhound, perhaps. But I'm not sure.'

He handed over the photographs and the documents. Tobiasson-Svartman also thought it could be a dog, but he too was unsure about the breed. The woman, who was most probably Karl-Heinz Richter's mother, looked cowed and scared. She seemed almost to be crouching before the photographer. And she was really fat.

'There are two possibilities,' Jakobsson said. 'Either it was a banal accident. A sailor falls overboard in the dark. Nobody notices. It doesn't even have to be dark for such an accident to occur. It could have happened in broad daylight. It only takes two or three seconds to fall into the water from the deck of a ship. Nobody sees you, nobody hears when you fall in with a splash and struggle with the sea that relentlessly sucks all the heat out of you and then pulls you under. You die from hypothermia, in a state of extreme panic. Anybody who's been close to drowning talks about a very special kind of fear that can't be compared to anything else, not even the terror you feel when making a bayonet charge on enemy forces shooting at you for all they are worth.'

He broke off, as if he had lost the thread. Tobiasson-Svartman could feel his stomach churning.

'But there could also be another explanation,' Jakobsson

said. 'He might have committed suicide. His angst had got the better of him. Young people most especially can take their own lives for the strangest reasons. A broken heart, for instance. Or that vague phenomenon the Germans call "*Weltschmerz*". But even homesickness is not unknown as a reason for servicemen taking their own lives. Mother's apron strings are more important than life. If you lose your grip on the apron strings, the only alternative is death.'

He reached for the miniature.

'It's not impossible that this woman has been overprotective as far as her son is concerned, and made his life without her impossible.'

He studied the image for a while before putting it down again.

'One could speculate about other reasons, of course. He might have been badly treated by his officers or fellow crewmen. I thought the lad looked little and scared even in death – he looked quite like a girl, in fact. All that was missing were the pigtails. Perhaps he couldn't put up with being at the bottom of the pecking order. Even so, it needs a special sort of courage to throw yourself into the water. Courage or stupidity. Often enough it boils down to the same thing. Especially among soldiers and sailors.'

Lieutenant Jakobsson stood up.

'I don't want the man on board any longer than necessary. Death weighs heavily on a ship. A crew gets nervy when they have a dead body as cargo. We'll bury him as soon as possible.'

'Doesn't there have to be a post-mortem?'

Jakobsson thought for a moment before replying.

'I'm in command of this ship and so I make the decisions. We can't be certain that the man hasn't been ill. People can carry an infection even when they are no longer breathing. I'm going to bury him as soon as possible.'

He paused in the doorway.

'I need some advice,' he said. 'You are presumably the best qualified person to give it in the whole of the Swedish Navy.'

'What?'

'I need a spot that's suitably deep. Ideally somewhere close where we can sink the body. Maybe you could check your charts and find somewhere?'

'That won't be necessary. I know a suitable place already.'

They went on deck and walked to the rail. It was strangely silent on board. Tobiasson-Svartman pointed to the north-east.

'There is a crack in the sea floor 250 metres from here. It never gets wider than thirty metres and it runs as far as Landsortsdjupet. As you know, that's the deepest part of the whole Baltic Sea, in excess of 450 metres. The location I'm talking about is 160 metres deep. If you want anything deeper than that you'll have to sail several nautical miles north.'

'That will be fine. On land they bury coffins only two metres deep. At sea, 160 metres should be more than enough.'

The body was sewn into a tarpaulin. Various pieces of

scrap metal from the engine room were lashed around the corpse. While the sea-coffin was being prepared, Lieutenant Jakobsson finished shaving.

The ship moved in accordance with the instructions given to the helmsman by Tobiasson-Svartman. It struck him that this was the first time he'd been in de facto command of a Swedish naval vessel. Even if it was only for 250 metres.

CHAPTER 36

The burial took place at nine thirty.

The crew gathered on the afterdeck. The carpenter had rigged up a plank between two trestles. The body wrapped in the tarpaulin was laid with the foot end next to the rail. The ship's three-tailed flag was at half mast.

Lieutenant Jakobsson followed the ritual laid down in his instruction book. He was holding a hymnal. The crew mumbled out the hymn. Jakobsson had a loud voice, but he sang out of tune. Tobiasson-Svartman only moved his lips. The seagulls circling the ship joined in the singing. After the hymn, Jakobsson read the prescribed prayer over the dead body, then the plank was tilted and the body slid over the rail and entered the water with a muffled splash.

The ship's foghorn sounded eerily. Jakobsson kept the crew to attention for a full minute. When they dispersed there was no sign of the body.

Jakobsson invited Tobiasson-Svartman to a glass of aquavit in the mess. They toasted each other and the lieutenant asked: 'How long do you think it took for the body to sink down to the mud or sand or whatever there is at the bottom just there?'

'It's mud,' said Tobiasson-Svartman. 'It's always mud in the Baltic.'

He made a rapid calculation in his head.

'Let's assume the body and the metal weigh a hundred kilos and the distance to the bottom is 160 metres. That would mean it would take two to three seconds for it to sink one metre. And so it will have taken the body about six minutes to reach the bottom.'

Jakobsson thought that over for a while.

'That ought to be enough to save my crew from worrying if he'll be coming back up to the surface again. Sailors can be as superstitious as hell. But the same applies to commanding officers if things are really bad.'

He poured himself another drink, and Tobiasson-Svartman did not say no.

'I shall spend a lot of time wondering about why he drowned,' Jakobsson said. 'I know I'll never know the answer, but I won't be able to forget him. Our meeting was brief. He lay on the deck of my ship under a piece of grey tarpaulin. Then he departed again. Even so, he will be with me for the rest of my life.'

'What will happen to his belongings? The miniature, the picture of the dog? His pay book?'

'I'll send them to Stockholm together with my report. I assume they'll eventually be sent to Germany. Sooner or later Frau Richter will find out what happened to her son. I know of no civilised nation where the procedures for dealing with dead soldiers and sailors are not meticulously observed.'

Tobiasson-Svartman stood up to prepare for resuming work. Lieutenant Jakobsson raised a hand to indicate that he had something more to say.

'I have a brother who's an engineer,' he said. 'He has been working for a number of years at the German naval yards in Gotenhafen and Kiel. He tells me that the German shipbuilders are considering making incredibly big vessels. With a deadweight of getting on for 50,000 tonnes, half of which is accounted for by the armour-plating. In some places that will be thirty-five centimetres thick. These ships will have crews comprising two thousand men and more, they'll be floating towns with access to everything you can think of. Presumably there'll be an undertaker or two on board as well. I suppose one of these days ships like that will come into being. I wonder what will happen to the human race, though. We could never have skin thirty-five centimetres thick, a skin that could withstand the biggest shells. Will the human race survive? Or will we end up fighting wars that never end, with nobody able to remember how they started, and nobody able to envisage them ending?'

Jakobsson poured himself another drink.

'The war that's being fought now could be the beginning of what I'm talking about. Millions of soldiers are going to die simply because one man was murdered in Sarajevo. Some insignificant Crown prince. Does that make any sense? Of course it doesn't. The bottom line is that war is always a mistake. Or the result of absurd assumptions and conclusions.'

Jakobsson did not appear to expect any comment. He replaced the bottle in its cupboard, then left the mess.

Just as he stepped out on to the deck he swayed and stumbled. But he did not turn round.

Tobiasson-Svartman remained in the mess, thinking over what he had just heard.

How thick was his own skin? How big a shell would it be able to resist?

What did he know about Kristina Tacker's skin, apart from the fact that it was fragrant?

For a moment he was overcome by utter panic. He was transfixed, as if poison were spreading all over his body. Then he got a grip on himself, took a deep breath and went on deck.

CHAPTER 37

They started work again and managed to complete eighty soundings before dusk.

That evening they were served baked flounder, potatoes and a thin, tasteless sauce. Lieutenant Jakobsson was very subdued and did no more than poke at his food.

Tobiasson-Svartman copied the day's notes into the main record book. When he had finished he felt restless and went on deck.

Once again it seemed to him that there was something glinting on Halsskär. As before, he put it down to his imagination.

That night he slept clutching his sounding lead. He cleaned it thoroughly every day, but he thought it smelled of mud from the bottom of the sea.

CHAPTER 38

He woke up with a start. It was dark in the cabin. The lead was next to his left arm. Water was lapping gently against the hull as the ship slowly rolled. He could hear the nightwatchman coughing on deck. It did not sound good, it had a rattling quality. The man's footsteps faded away as he moved aft.

He had been dreaming. There had been horses, and men whipping them. He had tried to intervene, but they ignored him. Then he understood that he was about to be whipped himself. At that point he woke up.

He checked his watch, hanging by the side of his bunk. A quarter past five. Not yet dawn.

He thought about the flash he thought he had seen on two occasions now. But surely Halsskär was just a barren rock? There could not be any kind of light there.

He lit the paraffin lamp, dressed, took a deep breath and examined his face in the mirror. It was still his own.

When he was a child – all the time he was growing up, in fact – he had looked like his mother. Now, as he grew older, his face had begun to change and he thought he could see more of his father every time he looked in a mirror.

Was there yet another face within him?

Would he ever be able to feel that he looked like himself and nobody else?

CHAPTER 39

It was hazy over the sea when he came out on deck.

The watchman with the hacking cough was sitting on the capstan, smoking. He jumped up when he heard footsteps. Hid his fag behind his back. Then he succumbed to a violent coughing fit. Scraping and rasping noises seemed to be tearing his chest.

Tobiasson-Svartman clambered into one of the tenders and untied the painter. The watchman, who had recovered from his coughing fit, asked breathlessly if the officer required an oarsman. Tobiasson-Svartman declined the offer.

The sun had not risen over the horizon as he rowed towards Halsskär. The rowlocks squeaked forlornly. In order to get to the skerry as directly as possible he lined his tender up with the starboard wing of the bridge, and did not need to change course at all. He rowed with powerful strokes and beached the boat at the same place as last time.

Halsskär gave the impression of having been crushed by a giant's hand. There were deep ravines and hollows, muddy soil had accumulated in depressions and provided a footing for moss campion and occasional clumps of wormwood. Lichens were creeping over the rocks, and sparse red heather.

He followed the shore northwards. Here and there he had to move inland when the cliffs became too steep. The terrain was in constant conflict with him, cliffs turned into precipices, rocks were slippery, every obstacle he overcame gave way to a new one.

After ten minutes he was covered in sweat. He was deep down in a crevice with steep rock walls on either side, and he could no longer see the sea. He was surrounded by stone. A snake had shed its skin at the bottom of the fissure. He continued clambering over the rocks, saw the sea once more and came to the edge of an inlet that seemed to have been carved out of the cliffs.

He stopped dead.

As far in as you could go was a rickety jetty. Moored there was a dinghy. A sail was furled around the mast, situated towards the bows. On the shore were some fishing nets hanging from hooks attached to poles that had been driven down among the stones. There was also a big washtub made of tarred oak, a heap of stones for weighing down the nets, and some floats made of bark and cork.

He stood motionless, taking in what he saw. He was surprised to find that a skerry so far out in the archipelago, next to the open sea, was being used by fishermen and bird-hunters. They could not very well be seal-hunters as there were no rocks or skerries in the vicinity of the Sandsänkan lighthouse where grey seals were known to bask. You would have to go further into the archipelago for that, to the shallows east of Harstena.

He continued walking along the shore towards the sheltered inlet, and noted that the dinghy was well looked after. The sail furled round the mast was not patched and the sheets were whole rather than being knotted together from odds and ends of line. The nets, hanging neatly from the hooks, were small-meshed and evidently intended for catching herring. Furthest in was a well-worn path leading towards dense thickets of dog rose and sea buckthorn. The path meandered on beyond the thickets and between two large outcrops. Beside it, to his surprised delight, he observed a freshwater spring.

Then he came upon a patch of level ground and a little cabin squatting in the shadow of a cliff wall. It had a brick chimney, and a thin wisp of smoke was rising skywards. The foundation was of rough stones, and the walls were made of grey planks, varying in width, none of them planed. The roof was patched with moss, but its base was a layer of turf. There was only one window. The door was closed. There was a little vegetable patch alongside the cabin. Nothing was growing in it at present, but somebody had made the effort of covering it with bunches of seaweed, to act as fertiliser. Further away, next to the cliff wall, was a potato patch. He estimated it to be twenty square metres. It too was blanketed in seaweed mixed with old, dried potato haulm.

At that very moment the door opened. A woman emerged from the cabin. She was wearing a grey skirt and a dishevelled cardigan; she was carrying an axe, and her hair was long, golden and braided into a plait tucked into her cardigan. She caught sight of him and gave a start. But she was not scared and did not raise the axe.

Tobiasson-Svartman was embarrassed. He felt as if he

had been caught in the act, without knowing what the act was. He raised his hand to the peak of his cap and saluted her.

'I didn't mean to come creeping up on you,' he said. 'My name is Lars Tobiasson-Svartman, I'm a commander but not the master of the naval vessel that's anchored off the east side of the skerry.'

Her eyes were bright and she did not lower her gaze.

'What are you doing? I've seen the boat. It anchors here day after day.'

'We're sounding depths and checking if the sea charts are reliable.'

'I'm not used to seeing ships lying at anchor out here among the shallows. Even less to finding people on the island.'

'The war has made it necessary.'

She did not take her eyes off him.

'What war?'

He could tell that she was genuine. She did not know. She walked out of the door of a cabin on Halsskär and did not know that there was a major war in progress.

Before answering, he glanced at the door, to see if her husband might put in an appearance.

'There has been war for several months now,' he said. 'A lot of countries are involved. But here in the Baltic it's mainly the German and Russian Fleets stalking each other and hoping to strike a telling blow.'

'What about Sweden?'

'We're not involved. But nobody knows how long that will last.'

Silence. She was young, could not have been thirty. Her face was entirely honest, like her voice.

'How's the fishing going?' he asked politely.

'It's hard.'

'No herring about, then? Any cod?'

'There are fish about. But it's hard.'

She put the axe down on a chopping block. Next to it was a collection of branches and driftwood for making firewood.

'I rarely have visitors,' she said. 'I've nothing to offer you.'

'Oh, that's all right. I'm going back to my ship now.'

She looked at him. He thought she had a pretty face.

'My name's Sara Fredrika,' she said. 'I'm not used to being with people.'

She turned and vanished into the cabin.

Tobiasson-Svartman stared for ages at the closed door. He hoped against hope that it would open and that she would come out again. But the door remained closed.

Then he went back to the *Blenda*. Lieutenant Jakobsson was smoking by the rail as he clambered on board.

'Halsskär? Is that what the skerry's called? What did you find there?'

'Nothing. There was nothing on it.'

They continued with their work, lowering and raising the sounding leads through the water.

All the time he was thinking about the woman who

had emerged from the cabin and looked him straight in the eye.

Towards mid-afternoon a wind got up from the south-west.

Just as they finished work for the day it started raining.

PART III

Fog

CHAPTER 40

The first snow fell on 15 November.

It was dead calm, the bank of dark cloud came rolling in from the Gulf of Finland. The snow was slight at first. The thermometer showed minus two degrees and the barometer was falling.

The previous evening Tobiasson-Svartman had noted in his journal that they had been working for twenty-one days and had three rest days. He calculated that they should have finished sounding the new route, from the Sandsänkan lighthouse to the Gryt area of the northern archipelago and the approach to Barösund, by 1 December. Then the *Blenda* would move south to Gamlebyviken where a small area of the approach channel needed to be measured again.

However, Naval Headquarters had issued a warning that this second stage might have to be postponed until New Year, 1915. In that case Tobiasson-Svartman and his colleagues would return to Stockholm and wait there.

He was still not sure whether it would be possible to shorten the whole route from Halsskär westwards. There was one area that worried him. It was a badly charted stretch where certain indications suggested dramatic irregularities on the seabed. But were these isolated projections which he could ignore? Or was there an underwater ridge that would force him to restrict changes that could be made to the route?

He was not sure. His worry was his alone. He shared it with nobody else.

When he settled down in his bunk and blew out the paraffin lamp, he wondered why he had still received no letter from his wife. The destroyer *Svea* had rendezvoused with them on six occasions. Every time, he had handed his main record book over to the cryptographers, spoken to Rake about the war and drunk a glass of brandy, and before leaving had passed over his letter. He had always been sure that this time she would have answered, but Rake never had any mail for him.

Another thought came into his head. It was now two weeks since he had met the woman on Halsskär. He felt an increasing need to go back to the skerry. Two mornings in succession he had untied the painter and set off in one of the tenders, but at the last moment changed his mind. The temptation was strong, but forbidden.

He wanted to go there, but he did not dare.

The snow became heavier. The sea was calm, blue-grey. The black clouds crept past. Lieutenant Jakobsson came out on deck with a scarf wrapped round his head and a peaked cap. One rating burst out laughing, then another, but Jakobsson was not angry: he seemed to be amused.

'This is totally against the rules,' he said with a smile. 'Scarves are for old women, not for ships' masters in the

Swedish Navy. But there's no denying that they keep your ears nice and warm.'

Then, to the general surprise, he bent down and scooped up some snow from the ship's deck and managed to shape it into a snowball despite his deformed hand. He threw it at Sub-Lieutenant Welander's back.

'Swedes practise to become soldiers or sailors by fighting snowball battles as they grow up,' he shouted, pleased with himself to have scored a bullseye.

Welander was surprised, shook the snow from his overcoat; but he said nothing, just turned on his heel and walked to the rope ladder and climbed down into his launch. Jakobsson watched him all the way. He frowned.

'Sub-Lieutenant Welander's launch has been given a secret nickname,' he confided to Tobiasson-Svartman. 'The crew think I don't know about it, but the most important task for a commanding officer, second only to making sure that his ship doesn't set sail for Hell, is to know what rumours and whispers are circulating among his crew. I have to be aware if one of the crew is being badly treated. I don't want a case like Richter's on my ship, somebody who gets bullied so badly that he prefers to jump into the sea. Sub-Lieutenant Welander's launch is known as "The Shilly-Shally". It's a malicious name, but an accurate one.'

Tobiasson-Svartman understood. Welander was sometimes in two minds about various sounding results and demanded, quite unnecessarily, a second measurement.

'What do they call my boat?' he said.

'Nothing. That's surprising. Sailors are generally an

inventive crowd. But your crew doesn't seem to have discovered a weakness in you that warrants the smashing of an invisible bottle of champagne against the bows and presenting the boat with a nickname.'

Tobiasson-Svartman felt relieved. He had not made himself vulnerable without knowing it.

Jakobsson suddenly pulled a face.

'I have a shooting pain in my arm,' he said. 'Perhaps I've strained it.'

Tobiasson-Svartman decided he would raise the matter he had been suppressing ever since coming on board.

'I sometimes wonder about your hand, of course.'

'Everybody does. But very few satisfy their curiosity. In my view it displays disgraceful cowardice not to dare to ask those you work with about their physical defects. The world is full of admirals who walk around with their heads under their arms, but no subordinate dares to ask them about their state of health.'

Jakobsson chuckled merrily.

'When I was a child I used to fantasise and say my hand had been injured in a pirate attack in the Caribbean,' he said. 'Or munched by a crocodile. It was too uninteresting and woeful to admit that it had always looked as it does now. Some people have a club foot, others are born with a hand that looks like a club. I still prefer to think that I came by it from a swarthy knave and his bloodstained cutlass, but it goes against the grain to tell lies to a fellow officer.'

The snow was now falling very heavily. Welander's launch was already on its way to the greyish white buoys that marked where the previous day's soundings had finished.

Tobiasson-Svartman boarded his launch, the ratings started rowing and he prepared his lead. As it was snowing he had his chart, notebook and pens in a waterproof oilskin wallet.

The ratings were shivering in the snow. Two of them had bad colds and their noses were running. Tobiasson-Svartman was furious. He hated people with runny noses. But, of course, he made no comment. He was one of the disgraceful cowards Lieutenant Jakobsson had recently referred to.

They rowed towards the buoys. He stood in the stern, gazing at Halsskär and thinking about Sara Fredrika. The thought of her husband made him jealous.

The snow continued falling.

He felt as if the sea were keeping watch on him, like a sharp-eyed animal.

CHAPTER 41

Shortly after ten o'clock Welander shouted that he had come across a significant underwater peak. Over twenty metres the depth of water had decreased from sixty-three metres to nineteen. It was like coming upon a cliff wall that had risen unnoticed beneath the surface of the sea. Tobiasson-Svartman sank his own lead. The last sounding, a mere ten metres astern, had been fifty-two metres. He held his breath, hoping for the same measurement again. But his lead came to a stop after only seventeen metres. What he had feared had come to pass. They had hit upon an underwater ridge that had not previously been marked on charts.

The sea had raised its voice and refused to cooperate.

Instead of continuing along the transit line, he requested readings at right angles to the course the launches had been following so far. They must find out if the ridge was a long one or just an isolated stack. They took soundings every three metres and shouted the results to each other. Welander found depths of 19, 16, 16, 15 and then suddenly 7 metres, thereafter 7 again, then 4, followed by another jump to 2 metres. For a further stretch of a hundred metres the distance to the seabed was between 2 and 3 metres.

Tobiasson-Svartman had the same result. This was no minor irregularity: they had come across a stretch of shallow water that for some reason had hitherto been missed. Off the top of his head he could not remember it being mentioned as a good place for herring fishing in old documents describing the best fishing grounds around the Sandsänkan lighthouse.

The snow was falling even more heavily. He felt disappointed. The sea had tricked him.

He shouted to Welander, instructing him to stop work for the day. The thoroughly soaked ratings came to life. One of them yawned noisily as he took hold of his oar. A lump of yellowish-green snot was trickling down his upper lip. Tobiasson-Svartman stood up abruptly and hit the sailor in the face with the chart pouch. It was a hard blow, and blood appeared immediately on the rating's lip.

It all happened so quickly that nobody had time to react.

Weakness, Tobiasson-Svartman thought. Now I have made myself vulnerable. I lost control.

The ratings carried on rowing. He sat with his eyes fixed on Halsskär. Nobody spoke.

Over dinner, which consisted of roast beef, potatoes and pickled gherkin, he told Lieutenant Jakobsson about the invisible cliff wall.

'What are the implications?' Jakobsson asked.

'I shall be able to relocate the navigable channel closer to the mainland, but it will not be as wide as I had hoped.'

'So it hasn't been a complete failure?'

'No.'

He went on to speak of the other incident.

'I gave a rating a good dressing-down today. It was necessary. He wasn't rowing as he should have been. I hit him with the chart pouch.'

Needless to say, Jakobsson knew about it already. He smiled.

'Naturally, the crew has to be punished if they don't obey orders or fail to carry out their work properly. I must ask you, though, from curiosity purely, what are you doing when you are not "rowing as you should be"?'

'He was lazy.'

Jakobsson nodded slowly, and eyed him quizzically.

'I didn't think a shipping lane could be such a personal matter,' he said. 'I can understand that a ship might be. I have seen old captains and bosuns weep when their ship has been towed away to the breaker's yard. But a navigable channel?'

Tobiasson-Svartman thought he ought to respond to that. But he could not think of anything to say.

CHAPTER 42

He finished his meal and left the mess. When he came out on deck he stopped to gaze in the direction of Halsskär, which was invisible in the dark. He tried to imagine what Sara Fredrika's husband looked like, and wondered if there were any children in the grey cottage.

A slight breeze had got up from the south. He could feel that the mercury had risen above freezing point.

It had stopped snowing.

He sat down at the table in his cabin and tried to deal with his disappointment. He had made a mistake, he had assumed that he would triumph. He had been convinced that he could change an arc into an almost straight line on the sea chart, give naval vessels more protection, and above all enable them to approach land or head out to sea at faster speeds. Although he knew from experience that a navigable channel was like an invisible obstacle course, he had allowed himself to approach the mission with too much confidence.

The sea had not tricked him. It was he who had failed to show sufficient respect. He had committed a grave sin: he had guessed.

* * *

The paraffin lamp started smoking. As he adjusted the flame a memory came to him. His father had once lapsed into one of his most furious rages when Lars arrived late at the dinner table because he had guessed the time and got it wrong. With a bellow his father had boxed his ears and sent him to bed without food.

To be late was to desecrate other people's time. Guessing could be an amusing game, but was never permissible in connection with dinner or other serious matters.

Such as being responsible for checking the depth of secret naval channels.

He wrote up the notes he had made during the day and worked out a plan for how they would continue their work. They would be forced to retreat about 150 metres. When they came to the previous course of the navigable channel they would start sounding again.

He calculated how long it would take. Provided nothing unforeseen happened, they should be finished by 1 December even so.

He put the main record book away, turned down the flame and stretched out on his bunk. There was a faint creaking from the hull. He could hear the watchman walking over the deck. Somebody coughed. He thought how there always seemed to be a coughing epidemic on board a naval vessel. It rattled like an echo through the collective chest of ships. When on board a warship you could be certain that the wind and the sound of the engines would always be accompanied by somebody coughing.

He pictured the crew of a big battleship, perhaps two thousand men, standing on parade and coughing in unison while their superiors looked on.

He thought about the sailor he had struck. What did he know about him? He was nineteen, came from inland, Vimmerby, and was called Mats Lindegren. That was all. The lad spoke an almost incomprehensible dialect, often smelled of sweat and gave the appearance of being frightened. He was an insignificant person with a pale, pimply face, and unnaturally thin to boot. There was something vague and elusive about him. It was incomprehensible that he should have joined the navy, even if he was not among the worst when it came to being seasick. He knew as much from Lieutenant Jakobsson, who always had people keeping a check on which members of the crew – himself included – became incapable of working during a bad storm. Mats Lindegren was one of those not affected. He was not sick, nor did he become dizzy.

There in the darkness Tobiasson-Svartman suddenly realised why he had been unable to control himself. The yawning sailor with the snotty nose had reminded him of the dead man Richter, the one who had been pulled out of the sea a few weeks ago. The similarity of their appearance, that and the fact that they had stumbled upon a big underwater ridge had shattered all his best-laid plans, had made him lose control.

* * *

He closed his eyes and thought about his wife. She was walking towards him through the darkness; he felt wholly calm deep down; the cabin was filled with a sweetish scent, and finally he managed to fall asleep.

CHAPTER 43

She followed him into his dreams.

It was 1905, they had just married and were on their honeymoon in Kristiania. The struggle over the 'to be or not to be' of the Swedish–Norwegian union was at its most troubled stage and he had made the naive mistake of going out for a walk with his wife along Karl Johan wearing his Swedish naval uniform. Just as they were passing the university somebody had shouted at him, and even in his dream he could hear that hot-tempered voice: 'Swedish bastard, go home.' He turned round, but there was no obvious culprit, just a crowd of people who looked the other way or smiled and looked down at the ground. They were staying at the Grand Hotel, and went back there immediately. Kristina Tacker had been fearful and wanted to leave right away, but he had refused. He changed into civilian clothes, they went out again and nobody had shouted at them. No one was hostile when they went to the Blom restaurant or the Grand Hotel's veranda, nor when they visited the newly built National Theatre. They saw Johanne Dybwad as Mrs Alving in a production of Ibsen's *Ghosts*, which his wife thought was disgusting. He agreed with her, to be polite, but in fact he had been disturbed and moved because the play reminded him of his own childhood and resurrected uncomfortable memories of pain and ignominy.

Thus far his dream was clear, a walk down memory lane. But then everything became chaotic. They become separated in a crowd at Bygdøy and soon afterwards he sees her with another man. He tries to pull the man away from her, but he is dead and his body is already decaying, the stink is something awful. Then suddenly everything is back at the beginning again. They walk along Karl Johan, stop at the entrance to the Blom restaurant and examine the menu, they talk about everyday things, she squeezes his arm and then the picture goes white, featureless, without content or meaning.

When he woke up he tried to interpret the dream. He had let it finish in nothing but whiteness. He had rubbed Kristina Tacker out.

His pocket watch showed three minutes to five. No hint of light yet. He lay with his eyes open, and in the darkness – the opposite of the whiteness of the dream – he decided to row to Halsskär that morning.

He had to. That was all there was to it. He had no choice.

The watchman was pacing up and down the deck.

Tobiasson-Svartman stretched out a hand and touched his sounding lead, which lay on the floor next to his bunk.

CHAPTER 44

The sea was wreathed in fog when he rowed over to Halsskär.

About halfway there the *Blenda* had faded away like a dark shadow amid all the white.

He wondered if the whiteness in his dream had presaged the fog. A fish broke the surface of the water alongside the boat with a plop. That's what pike do, he thought, but would a pike really be as far out to sea as this?

He rested on his oars and listened. The fog magnified the noises from the invisible ship. Some of the ratings had been ordered to scrape away rust. The blows of hammers and chisels bounced through the fog and reached his ears. There was no risk of his getting lost, he could navigate on the basis of the noises. He counted his strokes and when he looked ahead he saw he was close to land. He beached the tender as before, having considered rowing a bit further and tying up in the little inlet where the sailing dinghy was moored. That would save him having to clamber over the slippery rocks, but the inlet was not his, and he did not want to intrude.

He made his way to the protected natural harbour and paused to observe the dinghy. It was in the same place as last time, but the sail was not furled round the mast, it was flapping gently in the slight breeze. The nets were hanging as before, but as he approached he could smell fish. There were the remains of cod and a few flounders in the water next to the boat. He was surprised that the gulls had not already been there and eaten the lot. He walked on over the slippery rocks, slipped and cut his hand on a sharp stone. He had a handkerchief in one of his pockets, Kristina Tacker had embroidered his initials into one corner. He pressed it against his hand until the bleeding had stopped.

The door of the grey cottage was shut. Smoke was coming out of the chimney. He sat behind some large rocks and let his telescope glide over the building, the door, the walls, the window. The only moving thing was the smoke. He waited. Suddenly a black cat with a white nose appeared round one corner of the cottage. It paused and looked towards where he was sitting, one front paw poised. He held his breath. The cat moved on again and vanished into some bushes. The door opened. Sara Fredrika came out. She lifted up her skirt and squatted down. He had a glimpse of her white legs. He hesitated for a moment, then grasped the telescope and aimed it at her. Just as she stood up she looked straight at him. He jerked the telescope away and closed his eyes. She walked along the path towards the inlet where the sailing dinghy was moored, and disappeared behind an outcrop of rocks.

He stood up and half ran to the highest point of the skerry, where he could see down into the inlet. There was the creaking sound of an oar, some squeaking from a rowlock, and then he saw the boat moving away from land. She rowed with good, strong strokes, and the sail was hanging loose, flapping as if enjoying its freedom. He could see through the telescope that she had tucked her skirt above her knees, and that there were nets lying on the stern thwart. She emerged from the inlet but did not follow the line of the coast. Instead she headed for the inner archipelago where the nearest landmark was a group of bare rocks sticking up out of the water.

She tossed a cork float over the side and as the dinghy glided downwind at a fair pace she let the net go. The breeze was easterly, barely enough to cause ripples. He estimated the net to be forty-two metres long, and she quickly adjusted the flow whenever it threatened to become tangled. She knew what she was doing and wasted no time. Her blonde hair kept falling over her face, she kept blowing it away, shaking her head, and eventually hung on to a long strand with her teeth to keep it out of her way.

He lowered the telescope. Odd that she was out in the boat on her own. Was her husband ill? Was he in bed at the cottage, behind the closed door?

He made up his mind on the spot. It would be some time before she finished laying out the nets and came back to the skerry.

He walked down to the cottage. The door was still closed and there was no sign of the cat. He approached cautiously and peered in through the window. It was quite dark inside and difficult to see anything. A fire glowed in the hearth. Suddenly it flared up. There was only one room, a bed, a table and a chair inside the rough walls. He could not see anybody in there. He tried the door, knocked gently, then opened it. The room was empty. No sign of her husband. No boots, no overcoat, no pipe on the table, no shotgun on the wall. She lived there alone.

There *was* no husband. Sara Fredrika lived all alone on Halsskär.

He thought he heard the dinghy scraping against some stones in the inlet and hurried back to his hiding place behind the rocks. She soon appeared, walking towards the cottage. She glanced up at the sky then went inside.

The fog was lifting when he returned to the ship. He rowed so fast that his clothes were sticking to his body. Why was he in such a hurry?

Was he running away from something, or towards something?

CHAPTER 45

Lieutenant Jakobsson was standing by the rail, cleaning his pipe.

He smiled.

'You get up early.'

'I hope I didn't wake you?'

'If I manage to sleep, I dream I'm awake. Sometimes I don't know if I'm awake or asleep. But when I come out on deck it's the real world, and I saw that one of the tenders was missing and they said you had rowed off into the fog.'

'I need some exercise. The work in the boats isn't enough.'

He climbed up on deck and headed for the mess and breakfast. He had spent too much time on Halsskär. Work would be late in starting today.

Jakobsson followed him.

'Maybe I should accompany you,' he said, after lighting his pipe. 'Maybe you've discovered something?'

For a moment Tobiasson-Svartman thought that Jakobsson knew. Then he understood that it was an innocent question.

'There's nothing there. You can't even get ashore. But I enjoy rowing.'

'It's not something I try to do, not with my hand.'

Tobiasson-Svartman drained his cup of coffee then stood up, went back on deck and climbed down into his launch.

Sub-Lieutenant Welander gave him a clumsy salute. His launch had already cast off.

The rating Tobiasson-Svartman had struck in the face the day before had a swollen lip, but there was no snot hanging from his nostril. He had changed places and now had the oar furthest from the stern thwart. It would be harder for Tobiasson-Svartman to reach him there, should he have another fit of rage.

CHAPTER 46

Late that afternoon the *Svea* appeared on the horizon.

They stopped their work immediately. Tobiasson-Svartman had written up his notes by as early as six o'clock.

He made his way over the gangway that had been set up between the two vessels. Anders Höckert welcomed him aboard. While they were on their way to Captain Rake, he politely asked after Lieutenant Sundfeldt and Artillery Captain von Sidenbahn.

'Von Sidenbahn has done his stint and is back ashore,' Höckert said. 'That's where he prefers to be. He was damned annoyed, having to live on a moving floor. Sundfeldt is asleep – he was on bridge watch yesterday evening. He has an amazing ability to sleep, that man. Some of those who choose a seafaring life dream about being rocked to a sound night's sleep by their ship. I have a theory that says they are really longing for their mothers. So how's the work going?'

'Well.'

Höckert paused and eyed him up and down.

'Well? Neither more nor less? Just "well"?'

'Some things go brilliantly. Other days cause a few problems. Let's say, we're making progress.'

Höckert knocked on the door and opened it before Rake had a chance to respond. Then he stepped aside and vanished down a companionway.

Rake was waiting for him, his jacket unbuttoned.

He held a letter in his hand.

CHAPTER 47

He saw right away that it was from Kristina Tacker.

The handwriting was unmistakable, with marked, fancy flourishes on the capital letters. He would have preferred to leave Rake immediately and return to his cabin to read the letter.

Previously he had been worried because she had not written. Now that had changed and he was anxious to know what the letter said.

Rake picked up the brandy bottle. Tobiasson-Svartman noticed that he was wearing a black armband on his left arm.

Rake saw what he was looking at.

'My mother has died. I'll be going ashore in Kalmar and will hand the ship over to Lieutenant Sundfeldt for a few days while I deal with the funeral.'

'I'm so sorry.'

Rake filled his glass.

'My mother was 102,' Rake said. 'She was born in 1812, so if she had lived in France she might have met Napoleon. Her own mother was born sometime in the 1780s, I forget the exact year. But it was before the French Revolution. When I touched my mother's hand it often occurred to me that I was feeling the skin of somebody who in turn had touched the skin of people born in the eighteenth century. In certain circumstances it's almost incomprehensible how time can shrink.

'But it's hard to mourn a person who is 102 years old. For the last ten years she hasn't known who I was. Sometimes she thought I was her late husband, my own father, that is.

'Extreme age is a spiritual pitched battle fought in the dark. A battle that inevitably ends in defeat. The darkness and degradation of old age is something for which religions have never been able to offer us consolation or a satisfactory explanation.

'But death can come suddenly and unexpectedly even for one so very old. It might seem an odd thing to say, but death always disturbs us no matter when it comes. Although my mother was in spiritual darkness she had a strong will to live. She did not want to die, despite being so old.'

Tobiasson-Svartman made to leave, but Rake was not finished.

'There has been a military confrontation near the Gulf of Riga,' he said. 'Our clever radio operators who listen in to communications between the German and Russian ships and their high commands have been able to confirm the engagement. It happened at the end of last week. One German cruiser was damaged by torpedoes, but was able to limp back to Kiel. Two Russian vessels, a torpedo boat and a troopship, were torpedoed and sank.'

'Is there anything to suggest that Sweden might be drawn into the war?'

'Not a thing. But there are opinions, of course. Mine, for one. I think we should join in on the German side.'

Tobiasson-Svartman was astonished. The captain was openly declaring that he was opposed to Swedish neutrality, which had been decided on by parliament and the government. A vigorous Navy Minister would have stripped him of his command forthwith if he had heard what Rake had just said. But it was an open question whether a Navy Minister would dare to fall out with his senior officers.

Rake seemed to read his thoughts.

'Obviously it is forbidden to say something like that. But I'm not especially concerned about the consequences. If the worst comes to the worst, I can always plead diminished responsibility due to the sudden death of my mother.'

He stood up. The audience was over. He handed over the letter and opened the door leading to the deck. Rake accompanied Tobiasson-Svartman to the gangway sloping steeply down to the gunboat's deck.

'I keep thinking about that dead German sailor,' he said. 'There will now be lots of dead bodies floating around in the Gulf of Riga. All seas are graveyards, but there are no remains at the bottom of the Baltic. It is a big cemetery that is devoid of any human remains. The lack of calcium means that bodies and skeletons very quickly decay here, or so I've been told.'

They said their farewells when they came to the gangway. Rake asked how the work was going.

'Some days everything goes well, other days bring setbacks. But we are making progress,' Tobiasson-Svartman said.

On the way down the gangway he stumbled. For a moment he was in danger of dropping the letter.

CHAPTER 48

He shut himself away in his cabin and sat down to read the letter.

Suddenly he was overcome by the conviction that she had not written before because she had been unfaithful. The letter was bound to contain a confession that she had met somebody else. He sat for a long while with the letter in his hand, not daring to open it.

The letter contained nothing of what he had feared.

First she apologised for the delay in writing. She had been unwell for a few days and unable to write. Then their maid, Anna Beata, had left without warning. Perhaps she had got herself pregnant – it had not been possible to extract any sensible reason for her resignation. That had meant she was forced to turn to Fru Eber, who had an agency for domestic servants in Brahegatan, and then she had had to interview the applicants. It had taken several days and evenings before she was in a position to appoint a girl from Ödeshög who spoke in a funny dialect but had good references, including one from the head-master of the grammar school in Södertälje – she had worked for him, it seemed. She was also called Anna, was twenty-seven, and Kristina Tacker described her as 'on the chubby side, with large, foolish eyes, but she seems reliable and honest. She is also strong, which could be useful as our carpets are heavy.'

The letter ended with her saying how much she missed him, how empty and dreary the flat seemed, how frightened she was by the war, and how she hoped he would soon come back home. He put the letter down and felt guilty about having suspected the worst. He had a wife who opened her heart to him, a letter that had been delayed by a maid who might have been made pregnant in the bushes at Djurgården and no longer wanted to fulfil her duties. He had a bad conscience about leaving her on her own to take care of all the practical details that she might have difficulty in coping with. She was like one of her own china figurines.

It seemed to him that what he was feeling must be love. The tension that had eased, his bad conscience and her fragrance that filled the cramped cabin.

He wrote a reply immediately: he made no mention of Rudin's illness and death, nor did the dead German soldier feature in the letter. He was afraid that any such detail would only worry her the more. He wrote positive things about the sea that had a mind of its own, the endless hours in the launch, the lonely mealtimes. And how he longed for her and dreamed about her every night.

When he had finished, it dawned on him that not a word of it was true. Nothing he had written was genuine. It was all fantasy, empty poetry, nothing more.

It was as if something had come between him and Kristina Tacker. He knew what it was. Or, rather, who it was. It was Sara Fredrika, the woman who lived alone on Halsskär.

It was as if *she* was in his cabin here and now, with her skirt pulled up above her knees.

He went out on deck and gazed at Halsskär. It was hooded in darkness.

That was where he was heading for.

Late that night, just before midnight, Anders Höckert came across from the *Svea* and returned the main record book, which had been copied.

Tobiasson-Svartman handed him the letter he had written to his wife. Höckert invited him to join a game of cards that was in progress in the destroyer's wardroom.

He declined.

He lay awake. He was longing to be with the woman on Halsskär.

CHAPTER 49

The *Svea* weighed anchor during the night.

He was woken by the powerful vibrations as the destroyer backed away from the *Blenda*. The letter to his wife was on its way. The carrier pigeon was made of steel and instead of wings it had powerful steam engines.

CHAPTER 50

When he got up at dawn he was greeted by Lieutenant Jakobsson looking grim. He asked Tobiasson-Svartman to accompany him to the bows of the ship.

Lying among several large capstans was Sub-Lieutenant Welander. He was covered in vomit and smelled strongly of spirits. There was an empty vodka bottle between his feet. His hair was matted, his eyes bloodshot and when he tried to stand up he was incapable of maintaining his balance and fell backwards among the hawsers.

Jakobsson watched him in disgust.

'I suspected something like this,' he said. 'I could sometimes smell it, but he'd turn away and speak with his mouth almost closed. I've been waiting for the bubble to burst. Well, it has burst now. We'll let him lie here for the time being.'

They went to Welander's cabin. Beneath his bunk Jakobsson unearthed a collection of bottles, most of them empty, some unopened. He made a rough calculation.

'Sub-Lieutenant Welander has drunk a litre of spirits per day since he came on board. Only an advanced alcoholic can drink that much. He has done his job and not given himself away. But there are limits. He passed the alcoholic's meridian last night. Everything has fallen to pieces, he couldn't give a fig for his responsibilities or his reputation. He couldn't care less about his commission or his family. All he cares about is his damned bottles. It's tragic but not unusual. And very Swedish.'

They went back on deck. Jakobsson gave the order to carry Welander back to his cabin. They watched the sorrowful procession, with Welander's arms hanging limply between two strong ratings.

'He must leave the ship immediately, of course,' said Jakobsson. 'I'll send for the gunboat *Thule* to take him to port. But how are we going to resolve the business of his launch?'

Tobiasson-Svartman had started working on that problem the moment he saw the drunken officer sprawled among the hawsers. At the same time he was asking himself why he had not suspected that Welander was concealing his alcoholism behind a mask of correctness. He was irritated that Lieutenant Jakobsson had sharper eyes than he did.

He preferred not to wait for another naval engineer. One of the oarsmen in Tobiasson-Svartman's boat, Karl Hamberg, was older and more experienced than the rest. He could take over the responsibility until the soundings in this area were completed. The people in charge in Stockholm could come up with a successor to Welander for the next stage, the soundings at the approaches to Gamlebyviken.

Jakobsson listened to his proposals and gave his approval. Hamberg was a conscientious and energetic sailor from Öland. They called him in and explained the situation. He seemed to be honoured and not overawed by the responsibility he was being given.

Late that afternoon the *Thule* set sail from Slätbaken to fetch Welander. The crews of the launches watched with interest as Welander staggered over to the sister ship.

Tobiasson-Svartman could hear the oarsmen muttering contentedly among themselves. They made no attempt to conceal their *Schadenfreude* over the fact that an officer had been caught out.

Never again would Tobiasson-Svartman meet Sub-Lieutenant Welander. The thought scared him. It was like a cold wave hitting him from behind.

I will never learn how to cope with leave-taking, he thought. Never ever. Every leave-taking implies a threat.

CHAPTER 51

That evening he felt restless and started listing his assets.

He had settled into his bunk and snuffed out the paraffin lamp. Then it took possession of him, as if he were starving. He lit the lamp again and took out the black notebook in which he wrote up his accounts.

It was a habit he had inherited from his father. Throughout his childhood and youth, at the most unlikely times, sometimes at midnight, but just as often at dawn, Hugo Svartman would sit hunched over his black notebooks, checking his assets and the stock exchange index.

Hugo Svartman had left a fortune. When he died in 1912, his estate was valued at 295,000 kronor. Most of it was in equities, bonds and debentures. There was also a portfolio of industrial shares. He had invested mainly in Separator, Svenska Metallverken and Gasaccumulator.

His son calculated, checked, crossed out and started all over again. It was as if he were suffering from a fever. By two in the morning he felt satisfied. His insecurity had melted away.

Not only were his assets still there, they had grown. Since the death of his father the fortune had swollen to more than 300,000 kronor. The share index had shot up after the outbreak of war. Trenches and naval battles supplied the stock exchange with bloodstained energy.

He put out the light and lay down ready for sleep, on his left side, with his hands clenched by his crutch.

He was at peace.

CHAPTER 52

The next day it was grey and foggy again.

The temperature was plus two. He woke up with a start and saw that it was 5 a.m. He could hear the watchman walking on deck, but no coughing. It was a new watchman. They followed a rota drawn up by Lieutenant Jakobsson which, for some reason unknown, kept changing.

He stayed in his bunk until it started to get light. Then he got up and had coffee in the galley, where the cook was preparing breakfast. He climbed down into one of the tenders and pushed off, having turned down the offer of a rower.

The tender glided into the fog of its own accord. He established his course then started rowing. Somebody had oiled the rowlocks, which no longer squeaked like awkward children.

The silence was split by a desolate sound, a whining noise, possibly from birds gone astray in the fog.

When he came to the skerry he could not work out at first where he was. Nothing alters a shoreline so much as negotiating it in fog. He rowed cautiously alongside the shore, scraping the bottom now and then, and eventually found his usual landing place.

It was damp and he was freezing. The dinghy was

moored in the inlet. The sail was furled round the mast and the tiller was lying on the rocks. Nets hung wet from the hooks on the grey poles, and he gathered that she had already been out that morning and taken in the nets. He continued walking, but stopped dead when he heard a noise he could not identify. He waited until it had stopped then advanced with caution to his hiding place. He raised his head and looked down at the cottage. Fog was streaking in among the cliffs.

She was getting washed. She was naked, standing in a baler and facing him. Her hair hung down over her breasts, which were dripping wet. She was rubbing herself vigorously with a flannel, bending down for more water, quickly, as it was cold. The fog was a curtain that had been pulled aside and this performance was just for him.

A memory came to mind. A few months previously he and Kristina Tacker had gone to the Svenska Teatern and seen the young and highly praised actress Tora Teje in a play whose name he had forgotten. During one of Teje's big monologues he had undressed her in his mind's eye and she had stood there on the stage, just for him, belting out a monologue of which he could not remember a single word.

Sara Fredrika stepped out of the baler and wrapped herself in a grey linen sheet. She spent for ever rubbing her hair, it was as if she were drying a newly scrubbed floor. She emptied the baler, dressed and went indoors.

Crouching down he ran back along the path, slipped and stumbled on one of the rocks, but he did not stop until he had reached the tender. He rowed into the fog, the rowlocks had started squeaking again, he was sweating, and all he wanted to do was to get away.

What was he afraid of? He had no answer to that.

He lost his way in the fog and could not at first find the ship. Everything was strangely silent, he was forced to shout and only when he heard a response was he able to get back on course.

Jakobsson was smoking his pipe next to the rope ladder, waiting for him.

'You keep making your early-morning trips,' he said. 'Everybody has a right to their secrets. Welander had his, until the bubble burst. When will yours burst?'

Tobiasson-Svartman wondered yet again if Jakobsson knew something.

'I just row around in the fog,' he said. 'It might seem pointless, but it wakes me up, body and soul. I row myself into a state where I'm ready to do my work. It chases away all my ugly dreams. Rowing can be like getting washed.'

Lieutenant Jakobsson held out his pipe.

'I smoke. Without tobacco I wouldn't even be up to being in charge of one of the navy's old tugboats. I mean that metaphorically, I would never dream of saying nasty things about a tugboat. They are like Ardennes horses. Even if a tug doesn't have a heart or lungs, they wear themselves out in the end and eventually they are no longer capable of towing. Horses are sent to the knacker's yard, boats to the breaker's yard.'

Tobiasson-Svartman was growing tired of Jakobsson. He was a bit of a fusspot, tended to be ingratiating. And he was a damned chatterbox with bad breath and a smelly pipe. It was the same as the sailor with the snotty nose. Tobiasson-Svartman had an urge to punch him.

He had breakfast, then he went back to work. The rating who had taken Welander's place performed excellently. They broke the record that day, making 144 soundings before they had to stop work because of failing light.

All the time he was thinking about what he had seen that morning. It seemed to him more and more like a mirage, something he had not in fact experienced.

CHAPTER 53

Late that evening, when he had already fallen asleep, Lieutenant Jakobsson knocked on his door. He dressed quickly and went on deck.

Way out to sea, on the eastern horizon, tongues of fire rose up through the darkness. A naval battle was taking place.

'We have had radio telegrams to the effect that something big and possibly crucial was in the offing,' said Jakobsson. 'The Russian and German fleets have come up against each other. People will die tonight in a mixture of steam and fire, they'll be blown to pieces, drown.'

The flashes came and went, shooting up into the night sky. Distant rumbles and blasts could be heard.

Tobiasson-Svartman thought about the tragedy that was taking place. The heat of battle was hellish. An orchestra comprising the musicians of evil was playing out there in the darkness. Every flash in the night sky was a note that turned into a lethal projectile.

They stood on deck for a long time, watching the battle. Nobody said a word. Everybody was depressed, silent.

Shortly after three in the morning it was all over. The flames died away, the gunfire ceased. All that remained was the wind, which had veered to the east. The temperature had fallen again.

CHAPTER 54

Snow came, then drifted away. The wind remained light, alternating between east and north. They had just one day with a strong northerly gale. Tobiasson-Svartman forced the work rate up, the ratings were sometimes on their knees with exhaustion, but nobody complained.

The sea held its breath: there were fewer and fewer flocks of birds, and those, barely visible over the crests of the waves, heading due south.

The days became shorter.

All the time he was thinking about the woman on Halsskär.

CHAPTER 55

A week passed without his going back there.

He became more and more restless, wanted to go, but did not dare. Was he too close, or was the distance too far?

The *Svea* turned up, without Captain Rake, who had gone to Stockholm to bury his mother. Lieutenant Sundfeldt received him in the saloon. He had two letters. One was from his banker, Herr Håkansson at the Handelsbanken head office, and the other from his wife.

They conversed briefly. The cryptographers collected his record book.

When he returned to his cabin he first read the letter from Håkansson. The stock exchange was still reacting bullishly to the war. There was no reason to worry. The war meant rising share prices and stability in key industrial stocks.

His banker advised him to consider buying into Russian Telecom and Bofors Gullspång, both of which had just posted good profits forecasts.

He spent some time just holding the letter from his wife. Eventually he decided not to open it. It was as if he already knew what was in it, and it upset him. He tucked it into some pages in an old atlas he had in his travel archive.

Then he sat down at his little table. How should he reply to a letter he had not read?

He scribbled a few lines: he had a bad cold, a sore throat. Every evening his temperature varied between 37.9 and 38.8. But he was managing to cope with his work, which was now entering a crucial phase. He thanked her for her letter, and told her he loved her. That was all.

In his heart, he knew that he would soon return to Halsskär.

CHAPTER 56

By 27 November they had reached the point in their soundings where the new section of the navigable channel would join the old one.

It was further and further to row there from the mother ship. Lieutenant Jakobsson had offered to move the *Blenda*, but Tobiasson-Svartman had insisted that she remain where she was.

'My calculations regarding the new channel are based on the point where the *Blenda* has been anchored all the time. It would make matters more awkward if the ship were to be moved now,' he said.

Jakobsson accepted that response. He could not know that Tobiasson-Svartman did not want the *Blenda* to come too close to Halsskär.

On that morning he noted that the ship's barometer was falling. The slowness of the change might suggest that there was no major storm on the way, but he suspected that the weather would soon deteriorate significantly. The first dramatic storm of winter was looming.

This was the sign he had been waiting for. Swiftly he packed some of the dried food he always took with him on his travels, in case something unexpected happened. Without anyone noticing, he also paid a visit to the ship's store and took a few red flares. He rolled an extra sweater and some warm socks in an oilskin coat and placed the parcel in one of the tenders.

As he rowed away from the *Blenda*, the wind was gathering strength. He was sure that a storm would be over them from the north in an hour or so.

This time he decided to row into the little inlet where the tender would be less exposed. The dinghy was there. He beached the tender on the shingle and tied the painter round the base of a robust juniper bush.

It was just turned eight. There was a moment of calm, then the north wind set in. He waited in the inlet until he was certain the storm had come to stay. Then he clambered up to the highest point on the skerry and fired one of the flares. The crew of the *Blenda* would know that he was safe on the island and would stay there until the storm eased.

He hurried back to the tender, collected the parcel and followed the path to the cottage. The door was closed, smoke was rising from the chimney. He sat behind his rock, waiting for the rain. He stayed there until he was wet through. Then he emerged from behind the rock.

CHAPTER 57

She opened the door.

When she recognised his face she stepped to one side. No sooner had he entered the cottage than he wanted to turn and run out again. It was as if he had been enticed into a trap that he had set for himself. What was there for him to do here? This is madness, he thought, but a madness that I have been longing for.

She put a stool in front of the open fire.

'The storm blew up unexpectedly,' he said, holding his hands towards the fire.

'Storms always blow up unexpectedly,' she said.

She was keeping her face in the shadow, away from the fire.

'I was out rowing and didn't manage to get back to the ship. I took shelter here in the inlet.'

'They'll think you've been drowned.'

'I had a smoke grenade with me that I fired. So they'll know I'm here, on Halsskär.' He wondered if she knew what a smoke grenade was, but she did not ask him to explain.

She was wearing the grey skirt. Her hair was loosely tied at the back of her head, thick locks tumbled over her cheeks. When she handed him a cup, he wanted to take hold of her.

The coffee was bitter, full of grounds. She was still keeping in the shadows.

'You can stay here, of course,' she said from the darkness. 'I wouldn't turn anybody away in weather like this. But don't expect anything.'

She sat on the bunk along the wall. It seemed to him that she was concealing herself in the darkness, like an animal.

'I read in an old tax register that people used to live on this island,' he said. 'One, possibly two families settled here. But in the end it became too hard for them, and the skerry was uninhabited from then on.'

She did not reply. The wind was crashing into the walls. The cottage was draughty, although he could see that she had tried to fill the gaps in the walls.

'I can remember word for word what it said in that tax register,' he said. 'Maybe it wasn't a tax register, but rather an official letter from an enforcement officer. I think his name might have been Fahlstedt.' He recited from memory: '"They live on a barren skerry at the mercy of the sea, they are blessed with neither fields, meadows nor forest, but compelled to derive from the open sea, many a time in peril for their lives, all things they eat and require for apparel, or otherwise are in need of."'

'It sounds like a prayer,' she said. 'Like a priest.'

She was still in the dark, but her voice had come closer. Her voice had that special timbre that comes from being at sea and shouting from boat to boat, shouting in gales and headwinds. Her dialect was less pronounced than he had heard in others from these parts. There were sailors on board the *Blenda* who came from this section of the archipelago, one from Gräsmarö, and another was the son of a pilot from Häradskär. There was also a stoker from Kättilö and he spoke exactly as she did, like the voice from the dark.

Suddenly she emerged from the darkness. She was still sitting on the bunk, but she leaned forward and looked him in the eye. He was not used to that, his wife never did that. He looked away.

'Lars Tobiasson-Svartman,' she said. 'You are a naval officer and wear a uniform. You row around in stormy weather. You have a ring. You are married.'

'My wife is dead.'

It sounded perfectly natural, not the least bit strained. He had not planned to say that, but on the other hand, he was not surprised at it. An imagined sorrowful event became reality. Kristina Tacker had no place in this cottage. She belonged to another life that he was keeping at a distance, as if looking at it through the wrong end of a telescope.

'My wife Kristina is dead,' he said again, and thought that it still sounded as if he were telling the truth. 'She died two years ago. It was an accident. She fell.'

How had she fallen? And where? How could he bring about the most meaningless of deaths? He decided to throw her over a cliff. The woman sitting here in the darkness would understand that. But he couldn't let her die alone. Inspiration was flooding into him with irrestible force.

She would have a child with her, a daughter. What

should he call her? She must have a name that was worthy of her. He would call her Laura. That was the name of Kristina Tacker's sister, who had died young, coughing her lungs away with tuberculosis, Laura Amalia Tacker. The dead gave the living their names.

'We were travelling in Skåne. At Hovs Hallar, with our daughter Laura. She was six years old, an angel of a girl. My wife stumbled on the edge of the cliff, and happened to bump into our daughter, and they went hurtling down. I couldn't reach them in time. I shall never forget their screams. My wife broke her neck in the fall, and a sharp piece of rock dug deep into my daughter's head. She was still alive when they raised her up the cliff. She looked at me, as if accusing me, then died.'

'How can you bear such sorrow?'

'You bear it because you have to.'

She put some cut branches into the fire. The flames seemed to gather strength from the green wood.

He noticed that he was enticing her closer. It was as if he were directing all her movements. He could see her face now. Her eyes were less watchful.

It had been very easy to kill his wife and his daughter.

The storm was roaring into the cottage walls. There was a long way to go before it reached its culmination.

PART IV

Autumn, Winter, Loneliness

CHAPTER 58

Their conversations were spasmodic.

He was close to her all the time in the cramped room, but it felt to him as if the distance between them grew.

Late in the afternoon she stood up and left the cottage. He made no move, but glanced surreptitiously at the window. He expected her to be standing there, watching him.

The window was empty.

He did not understand it. She was not behaving as she ought to have done. All the time when he was growing up he had kept his parents under constant observation. He would peer furtively through half-closed doors or use mirrors to see unnoticed into rooms where his parents were, together or alone or with others. In his imagination he bored invisible holes in the upstairs floor of the house they lived in at Skeppsbron, so that he could see down into his father's office.

He had learned not to reveal his presence when he listened to their angry exchanges, watched them drinking themselves silly or, as was often the case with his mother, sitting alone, sobbing.

His mother always wept silently. Her tears seemed to tiptoe out of her eyes.

These memories shot through his mind, one after the other. He walked to the window, which was coated in a thin layer of salt spray.

He caught a glimpse of her walking along the path to the inlet. He assumed that she wanted to make sure her boat was securely moored.

He looked around the room. She had just put more wood on the fire. It smelled of juniper. The light from the flames danced round the walls. In one of them was a low door, closed. He tried the handle. It was not locked and led into a windowless closet. In one corner were a few wooden barrels; sheep shears and broken carding combs were scattered on the floor as well as some folded sacks for flour. On one of the walls hung a herring net, half finished. He made a mental inventory of the room and its contents, as if it were important to remember every detail.

Sara Fredrika still had not returned. In the big room was a corner cupboard, rickety, with rusty hinges. Did he dare to open it? Would the door fall off if he did? He pressed his hand against the cupboard frame and turned the key.

On the only shelf were two objects: a hymn book and a pipe. The pipe was similar to the one Lieutenant Jakobsson usually had in his mouth. He picked it up and sniffed at it. It seemed not to have been used for a long time. The remains of the burned tobacco were rock hard. It still smelled of old tar. He put the pipe down, eyed the hymn book without touching it, then closed the door.

He squatted down and felt under the bed. There was something there. He could feel that it was an old-fashioned shotgun, but he did not take it out. He pressed his face against the pillow, trying to find traces of her smell. All he could feel was that the pillow was damp.

Damp loneliness, he thought. That's her fragrance. The thought excited him.

There had been a man in the house, a man who had left behind a well-used pipe and an old shotgun. Perhaps he was not gone altogether. Perhaps he was away selling fish in Slätbaken on the way to Söderköping. Autumn was ending, and there were markets all over Sweden.

The storm was still battering the walls. He tried to imagine the man, but was unable to give him a face.

The door flew open. Sara Fredrika was back. The cold wind rushed into the room.

'I went to check the boats,' she said. 'I've never seen one like yours before.'

'It's a tender. We have four of them, in case we need to abandon ship. And we also have two quite big launches. If the ship starts to sink, nobody need be left behind. You may find it hard to believe, but the tender is classified as a warship.'

She poked at the fire. Her movements were precise and purposeful, he noticed, but she was trying to conceal a degree of worry or impatience. She sat down on the bunk. The fire was blazing away again, and he could see her clearly. Something was welling up inside him that he could not put his finger on. Somehow or other he felt tricked, deceived. The pipe in the corner cupboard belonged to somebody who had been in this cottage, who might even have built it, who had shared her bed and who might come back.

He eyed her as he had looked at the sailor with the snotty nose. He wanted to hit her. Quickly he moved his stool back to avoid that happening. In order to have something to say he said: 'Do you not have any animals? I thought I saw a cat with bluish-grey fur. If there is such a thing as a cat with a touch of blue in its fur.'

'There are no animals here.'

'Not even a cat?'

'I wouldn't mind having a dog that could swim out and fetch the birds I shoot.'

'But I thought I saw a cat?'

'There is no cat. I know what there is on this skerry. There are two adders, one male and one female. I kill the young ones every spring. Maybe I ought to let one or two live so that the skerry doesn't become snakeless if the parents upped and died or are caught by an eagle. There was a fox here once.'

She pointed to a fox fur lying on a bench.

'Had it swum here?'

'Sometimes the winters are so cold and long that ice forms on the sea even as far out as this, and occasionally further – as far as the outermost herring grounds. That's when the fox came. It stayed when the ice melted. I shot it through the door when it was scavenging for food. It had seaweed and bits of stone in its stomach. I think it had gone mad and started chewing stones in desperation. I suppose it's worse for a fox than for a person to be all alone. But it may be easier for animals to do away with themselves.'

'Why?' he said, surprised.

'They have no god to be afraid of. Unlike me.'

He hoped she would start talking about herself. He did not care about the snakes and the fox. But she kept on about the animals.

'Seals sometimes bask on the reefs north-west of Sandsänkan if it gets too crowded on their usual rocks. Occasionally a seal comes ashore here. But there are no animals apart from those. I think this is the only skerry out here where there aren't any ants. I don't know why.'

'I see no sign of a rifle,' he said. 'But you say you shot a fox?'

She pointed under the bed she was sitting on.

'I have a shotgun. And crampons for my boots. And also a seal club. My father made it. He was born in 1851 and died when I was a little girl. No picture of him exists, nothing. A photographer from Norrköping visited the islands in the 1890s, but my father didn't want to have his picture taken. He ran away and hid in a rock crevice somewhere. Some of the old men out here used to believe they would lose the ability to aim straight at seabirds if they had their photo taken. There was a lot of superstition in the archipelago when I was a girl. That seal club is the only thing I have that belonged to my father. A club covered in dried seal blood instead of a face.'

He tried cautiously to wheedle out an answer to what really interested him.

'Are there any other people on this skerry?'

'Not any more. There used to be.'

'That's hard to understand.'

'Understand what? That anybody would stay here? I've stayed here. But there'll be no one when I've gone. When I leave, the island will revert to what it used to be. The snakes will be able to live in peace. They might multiply. There might be so many of them that no humans will dare to land here any more. Once, a long time ago, people rowed out to here. They used their ribs as oars. Now they've all gone. Even the stones that were carried up here from the shore to make the foundations for the houses have started to go away. I go out and look at them. It's like trying to watch the elevation of the land. You would have to stand in the same place for very many years to check if the land really was rising. It's the same with the stones they lugged up here, the first of the people who came to the skerry hundreds of years ago. Now the stones are slowly sliding back again, to the places they were taken from.'

He listened in astonishment. Ribs used as oars? Stones that move? What was she talking about?

'I'm not used to people,' she said. 'Not since I became alone.'

'Why do you live here on your own?'

'Is there more than one answer?'

'Either you have chosen to do so, or you haven't.'

'Who would choose loneliness?'

'Some people would. You can shut yourself away in a house, but you can also do it on an island where the sea is a sort of terrifying moat.'

'I don't understand that. I'm twenty-seven years old, nothing can scare me any more.'

'I just wonder what happened.'

A massive gust of wind shook the cottage to its foundations.

'One of these days it can simply collapse,' she shouted, in a sudden burst of emotion. 'I'll let it fall to bits all round me.'

She went on talking, in long sentences. She expressed herself clearly, as only people who talk a lot to themselves can. Afterwards, when she had fallen silent, abruptly, as if she regretted having spoken, he realised that he could no longer hear the wind. Had the storm blown over so soon?

He listened. She had shrunk back into the shadows again.

Then the wind started once more.

She had spoken without hesitation, known in detail exactly what she wanted to say. It was as if she had told the story many times, but only to herself, the story of why she was alone on Halsskär. Or perhaps, in the evenings, in the darkness, she had practised so that she could tell the story to somebody she hoped might one day come to the skerry.

He had the feeling that he had come to Halsskär for one specific reason. He had come so that she would have somebody to listen to her.

CHAPTER 59

The man whose pipe was here was called Nils Ferdinand Persson.

He had been Sara Fredrika's husband.

The story began several years ago when they were newly married and worked as domestic servants for a relative of hers, Axel Theodor Homeros Lundberg. He was well-to-do, owned farms in both Gusum and in the archipelago near Finnö and as far north as Risö. They did not enjoy working for Lundberg. He was miserly and vindictive, and the only things he seemed to like were his riding boots, which he was forever treating with seal fat. No one was allowed to touch them, not even his wife, who was scared stiff of getting a beating. They stuck it for a year, but left in acrimonious circumstances and went to live on one of the islands near Turmulefjärden. It was a very poor smallholding, but at least there was nobody there polishing boots and shouting at them. They stayed there for a year, then heard that there was an abandoned cottage on Halsskär. They were able to secure the lease cheaply, for practically nothing – a barrel of herring every spring and autumn, that was all.

They sailed out to Halsskär one chilly Sunday in March. It had been a severe winter and the ice had not altogether loosened its grip. Her husband said that nothing could be worse than loud-mouthed gentleman farmers. Houses could be made windproof, nets and drift nets could be patched up and repaired, but nobody could shut the mouth of a gentleman farmer who bellowed and yelled.

They moved in as summer approached, made repairs on the house and started to prepare for whatever was in store: autumn, winter, ice, isolation.

Every now and then farmers from the inner archipelago would appear, sailing along the channel known as Märsfjärden that led to Halsskär and Krampbådorna. They were heading for the herring fishing grounds or shooting birds, and were astonished to see Sara Fredrika and her husband. Hadn't Halsskär been abandoned a century ago? In 1807 an old spinster lived there, but she froze to death and was pecked to the bone by gulls and crows. Ever since then the skerry had been uninhabited. The outhouses had collapsed, the jetties in the inlet had rotted away and the houses that could be dismantled were moved, plank by plank, to the green islands closer to the mainland.

It was said that Nils Ferdinand Persson and his wife Sara Fredrika had their noses in the air, and people with noses in the air were the first to fall.

They were also visited by people from Åland and Finland, who were hunting seals illegally. They would shake their heads and shout warnings to them in their incomprehensible language.

Autumn arrived in September. The first storm was quite unexpected, it blew in from the east in the middle of the night and it was sheer luck that they did not have any nets out. They soon learned their lesson, and every day as night closed in they would keep a close eye on the sea, and try to identify signs indicating that dangerous winds might be approaching.

In November one of the sheep – they had two, but no cow – slipped from a rock and broke its leg. Then the surviving one died, and they were even more isolated, if that were possible.

On the morning of Christmas Day, six months after they had settled on the skerry, catastrophe struck. They had laid out nets a few days earlier when the weather was cold and clear with virtually no wind, just a gentle breeze from the south. The nets were in two shallows and did not need too many heavy stones to anchor them. They had experienced good catches there ever since early December. As the shallows had no name, Nils Ferdinand christened one of them Sara Rocks and the other Fredrika Shallows.

The storm came late on Christmas Eve. It attacked from the south, charging towards them with a dense blizzard as the first line of assault. When dawn came it was obvious that if they were not to lose their nets they would have to go out and take them in. The winds were storm force, but that couldn't be helped, they had no choice. They launched the boat and managed to haul in one of the nets. Then came a colossal wave that crashed into the starboard side of the boat and capsized it.

When she managed to get out of the floating coffin she saw her husband. He had become enmeshed in the net he had been trying to take in, and it was writhing around him like a sea monster. He fought and screamed, but was dragged down and she was unable to do anything except cling to an oar and the stern seat that had broken loose, struggle back to land and crawl to the cottage, half frozen.

That was her story. She had hewn it from deep inside her as if sculpting a block of stone with violent blows from a chisel. A block of stone, a headstone for her husband.

She said no more. It was getting dark when she finished. The shadows were lengthening.

He sat on his stool and watched while she made a soup. They ate in silence.

Tobiasson-Svartman thought: It must be like staring straight into Hell, watching somebody you love die screaming.

CHAPTER 60

That night he lay on the floor close to the fire.

His 'bed' comprised the pelt of the mad fox, some rag mats and sealskins. His 'pillow' was some logs of wood covered by his sweater. He spread the oilskin coat over him and worried that the draught would make him ill.

She had offered him the bunk. For one intoxicating moment he had thought she was inviting him to share it with her. Did she suspect what he was thinking? He could not be sure. She stroked her hair away from her face and asked him again. He shook his head, he could sleep on the floor.

She wrapped herself up in a thick quilt that he assumed was stuffed with feathers from the birds she had shot. She turned her back to him. Her breathing became deeper. She was asleep. When he adjusted the logs under his head he could hear that she had woken up, listened, then gone back to sleep.

I am not a danger as far as she is concerned, he thought. I'm not a temptation, I'm nothing.

The embers in the fire died down. He opened his pocket watch and managed with difficulty to make out the hands. It was half past nine. The cold from the floor had already started to penetrate through the skins.

The storm was still raging. The wind came and went in powerful gusts.

CHAPTER 61

His thoughts wandered to his wife moving around in their warm flat in Wallingatan. No doubt she was still awake. Last thing at night she would usually walk around from room to room, smoothing the heavy curtains in the windows, adjusting cloths and covers, straightening out a crease in a carpet.

He worked out distances, lived by checking where he was in relation to others. His wife looked for irregularities, in order to put them right. Before shutting the bedroom door behind her she would check that the flat's front door was locked and that the maid had put the light out in her room behind the kitchen.

He realised that he was having difficulty in picturing her face here in the darkness. It was in the shadowy part of his memory, he could not get through to her. Nor could he conjure up her voice, that tense, slightly harsh tone with just a hint of a lisp, barely noticeable.

He sat up. The woman in the bunk gave a snore. He held his breath.

'I love my wife,' he whispered softly, 'but also the woman in the bunk next to me. Or at least, I desire her and am jealous of the man who died screaming, tangled up in a herring net. I hate that accursed pipe she keeps hidden in her cupboard.'

Again he was tempted to creep into her bed. Perhaps that was what she expected, perhaps he had not grasped her intention when she spread the skins out on the floor. Perhaps something he could never have imagined was in store for him in this draughty little cottage.

He recalled with dismay his and Kristina Tacker's wedding night. They had spent it in a hotel, one of the suites at the Grand Hotel, paid for by her rich father. They had groped after each other in the darkness, tried to ignore each other's angst over what was about to happen. All he had hitherto experienced was some torn and well-thumbed photographs, which had been passed round furtively in various wardrooms, pictures taken in French photo studios. They showed fat women, their legs wide apart and their mouths open wide, with stuffed lion heads on the walls behind them. And he had undergone a degrading experience in a squalid room in Nyhavn. He was serving as a cadet on board the *Loke*, an old frigate that was due for the scrapyard but was making an official naval visit to Copenhagen. One evening he was off duty and got drunk in several harbourside cafés, together with the ship's mate and a petty officer. Late on he had become separated from the others, and in his drunken state had ended up in a room with a toothless old whore who dragged off his trousers, and kicked him out with a mocking laugh when it was all over. He had vomited in the gutter, a group of Danish urchins had stolen his cap, and for that he had received an almighty dressing-down from the captain the following day.

That was the sum total of his experience, and he had never asked his wife how much she knew about what was coming. It deteriorated into a convulsion with both of them scratching like tigers and in the end they had retreated to opposite sides of the bed, she crying and he confused. But as time went by they had worked it out and sealed a relationship, always in the dark, not very often.

He lay awake, listening to Sara Fredrika's breathing. He could hear that she was not asleep. He stood up, went to her bed and crept inside. To his surprise she received him willingly, naked, warm, wide open. It was, soon afterwards, as if all distance had ceased to exist. The storm could carry on raging for another day, perhaps more.

He had time. He had come close to her.

CHAPTER 62

When he opened his eyes the next morning, the storm had abated.

All was silent, and he tried to orientate himself. Silence could be large or small, but it always came from somewhere; there was a southern silence, and a northern one, and an eastern and a western.

Silence was invariably under way.

Sara Fredrika's bed was empty. She must be a very silent person. He was a light sleeper and normally woke up every time his wife got out of bed. But he had heard nothing when Sara Fredrika left the cottage.

It was cold, the embers had gone out and turned white. Without warning, the room was filled with Kristina Tacker's fragrance. He knew that she would never discard him, she would never turn in secret to another man. In the early years he had followed her like a shadow when she woke up in the middle of the night and slunk out of the bedroom. But all she ever did was go to the bathroom or pour herself a glass of water from the carafe that was on the table in the drawing room. Sometimes she would pause in front of the shelves containing the china figurines: lost in thought, so far away that he thought she might never return.

He never said anything to her. He did not think she noticed him following her.

He sometimes thought that they were like ships in crowded channels. Channels with leading lights, meaning that you had to keep a lookout straight ahead and astern, but not to either side.

The floor was cold. He stood up, put on his boots, jumper and jacket and went out. The wind had not died down completely, it still crashed into the rocks at irregular intervals. He looked around, but could not see her. He walked to the inlet where the boats were moored. Before he reached there, he took cover in a hawthorn thicket.

She was sitting in the stern of her boat, baling it out. Her skirt was hoisted over her knees, and she was holding on to a lock of hair with her teeth. He observed her and decided to christen her Sara Fredrika Kristina. But he could not imagine her in the silent rooms in the flat in Wallingatan. He could not picture her wearing a long skirt, adjusting with deft fingers the china figurines. He could not conjure her up with her skirt hoisted above her knees when he said goodbye to her in the hall before setting out on one of his missions.

Not being able to find a place for her in his life made him so upset that he started panting. He backed out of the bushes and clambered up on to a rock from which there was a more open view of the sea, and where the wind was more biting.

He thought about what he had said to her the

previous evening, about his wife and daughter being killed. Whenever he lied to his father he felt ill or suffered diarrhoea. Terror was at home in his stomach, and always tried to flee through the dark passages of his guts.

But now? Having killed off Kristina without her knowing was a special triumph.

He contemplated the *Blenda*, riding the waves some way out to sea. He tried briefly to erase the ship from his consciousness. No Lieutenant Jakobsson, no crew, an empty sea, navigable channels meaningless. The only thing in existence was this rock, and Sara Fredrika. But it was not possible to erase the ship, nor the ship's master, nor the navigable channels; it was not possible to erase himself.

He went down to the path again, stamped on the stones so as not to surprise her. When he got there he saw how dirty her skirt was. There were layers of muck. The light was clearer now that the clouds had scudded away, and it was not possible to disguise the filth. He could see that her hair was matted and sticky thanks to all the grease and sea salt. Her hands were black, her neck coated in dirt. But she did wash, he thought, confused. I saw her naked. The dirt must have some recent cause.

She had stowed away the baler and left the boat. As he approached her now, he noticed that she smelled of everything associated with being unwashed, of sweat and urine. Why hadn't he noticed that before, in the cottage? Why now, out in the open?

'It wasn't much of a storm,' she said. 'The weather was impatient.'

'They say that a storm lasts for three days,' he said. 'It takes three days for a storm to declare itself the winner.'

I'm talking rubbish, he thought. I know nothing about a storm lasting for three days, I know nothing about what people ought to believe or not believe about a storm.

'Now you can row back to the ship,' she said.

He held out his hand. She hesitated before shaking it. Then she took back her hand, like a shot. Like a fish that changes its mind and spits out the bait it has tasted.

She went back to the cottage and fetched his oilskin coat. He untied the painter, the boat scraped over the stony bottom and he jumped aboard.

There is still a possibility, he thought. A moment when everything could change. I can confess that what I told her yesterday was a lie.

But, of course, he said nothing. She remained on the shore, watching him.

She did not raise a hand to wave. A bit like when you know that somebody who is leaving will never return, he thought.

CHAPTER 63

The days grew shorter, darker, and the sea more choppy.

One afternoon a lone seal swam past, on its way to a distant reef. Flocks of migrating birds headed south, especially at dusk.

Lars Tobiasson-Svartman used the term 'chapter' in his private diary concerning the various stages of the depth-sounding mission. Now the chapter involving Sandsänkan and Halsskär would soon be concluded. The new navigable channel would reduce the north–south passage by a little more than one nautical mile. Another advantage was that ships would be able to come rather sooner into the protection afforded by the islands from mines and U-boat attacks.

So far his mission had enjoyed good fortune. Apart from the matter of the unanticipated underwater ridge, his soundings had gone far better than expected.

But there was one thing that disturbed Tobiasson-Svartman. When he returned to the mother ship after the storm, Lieutenant Jakobsson had made no attempt to conceal his anger at Tobiasson-Svartman's absence. He was openly sceptical, hardly bothered to speak to him and asked no questions about the night spent on the skerry. At first Tobiasson-Svartman thought that his superior's unsympathetic behaviour was a passing phase, but it persisted. He made cautious attempts to find out why. Jakobsson went into his shell, and did not speak over dinner.

Captain Rake had returned to take charge of his ship. Tobiasson-Svartman wrote a long letter to Kristina Tacker and handed it over for delivery three days after his night on Halsskär.

When he read through what he had written, he had the sense that what he was putting into the envelope was a packet of silence. The words had no meaning. He had written about the storm, but nothing about the night on the skerry. He wrote about life on board ship, the food and the outstandingly good cook, and nice things about Lieutenant Jakobsson. But none of it was true, none of it about what he was thinking. He was mapping navigable channels so that other people would be able to travel in safety, but the charts he was mapping for himself led to chaos.

When he sealed the envelope he had the vague idea that he was lying to avenge himself, to get his own back because his wife never dropped any of her china figurines.

CHAPTER 64

Captain Rake had a very nasty case of eczema on his cheeks and forehead. Tobiasson-Svartman felt uncomfortable when he saw Rake's face. Red patches fused together forming raised islands; yellow abscesses seemed on the point of bursting in this archipelago of spots.

Rake himself appeared unconcerned. He spoke enthusiastically about the war. The German invasion of France was going exactly as intended under the so-called Schlieffen Plan.

'It's one of the most detailed war strategies ever made,' Rake said. 'General Schlieffen devoted the last part of his life to working out the best way for Germany to crush France once and for all. He found the solution in the end. The route through Belgium, the closing in on Paris by armies forming an extensive right flank. Every eventuality is covered in this unique plan. How many railway wagons are needed to transport the troops, horses, guns and stores; precise calculations of how fast each train must travel so as to avoid jams. A great many military engineers have been turned into advanced railway administrators. Sadly, Schlieffen died some years ago and so is unable to see his strategy realised. Everything is going well. Too well, some might think. There's just one thing missing in Schlieffen's plan. Recognition of the fact that not everything can be planned. No war can be won without a moment of improvisation. Just as no significant work of art can be created without that element of irrationality that is in fact the artist's talent.'

They were drinking brandy. The cryptographer collected the main record book, Rake continued talking about the war and took Tobiasson-Svartman's letter. He had no letter from Kristina Tacker to deliver.

They shook hands on the port wing of the bridge. It was cold, and dead calm. The sky was clear.

'Sweden will probably stay out of the war,' Rake said. 'Only time will tell if that's the best thing that could have happened.'

Tobiasson-Svartman negotiated the steeply sloping gangway on to the deck of the *Blenda*. He was about to go into his cabin when he noticed the smell of pipe tobacco. He turned and saw Lieutenant Jakobsson standing by one of the gun turrets. His face was in shadow. His pipe glowed. Tobiasson-Svartman found himself feeling uneasy. The shadow of the commanding officer alarmed him.

CHAPTER 65

Four days before they were due to complete the soundings at Sandsänkan he rowed out to Halsskär again. He did not know why he wanted to see her again: the smell of sweat and urine was a kind of barrier between them. Nevertheless, he was tempted by it.

The sea was calm, dark clouds came rolling in from the south-east, the thermometer was falling. The water had an acrid smell to it, as if it were secreting some unknown substance.

He moored the tender in the inlet. The nets were hanging on the drying rack, damp and smelling of fish. He lifted the lid of a corf kept firmly in place by some stones at the side of her boat. There was a thrashing and splashing inside. He stuck down his hands and felt the scales of the writhing fish. Something stung him in the palm of the hand, a dorsal fin or a pair of teeth. He pulled his bleeding hand away. Reacting in fury, he struck out like a reptile. He overturned the corf and let the fish wriggle their way to freedom.

He remembered the drift net he had seen on one of the first mornings as he leaned over the *Blenda*'s rail. That was in the distant past now, a vague memory of an image standing for the impossible terms of freedom.

He stood the corf up again and walked away. He went to rinse his hand in the spring water, and then he lay down behind the usual rocks and aimed his telescope at the cottage. There was no smoke coming out of the chimney, the door was closed. It started to snow, a faint white glimmer in the air.

She had made no sound, but she was immediately behind him when he turned round. She was looking him straight in the eye, as if ready to pounce.

'Why are you lying here? What do you want? What have I done to you?'

'Nothing. I was looking for you, I lay down here to wait.'

'With a telescope?'

'I like to study details.'

'What have I done?' she repeated.

'Nothing. I didn't mean to frighten you.'

'You don't frighten me. What could frighten me, after all I've been through?'

She grabbed hold of his arm.

'Help me get away from here,' she said.

Her voice was hoarse, almost snarling. He could see the change in her face.

'I'm dying here,' she said. 'Help me to get away. Let me come with you on the ship. Take me anywhere, as long as it's away from here. I can't live here any longer.'

'I can't take you on a warship. Don't you have any family?'

She shook her head impatiently.

'My family is at the bottom of the sea. I row around

and fish feed at the site of my husband's grave. I sometimes expect bits of his body to come up with the nets. An arm, a foot, his head. I can't put up with that thought. I have to get away.'

'I don't think I can help you.'

Her face was close to his. It was like during the night. All the smells had gone.

'I'll do absolutely anything to avoid having to stay here.'

She ran her hands over his body. He pushed her gently away and stood up.

'I'll come back,' he said. 'I must think this over. I'll come back. In a few days. Three days, four at most.'

He hurried down to his boat. There was still snow in the air. He rowed away from Halsskär and could see her on a rock, watching him go.

She would have to wait for four days. After the fifth day the ship would already have left.

He rowed with long, vigorous strokes and longed to be back at home. Kristina Tacker sat on the stern seat, smiling at him.

His mission would soon be over.

CHAPTER 66

The next day he completed the last of the soundings.

All that was left to be done now was a final check of the area sounded. It would take two days if thc weather stayed fine.

The barometer was climbing, the worst of the snowy weather had moved away southwards.

For the last time he sent his lead plunging down to the bottom. Once again he had the overwhelming hope that this would be the moment when he discovered the place where there was no bottom, the point where the whole of his life would be dismantled and changed, but also be given a meaning. The lead stopped at nineteen metres. He made his final note. He had sent his lead down to the seabed 5,346 times since they started work on this mission.

They rowed back to the *Blenda.* The ratings seemed exhilarated, and rowed at full speed. Tobiasson-Svartman knew that for ages they had spent much of their free time cursing under their breath this boring task they had been ordered to perform.

Mats Lindegren, the sailor Tobiasson-Svartman had hit, still sat as far away from him as possible. His lip was no longer swollen, but he never looked Tobiasson-Svartman in the eye.

Lieutenant Jakobsson was standing, pipe in hand, as they winched the two launches on board. He was still uncommunicative. Tobiasson-Svartman was pleased that they would soon take leave of each other and never meet again.

He reported that the mission was complete. Jakobsson nodded, without speaking. Then he lit his pipe, inhaled deeply, coughed, and fell down on to the deck as if he had been struck a violent blow by an unseen fist.

He fell without a sound. Everything came to a standstill, the ratings stopped operating the winch's ropes and tackle, Tobiasson-Svartman was holding his notebook and lead in his hands.

The first to react was Lindegren. He knelt down and placed his fingers on the officer's neck. Then he stood up and saluted. His dialect was so hard to understand that he had to repeat what he said before Tobiasson-Svartman could understand.

'I believe Lieutenant Jakobsson is dead.'

Tobiasson-Svartman stared at the man lying on his back. He was holding his pipe in his right hand, staring fixedly at a point over Tobiasson-Svartman's head.

Lieutenant Jakobsson was carried to his cabin. Fredén, who had had some medical training, took Jakobsson's pulse in several places before confirming that he was dead. The time of death was entered into the logbook. Fredén took over command of the ship. His first duty was to write a report of what had happened for Naval Headquarters in Stockholm.

The radio telegraphist went to his cabin to send the message.

For a moment Fredén was alone with Tobiasson-Svartman. Both were shaking.

'What did he die of?'

Fredén pulled a face.

'Difficult to say. It happened so quickly. Jakobsson was still comparatively young. He drank no more than anybody else, didn't get blind drunk in any case. Didn't exactly overeat either. He occasionally used to complain about pains in his left arm. Nowadays some doctors regard that as an indication that the heart is not as healthy as it might be. The way he simply fell over could suggest a massive heart attack. Either it was his heart or a blood vessel burst in his brain.'

'He always seemed to be healthy.'

'Hymn 452,' Fredén said. '"My life's a journey unto death." We sing that whenever we have a burial on board. We sung it for the German sailor we picked up. Strangely, not many people seem to realise that Wallin, the man who wrote it, knew what he was talking about. He reminds us all of what is in store for us, if only we listen.'

He excused himself and went on deck to assemble the crew and tell them what they already knew, namely that Lieutenant Jakobsson was dead.

Tobiasson-Svartman looked at the dead man again. This was the third dead person he had seen in his life, the third dead man. First his father, then the German sailor and now Lieutenant Jakobsson.

Death is silence, he thought. That's all. Trees fallen, their roots exposed.

Above all silence. Death announces its approach by silencing men's tongues.

For a second he felt as if he himself were falling. He was forced to grab hold of the chest of drawers and close his eyes. When he opened them again, it looked as though Lieutenant Jakobsson had changed his position.

He hurried from the cabin.

CHAPTER 67

An invisible veil of mourning was being pulled over the ship.

It was dusk when Fredén assembled the ship's crew on the foredeck, and some of the searchlights were already lit. The arc lamps crackled away as night-flying insects flew into the filaments and were roasted.

Tobiasson-Svartman thought it was like watching something on a stage. A play was about to begin. Or, perhaps better, the last act and epilogue. The end of Lieutenant Jakobsson's story.

Lieutenant Fredén spoke very briefly. He urged the crew to master their emotions and maintain discipline. Then he dismissed them.

Tobiasson-Svartman could not sleep that night, even though he was hugging his lead. He got up at midnight, dressed and went out on deck. His mission was over, he was surrounded by death, there was a woman on a skerry when he desired and he both longed for and dreaded the imminent meeting with his wife. He had measured the depth of the sea around the Sandsänkan lighthouse, but he had not succeeded in coordinating his discoveries with the navigable channels inside himself.

The ship was rocking gently in the swell. He had the feeling of being a large animal padding round a cage. The cold night made him shiver. He set off round the ship. The sailors on watch saluted him, and he nodded in reply. Suddenly he found himself outside the door of Jakobsson's cabin. Now that the ship's master was dead he no longer felt he needed to use his title when he thought about him.

He wondered where Fredén was sleeping. Until now he had been sharing a cabin with Jakobsson.

The dead man was still there. There was a lantern on the table, he could see the light under the door. He opened it and went in. Somebody had placed a white handkerchief over Jakobsson's face. The pipe had been taken from his grasp before his hands had been crossed over his chest. Tobiasson-Svartman contemplated Jakobsson's chest, as if there might be a trace of a forgotten breath.

He opened the drawer in the bureau attached to the wall. It contained a few notebooks and a framed photograph. It was of a woman. He looked furtively at the photograph. She was very beautiful. He stared at the picture as if bewitched. She was one of the most beautiful women he had ever seen. On the back was the name Emma Lidén.

He sat down and started thumbing through the notebooks. To his surprise he saw that Jakobsson had been keeping a private diary in parallel with the official logbook.

Tobiasson-Svartman glanced at the man lying with a handkerchief over his face. It felt both dangerous and amusing to penetrate his private world. He leafed through to the date when he had joined the ship.

It took him an hour to read to the end. Jakobsson had made the last entry only a couple of hours before he died. He had noted 'a pain in my left arm, some slight pressure over my chest' and reflected on why his bowel movements had been so sluggish these last few days.

Tobiasson-Svartman was shaken. The man who ended his life with a worried comment about a stomach upset had been in possession of colossal strength, of both love and hatred.

Emma Lidén was his secret fiancée, but she was already attached to another man and had several children. The diaries were full of notes about letters exchanged and then burned, of a love that exceeds all bounds, that is a blessing without equal, but can never be anything but a dream. The phrase 'woke up in tears again this morning' was repeated at regular intervals.

Tobiasson-Svartman tried to picture it. The man with the pipe and the shrivelled hand, weeping in his cabin. But the image was no more than a blur.

He could never have imagined that Jakobsson had hated him so intensely, but the lieutenant had taken a dislike to him the moment he stepped on board. 'I will never be able to trust that man. Both his reserved manner and his smile seem to be false. I have an illusion on board.'

Tobiasson-Svartman tried to recall the moment when he had met the *Blenda's* master for the first time. His own impression had been quite different. Jakobsson must have been a man turned inside out. He had not been who he was.

Tobiasson-Svartman read every diary entry for the period that he had been on board. Jakobsson never referred to him by his name, only as 'the sea-measurer', a term exuding deeply felt contempt. It sounds like a grub, he thought. A beetle that hides in the cracks of his ship.

The hatred that emerged from the diary was shapeless, like a lump of mud that spread out over the pages. Jakobsson never vouchsafed the reason for his antagonism and hatred. Tobiasson-Svartman was no more than 'a mud-dipper, repulsive, stuck-up and stupid. He also smells like sludge. He has mud in his mouth, he is a man rotting away.'

It was almost one thirty by the time he closed the last of the diaries. A half-empty bottle of brandy was sticking up out of a jackboot. He removed the cork and drank. He pulled the handkerchief aside and tipped some drops of brandy into Jakobsson's nostrils and eyes. Then he opened Lieutenant Jakobsson's trousers, eyed his wrinkled, shrivelled penis and poured brandy over that as well. He put the bottle back in the jackboot, put the handkerchief back in place and left the cabin with the diaries in his hand.

Once back in his own cabin he took out the oilskin pouch he used for his sounding notes, put the diaries inside it, together with some steel edging he had kicked loose from the floor.

He went out on deck, walked to a point by the rail where none of the lookouts could see him, and dropped the diaries into the sea.

Somewhere in the distance one of the watchmen started coughing. The moon was half full, and its reflection formed a path over the water between the ship and the Sandsänkan lighthouse.

He remained by the rail for a long time. Even if he did not recognise himself in what the diaries had said about him, he could not get away from the fact that, as far as Jakobsson was concerned, it was the truth. It was what he had taken with him into death. No one could bring it back.

CHAPTER 68

On 2 December an easterly gale was blowing over the sea to the north of Gotland.

The *Svea* had appeared on the horizon at about nine in the morning. That afternoon Tobiasson-Svartman packed his bags and said goodbye to the officers. He thanked the ratings who helped him with his work the previous day. Mats Lindegren did not put in an appearance, however; but Tobiasson-Svartman had not ordered him to turn up.

Later in the evening he was invited to a little party in the gunroom. Fredén, the new commanding officer, had given his permission on condition that they were not too noisy, in view of the fact that they had a dead man on board. One of the petty officers and the chief engineer had good singing voices and performed some sea shanties. They had drunk punch laced with liberal quantities of aquavit. When they were all drunk, of course, they started talking about the dead man. Several of the officers present maintained that Lieutenant Jakobsson had approved of and been impressed by Tobiasson-Svartman's work. He did not need to make an effort in order to appear surprised. But he did not feel up to staying long at the impromptu party and withdrew, saying he had some reports to finish.

The last he heard before dropping off to sleep was the deep but unclear male voices singing, possibly in Italian.

When he left the gunboat and walked along the gangway for the last time, he glanced over his shoulder, as if to make sure that Jakobsson had not returned to life.

Two ratings helped carry his bags to the same cabin as he had occupied at the beginning of his mission.

He stood quite still in the cabin. He was back at the beginning once more.

Captain Rake welcomed him on board. He had shaved off all his hair and gave the impression of being very tired. His left eye was infected and running. His eczema was in full bloom.

They sat down. Captain Rake served brandy, despite the fact that it was not yet noon.

'I'm a man who lives in accordance with strict routines,' Rake said. 'I hate any form of lax discipline. People can never achieve dignity if they don't recognise the importance of obeying both themselves and others. But now and then I allow myself one little step from the straight and narrow. One example is the occasional indulgence in a glass of spirits before lunch, and possibly even two.'

They drank each other's health.

'All these dead bodies,' muttered Rake out of the blue. 'On the way here my bosun Rudin died. Then you fished up that corpse wearing the uniform of a German sailor. And now Lieutenant Jakobsson. Was it his heart?'

'His heart or his brain.'

Rake nodded and stroked his shaven head. Tobiasson-Svartman noticed that Rake's finger was shaking.

'It's the tiny blood vessels we can't see that can be our weakest point,' Rake said. 'When they burst we are sent into free fall, which leads to death and the grave, or paralysis and an iron lung, to an instant's agony or long-drawn-out and horrific suffering.'

He screwed up his eyes and stared hard at Tobiasson-Svartman.

'What is your weakness? You don't need to tell me if you don't want to, of course. It's a man's right not to reveal the misery he is saddled with. Weakness and misery are the same thing in my book. It's merely a question of which word you choose.'

It seemed to Tobiasson-Svartman that his weakness was a woman who lived alone on a skerry half a nautical mile south-west of the destroyer he was on. But he did not say so. Rake was somebody he was now looking forward to saying goodbye to for ever.

'I have many weaknesses,' he said. 'It's not possible to pick just one.'

Rake stood up to indicate that the conversation was over.

'My question was a general one. We are expecting to dock at Skeppsbron tomorrow at nine in the morning. I'm afraid we can't travel at top speed.'

'Engine trouble?'

'An unfortunate decision made by Naval Headquarters. In a mistaken attempt to nurse the engines, top speeds are allowed only in actual battle situations. There are very few engineers and officers with technical qualifications at headquarters. Engines need to be stretched, not often but regularly. Otherwise there is a bigger risk of engine trouble when it really matters.' Rake gave a laugh. 'It's the same with people. We too need to be forced to work at the limit of our abilities. The difference between a machine and a person isn't all that great.'

Rake opened the cabin door and looked forward to seeing him at table that evening.

Tobiasson-Svartman went back to his cabin and lay down on his bunk. He was soon fast asleep.

He awoke with a start an hour or more later. A plaintive scraping sound was spreading through the ship's hull, indicating that anchors and cables were being pulled aboard. He got up, put on his jacket and went out on deck. The *Blenda* was out of sight. The *Svea*'s engines were throbbing, smoke was pouring out of the four big funnels. The ship turned slowly on its own axis and then set course to the north-east.

He stared hard at Halsskär, but could see nothing. The sea was frighteningly deserted.

There's something I don't understand, he thought. A warning. I am right now making a mistake, but I do not know what it is.

Halsskär faded into the mist.

Tobiasson-Svartman thought about the spot he had been looking for, the point where his sounding lead never reached the bottom of the sea.

PART V

The Dead Eyes of China Figurines

CHAPTER 69

He had slept badly the night before he arrived back in Stockholm. When he blew out the paraffin lamp he began to feel that a catastrophe was approaching. It could arrive at any time: a single German torpedo fired by an unseen submarine racing through the dark water. He lay in his cabin with sweat pouring off him and listened to the sound of the powerful engines. Rake's assurance that he would not expose the engines to undue strain did not help him. The boilers could explode without warning, create big holes under the waterline and sink the ship in less than thirty seconds.

That was his greatest dread: being trapped inside a bubble of air deep in the innards of a ship that was sinking to the bottom. Not even his screams would leave any trace. He was afraid that death would be totally silent.

It was not until dawn when the vibrations had lessened and the ship was in the inshore channel of the Stockholm archipelago that he managed to fall asleep. But the vibrations followed him into his dream.

He was in an engine room. The heat was unbearable, he was surrounded by groaning and screaming stokers with black faces, backs covered in oil, and he knew everything would soon be over. Then he noticed that one of the sweating stokers was the dead German sailor. He had a shovel in his hand, but his eyes were missing, there were only two bloody sockets.

At that moment he managed to kick himself free of the dream and rise to the surface.

He was very tired, but he got dressed and went on deck. The sea was grey, the dark, rocky skerries came and went through the mist. His exhaustion led to his eyes playing tricks. Sea and sky merged to form vague points of light, an interplay of light and shade.

The temperature had fallen during the night. He moved to the spot where nobody could see him. He stayed there until they had passed Oxdjupet. Then he returned to his cabin, closed his suitcases and examined his face in the mirror.

His father was more evident now, the wrinkles drawing his eyebrows closer together, a feature that made him look bitter and had always frightened him as a boy. Against his will he was on the way to inheriting his father's tortured face. His father was trying to reclaim the power he used to have, to resurrect himself in his son's face.

He breathed on the mirror until it misted over, and the face disappeared.

I am drawing a line under this journey, he thought. It is over now. I fulfilled my mission. I have done what was expected of me. I will not get much thanks for it, that is hardly the done thing at Naval Headquarters. But I shall be given new jobs to do, more responsibility, and sooner or later I shall be promoted. I am proceeding up life's invisible staircase.

He checked his suitcases, made sure he had not forgotten anything and left the cabin. It was lighter now, the archipelago stepped forward out of the mist. Corves full of fish in little cargo boats sailing towards Stockholm to unload their catches. Grey men hunched over tillers and leaning against masts.

He had a quick breakfast in the officers' mess. Without joining in, he listened to a heated discussion between a lieutenant and an engineer officer. The lieutenant, who was red-haired and pale, insisted in a shrill voice that the outcome of the war was obvious. Germany would win, since that nation was driven by a fury that the English had lost. The first engineer maintained that the Germans and Russians were arrogant, they wore 'Napoleon's boots', he claimed, which meant they would be punished and defeated.

Tobiasson-Svartman left the mess and went on deck. What kind of boots am I wearing? he wondered. They were now approaching Djurgården. He remembered his dream. What did it mean? The German sailor who had returned from the bottom of the sea off Sandsänkan, what did he want?

A warning, he thought. Don't proceed too quickly, don't forget too quickly.

That was as far as he got. His thoughts got in each other's way, short-circuited his power to reason.

CHAPTER 70

The *Svea* had docked. Captain Rake bade him farewell. A rating had already carried his suitcases down to the quay, where he was hailing a man with a wheelbarrow.

Rake looked hard at Tobiasson-Svartman. The dawn light was very bright.

'You look pale,' he said. 'Paler than you did.'

'Perhaps exhaustion is taking its toll.'

Rake nodded thoughtfully. 'Like when there's been a battle at sea,' he said. 'While it's happening you notice nothing. Doctors have maintained that it's a purely physical process. Something they call "adrenalin" is pumped around the body. A chemical or biological name for human bloodthirstiness. When the battle is over you are either dead or alive. If you are dead the bloodthirstiness was pumped round in vain. If you are alive you are overcome by exhaustion. Whether you have won or lost is of no great significance. Or rather, if you have survived you have won, even if you are on the losing side.' He stopped abruptly, as if he had realised he was uttering something inappropriate. 'I talk too much sometimes,' he said, embarrassed. 'I often tell people around about me to hold their tongues, but I don't always practise what I preach.'

He stood erect, saluted and shook hands.

'Good luck.'

'Thank you.'

Tobiasson-Svartman walked off the gangway. He turned, but there was no sign of the captain. He took a few hesitant steps, almost stumbled. He had experienced the same dizziness each time he landed on Halsskär. On board ship he had to work actively to keep his balance, whereas on dry land it was up to the earth or the stones under his feet to prevent him from falling.

The rating saluted and returned to the ship. The man with the wheelbarrow full of luggage was old and toothless. His cheeks were hollow, he wheezed when he breathed. Tobiasson-Svartman had to help him to get the wheelbarrow on the move.

Stockholm was all hustle and bustle. It seemed to him rusty, covered in mud and dirt, all these houses, trees, streets and people that suddenly surrounded him. The city gushed all over him, unexpectedly; perhaps it was frightening, perhaps beautiful.

CHAPTER 71

He did not go directly home.

He had in him something of the sluggishness of a large ship, the need to reduce speed slowly, to yaw without excessive impetuosity. He could not walk through the door of his flat in Wallingatan too soon. That would be like losing control and crashing your bows into the quay.

The first time he had been away on a mission after marrying Kristina Tacker he sent a telegram saying when he expected to be home. That was the only time. He had never repeated the mistake.

He parked the toothless man outside the building in Wallingatan and went to a modest licensed café in the next block. It was early in the day, but he knew the owner, the widow of a sailmaker who had spent his life working for the Crown. Her name was Sally Andersson and she was full of life. He could go to her place and get drunk at six in the morning if he wanted to. She was still young, this merry widow, and he never ceased to be surprised by her gleaming white teeth.

Sally was standing among her cups and beer mugs and saw him coming.

'I haven't seen you for ages. You must have just returned from a long voyage,' she said, wiping down the corner table where he usually sat. 'Can you tell me why the navy employs such wretched cooks?'

'What makes you say that?'

'You are too thin. A ship's master can't be as thin as that. One of these days the wind will blow right through you. You'll be seagull meat.'

'The cook was good. But the sea wears you down. You don't grow thinner, you get worn down by all the salt and the constant motion of the sea.'

She laughed, flicked at the arm of a chair with her cloth and served him his usual glass of aquavit with a beer chaser.

A couple of years back, in May 1912, after a lengthy mission checking the depths of the secret channels around the north of Gotland and Fårön, he had drunk far too much when he got back home. He was very drunk by ten in the morning and started talking non-stop. He had lost control of himself, and Sally Andersson saved him from making a fool of himself. When he started saying things about the naval chiefs of staff that he would later regret, she piloted him to a room behind the kitchen and laid him down on a wooden bench. Although she employed two waitresses, Sally always served him herself. Nobody else was allowed to come near him, recharge his glass, wipe up when he was drunk and started spilling beer. She gave him what he needed to drink, never more than that, and she was always the one who would eventually tell him he had had enough.

'You've come back,' she would say. 'You can go home now.'

He had never questioned her judgement, simply settled his bill, and left.

CHAPTER 72

She gave him watered-down aquavit and beer that morning, and made him eat some sandwiches with lots of butter and thick slices of ham.

He drank quickly. He was merry after only half an hour. Sally sat down at his table and looked hard at him. Her white teeth glistened. They were like seashells. Straight, polished seashells in a row, stuck down in dark red sand.

'How close is the war?' she wanted to know.

He searched in his befuddled brain for an answer.

'Firelight,' he said eventually. 'In the distance, over the sea. A terrible silence.'

'I asked how close the war was, not what it looks like.'

He pointed to his forehead.

'Inside here,' he said. 'That's how close the war is.'

'How can a clever man like you talk such a lot of crap?' she said.

He emptied his glass, but she shook her head when he asked for more.

'If you have any more now, you'll pass the limit.'

'What limit?'

'The limit where a woman no longer recognises the man she married.'

He put what he owed her on the table. There was a strong smell of old leather and wet wool as he left the room and its tobacco-laden fug. He stumbled, emerging into the street. He walked round the block and stopped at his front door in Wallingatan. The man who was supposed to be guarding his luggage had fallen asleep, propped up against one of the wheels. Tobiasson-Svartman gave him a kick. The man jumped to his feet and unloaded the cases.

He opened the door. He left everything that had happened in the bright light of the street. In the darkness of the stairwell he had the feeling that he had docked at the Wallingatan quay.

CHAPTER 73

Kristina Tacker was waiting for him in the dim hall.

That made him feel insecure, it went against his plans. He had not sent her a telegram, nobody else would have had a reason for letting her know when he was due. She noticed his confusion, also of course that he was a bit drunk.

'I saw the wheelbarrow with your luggage. I could almost smell it from the flat window. But I was beginning to wonder when you were going to appear.'

'I went for a walk round the block to shake off the spray and the seaweed and the smell of mud. Leaving a ship is a complicated process.'

He embraced her, sucked in all her fragrances, the wine, her perfume with the hint of lemon zest. She didn't hug him tightly, there was a gap between them, but he hoped she was pleased to have him home.

Somebody started giggling behind them. His wife gave a start, whipped round and dealt the maid a mighty box on the ear.

'Go away,' she said. 'Leave my husband and me in peace.'

The girl ran. Her rapid footsteps made no sound. He had never known his wife physically violent before and was scared by the force of the blow, as if he had been on the receiving end.

'Did you get my letter? The one where I wrote about her?'

'I got all your letters.'

Nothing was said as he hung up his naval overcoat, removed his shoes and followed her into the living room where the china figurines were standing on their shelves.

Nothing had changed. It was like entering a room that nobody lived in.

They sat on the chairs by the window. The light from the low sun came in through the thin curtains.

He told her about his mission in great detail. He could hide among the details. Everything he said was true, and he only omitted one detail: the existence of an island in the sea called Halsskär.

He erased it from the map, let the skerry sink down to the seabed.

Recalling that he had said his wife and daughter were dead upset him for a moment. He felt a pain in his stomach.

She was as sharp as a bird.

'What's the matter?'

'Just a shooting pain in a tooth.'

'Where?'

'My lower jaw.'

'You must go to a dentist.'

'It's gone. It was only a shooting pain, nothing to worry about.'

He continued with his story as if nothing had happened.

When she got up to instruct the maid to serve coffee, it seemed to him that he had measured out a considerable distance between himself and his wife.

He had planted a lie between them. A lie that would continue to grow, even if everything else he had told her was true, or at least honestly meant. The lie did not need feeding. It would continue to grow of its own accord.

He wondered if it were possible to live without lying. Had he ever met a person who did not tell lies? He searched his memory, but he could think of no one.

CHAPTER 74

They sat by the window drinking coffee.

The maid who had had her ears boxed seemed timid and scared. He felt sorry for her, and remembered the snotty-nosed oarsman. We are people who hit others, he thought, that is one thing, at least, we have in common, my wife and I, we deliver powerful blows that resound against people's heads. But one can always discuss the servants. We have to keep quiet about everything else, for the time being anyway.

'I find her so annoying,' Kristina Tacker said. 'She smells of sweat despite my telling her over and over again to wash herself properly, she doesn't dust the top of picture frames, it takes her ages to empty the bins or to go shopping and she can never get the amounts right in recipes.'

She spoke softly so that her words could not be heard outside the room.

'I'll have a word with her, of course,' he said. 'If necessary we shall have to sack her and find somebody else.'

'People don't want to be in domestic service any more,' Kristina Tacker said. 'We live in an unwilling age.'

CHAPTER 75

They had a candlelit dinner.

The heat from the tiled stove spread all round the room. Tobiasson-Svartman would have dearly liked to find peace, and for everything that had happened around the Sandsänkan lighthouse to slip out of his memory. Then there would be no truths or lies, just the navigable channel he had redefined.

He drank wine with the dinner and afterwards port. Kristina sat in the low light embroidering a tablecloth. He could feel that he was not yet ready for bed.

She stood up soon after ten. He waited until he heard her settling down in bed, then he drank two glasses of cognac, washed, drank two more glasses of cognac, brushed his teeth and went into the dark bedroom. The alcohol made his desire stronger than his insecurity.

When it was over, the act that had taken place in total silence, it seemed to him that their love was a bit like running for your life. What he felt most was relief. He tried to think of something to say, but there was nothing.

He lay awake for a long time, knowing that she had not gone to sleep either. He wondered if there was a greater distance than the one between two people in the same bed pretending to sleep. It was a distance he was not able to assess, using any of the measuring instruments at his disposal.

CHAPTER 76

It was almost three before he was sure that she was asleep.

She was breathing deeply, snoring slightly. He got out of bed, put on his dressing gown and left the room. He took a pair of white gloves out of a cupboard.

He poured himself a glass of cognac and went over to her escritoire. He listened to be sure she had not woken up, carefully turned the key and took out her diary. It seemed to him that the white gloves would lessen the gravity of his intrusion, not touching the pages with his hands.

She had made an entry every day since he left. She had not recorded her sudden unwillingness to accompany him to the quay. It just gave the time, the weather, and said: *Lars has left.*

He leafed through the pages, listening all the time for her padding footsteps. In the street outside a drunken man gave vent to his anger and cursed God.

Her notes were usually short, non-committal. *I have had a letter from Lars.* But nothing about the contents, nothing of her reaction to what he had written. Her life is like a slow sinking process, he thought. One day she will drag me down into the depths with her. One day she will no longer be the lid over the abyss on whose edge I am balancing.

When he came to 14 November he found something that broke the pattern. She had recorded the temperature, the wind direction, *a light snowfall at about nine that soon passed over*, but then something more, the first personal comments.

She described a dream she had had that night. It had woken her up and she had immediately got out of bed and written down what she could remember. She concluded with the words: *Some nights the silence is cold and unresponsive, other nights it is soft and inviting. Tonight the silence has gone away.*

After that the entries reverted to the previous pattern. Falling temperatures, gusts of wind, having a new water pipe installed in the kitchen.

During the night of 27 November she had another dream:

> I wake up with a start. In the dark bedroom I think I can detect the presence of some person, but when I sit up there is nobody there, only the white glint of the moon on the door. I remain sitting up, and I know the dream is important. Suddenly I find myself standing in a street in an unknown town, I have no idea how I got there or where I am going. Nor do I recognise the town. The people all around me are speaking a foreign language I cannot understand. I start walking down the street, the traffic is lively, it's very hot and I have a thick black veil over my face. I come to a big open square where there is a cathedral. People are bustling back and

> forth over the square, they are all blind, but they are playing a violent game, bumping into one another, crashing into the cathedral walls or the fountain in the middle of the square and drawing blood. So as not to be in the way I go into the cathedral. It is cold and dark inside there. The floor is covered in newly fallen snow, individual flakes are still drifting down from the high-vaulted ceiling. It is a gigantic church, like a vast expanse of ice. A few people are sitting in the pews. I walk down the centre aisle and sit in a pew. I don't say any prayers, just sit there; I still don't know what town I'm in, but I'm not afraid. That surprises me because I'm always made anxious by unfamiliar things, I can never bring myself to travel alone but must always have a companion. I sit in the pew, it's still cold, snow is swirling around over the stone floor, then somebody sits down in front of me. I can tell it is a woman, but am unable to see what she looks like. She turns round, and I see that it is in fact me sitting there. She whispers something I can't understand. Who am I, if that really is me sitting in front of me? Then I wake up. I have some idea of what the dream means, of course, perhaps I am unsure about what is the real me. But the most important thing is that I wasn't afraid in the dream

That was the end of the entry, there wasn't even a full stop.

He put the diary back and locked the escritoire. He stood in a window and looked down at the street. A rat ran along the bottom of the house wall and disappeared through a basement window. He thought about the dream his wife had described in her diary. A dream that got the better of her comfort, he thought. It takes a lot to make her get up once she's in bed, unless she really has to. She leads a very lazy life. But a dream about visiting a cathedral, an unexpected mirror image of her own face, makes her get out of bed and make an effort.

He paused on the words. His wife had *made an effort.* How often had she done that? When she dusted and polished her china figurines. But other than that?

He tried to interpret the dream. It was like breaking and entering her in secret. He sat in a rocking chair, cognac in hand, and rehearsed the dream in his head. But he could not find a way in. The moment she stepped inside the snow-filled cathedral, the dream closed its doors.

He drank another glass of cognac, realised he was becoming very drunk but continued walking around the apartment. He paused to listen outside the maid's door. He could hear her snoring. Very gently he opened the door and peered inside. The girl was sleeping on her back with her mouth wide open. The quilt was pulled right up to her neck. For a moment he was tempted to lift it up and see if she was sleeping naked. He closed the door and went to the room where his wife kept her china figurines. He overcame his urge to smash one of them. What an awful indictment, he thought – I am jealous of a collection of lifeless, mostly badly made china figurines.

Their lifeless eyes stared at him in the pale light seeping in through the windows.

CHAPTER 77

On the morning of 17 December the city was covered by thick fog, the temperature was a few degrees above zero. He felt nervous in advance of the meeting he had to attend at Naval Headquarters. The measurements he had carried out had been conducted and reported in exemplary fashion, and he had no reason to think that they would not be pleased with his work. Even so, he was on edge.

The invisible torpedo was still hurtling towards him.

He went for a long walk through the town, having left home before six without waking his wife. Nor had he roused the maid, but made his own coffee. She had pressed his uniform the day before, supervised by Kristina Tacker. He strolled up the hills to Brunkebergstorg where the coachmen had set up braziers to keep warm, as usual. He crossed the bridge at Strömbron and continued through the alleys of the Old Town, where shadowy figures scuttled in all directions. He was going through everything that had happened at the Sandsänkan lighthouse. It was all there: Captain Rake, Lieutenant Jakobsson, Welander with his vodka bottles, the sailor Richter with no eyes.

The only thing missing was Sara Fredrika.

The woman who, day after day, dreaded catching her own husband in her nets.

CHAPTER 78

At eight o'clock he walked through the main entrance to the Swedish Navy Headquarters on Skeppsholmen. An adjutant invited him to sit down and wait as not everybody on the committee had arrived. A vice admiral who lived out at Djursholm had telegraphed to say that he would be late.

Tobiasson-Svartman shuddered in the cold corridor. He listened to some bugle calls drifting in through the window, followed by the dull thud of a single artillery shot.

After half an hour or so the adjutant informed him that the committee was ready to receive him. He entered a room with previous Admirals of the Fleet staring down at him from the walls. The committee comprised two vice admirals, a captain and a lieutenant whose job it was to keep the minutes. A chair had been placed in readiness for him, in front of the committee who were sitting in a row behind a table covered in a green baize.

Vice Admiral Lars H:son-Lydenfeldt was the chairman. For many years he had been the driving force behind efforts to increase the Swedish Navy's operating capabilities. He had a reputation of being impatient and arrogant, and dominated all those around him by means of sudden outbursts of fury. He invited Tobiasson-Svartman to sit down.

'Your work is impressive,' he said. 'You seem to have that rare thing, a passion for secret military navigable channels. Is that true?'

'I just try to do my job to the best of my ability.'

The vice admiral shook his head impatiently.

'Every single member of the Swedish Navy does his job to the best of his ability. Or at least one can assume that there are not too many idlers and layabouts. I'm talking about something different. Passion. Do you understand?'

'I understand.'

'Then perhaps you would be kind enough to answer my question?'

Tobiasson-Svartman thought about his dream of finding a depth too deep to measure.

'It is exciting to record things that cannot immediately be taken in and comprehended.'

The vice admiral looked doubtfully at him, but decided to accept the answer.

'What you say is understandable. I thought something similar myself in my younger days. But what you thought in your youth, you forget in your manhood and only recall it in your old age.'

The vice admiral sat up straight and held up a chart.

'Our commander-in-chief will receive the chart with the new stretches of channel at Sandsänkan in the new year. A couple of our frigates will test them out during night manoeuvres in differing weather conditions.'

He reached for another chart.

'Gamlebyviken,' he said. 'The approach to the narrow bay. Cramped, existing depth soundings doubtful, constant silting up that hasn't been checked since the 1840s. Well, Commander Svartman, have you been informed that we are counting on you to undertake this mission in the new year?'

'Yes, I have been informed.'

'In our judgement this mission is important and will be given priority. Other measuring operations will be postponed for the time being, since the war means that vessels are needed for other duties.'

'I am ready to start at once.'

'Excellent. You will receive your instructions immediately after Christmas.'

The vice admiral glanced at the lieutenant who was keeping the minutes.

'On 27 December, 08.45 hours,' the lieutenant said.

The vice admiral nodded.

'So, that's that. Has any member of the committee any questions?'

Captain Hansson, who was the oldest person present, with experience dating from the age of sailing ships and always overlooked when it came to promotion, raised his hand.

'You seem to be surrounding yourself with a series of peculiar deaths,' he said. 'It's not exactly commonplace for dead sailors to be fished up out of the sea, for regular bosuns to pass away and ships' captains to fall down dead on deck.'

'I didn't catch the question,' Tobiasson-Svartman said.

'It wasn't a question,' Hansson said. 'It was just a comment that doesn't need to be recorded in the minutes.'

'Can I declare the meeting closed, then?' Vice Admiral H:son-Lydenfeldt inquired.

Tobiasson-Svartman raised his hand.

'I have a question. There will probably be a layer of ice at the approach to Gamlebyviken in January. Is it the intention that I should make soundings through boreholes?'

'All your work will be concentrated in an area less than half of a nautical mile,' the vice admiral answered. 'Which means that boring holes through the ice will be a satisfactory method of proceeding.'

Tobiasson-Svartman nodded. The vice admiral smiled.

'I've bored holes through the ice myself in my time,' he said. 'I remember when we were sounding a channel in the far north of the Gulf of Bothnia. The ice was a metre thick. It was so cold that the lines froze stiff in the boreholes. It's strenuous work, but you can console yourself with the thought that your task will only take three to four weeks at the most.'

The meeting was over. Everyone stood up. Tobiasson-Svartman saluted and left the room. The adjutant handed him his black overcoat. He left through the front door of the headquarters building and felt mightily relieved.

But Captain Hansson's words gnawed away inside him. Was it mere coincidence that he had been surrounded by so many peculiar deaths? Or was there a message involved? A warning?

Stockholm was still enveloped in fog.

CHAPTER 79

Something strange happened on the Sunday before Christmas. Tobiasson-Svartman was bewildered by it, and also by Kristina Tacker's reaction.

It was as if, out of the blue, she had leapt ahead and left him far behind her.

They had gone for a walk to the traditional Christmas market in Stortorget. They left home late in the afternoon, as it was rapidly getting dark. It was mild, a week of freezing cold weather had been followed by a thaw. They left their flat in Wallingatan even though the streets and pavements were slippery and covered in slush. Kristina Tacker insisted, they needed some exercise and he did not want to disappoint her even though he would have preferred to take the tram or a cab.

In the Old Town the square and all the alleys were swarming with people. They examined the goods for sale at the various stalls, his wife bought a little goat made of straw, and after strolling around for an hour they decided to make for home.

When they came to Slottsbacken they suddenly heard a little girl screaming. In the shadow of the royal palace, a man was smacking his daughter. He raised his heavy hand time and time again and smacked her. Kristina

Tacker ran up to the man and dragged him away from the girl. She was yelling something neither the man nor her husband could make out, and wrapped her arms round the girl who was howling in pain and fear. She let go of the girl only when the man had promised faithfully not to beat his daughter any more.

The whole incident, from the moment his wife had run ahead of him until the man and the girl disappeared down Skeppsbron, lasted for four minutes and thirty seconds. He had switched on his inbuilt timer then stopped it when she came back to him, out of breath and trembling.

They continued walking home without exchanging a word.

They made no reference to what had happened later that evening either. But Tobiasson-Svartman wondered why it was his wife who had reacted and not him.

CHAPTER 80

Kristina Tacker's parents lived in a large apartment on the corner of Strandgatan and Grevgatan. Tobiasson-Svartman hated having dinner with them on Christmas Day. It was one of the Tacker family's fixed rituals. Kristina's grandfather Horatius Tacker, a mining consultant, had established this ritual, and nobody in the family dared stay away.

The Tacker family had a well-to-do branch that had made a fortune out of the discreditable acquisition of forests in the north of Sweden in keen competition with the better-known Dickson family, and a less well-off branch comprising a number of wholesalers, low-grade civil servants and officers, none of whom had attained a rank higher than commander.

The poor relations were browbeaten at the Christmas dinner, and the men and women who had married into the family were scrutinised as if they were cattle in a show. He disliked this dinner intensely, and knew that his wife hated it too because she could tell how much he was suffering. But nobody could escape. Those who tried were punished severely by being excluded from the family's financial circle that paid dividends every time one of the wealthy relations died and the will was read.

Kristina's father, Ludwig, had displayed proof of considerable careerist agility in the Civil Service and a few years ago had achieved the ultimate triumph of being appointed a lord chamberlain in the King's household. Tobiasson-Svartman considered him to be a clockwork doll that never stopped bowing and scraping, and his instinct was to pull the key out of his father-in-law's back. He derived great pleasure from imagining unwinding the spring as torturers used to do in the olden days with their victim's guts.

Ludwig Tacker for his part no doubt regarded him as an acquisition to the family of doubtful value. But he never said anything, of course. The Tacker family dominated by means of silence that ate into people like acid.

Kristina Tacker's mother was like the figurines on the shelves in her daughter's flat. If Fru Martina Tacker were to trip over a rug or lose her balance on a polished floor she would not simply hurt herself, she would shatter like a china sculpture.

Thirty-four persons were assembled round the dinner table on Christmas Day, 1914. Tobiasson-Svartman had been placed between one of Kristina Tacker's sisters and her grandmother. He was more or less in the middle of one of the long sides of the table, and still had a long way to go before reaching one of the sought-after places close to his father-in-law. The elderly woman on his right was asthmatic and had difficulty in breathing. She was also hard of hearing. She did not reply when he spoke to her;

he could not make up his mind if that was because she had not heard, or because she did not consider it worth the trouble of responding. Now and then she would shout to somebody on the other side of the table, usually a line from a poem by Snoilsky, expecting to hear the next line in return.

Nor did he manage to conduct a conversation with his sister-in-law, who was deeply religious. She was lost inside herself, and hardly touched her food.

It was like being cast away on a barren reef.

He drank a lot of wine in order to survive. He looked at his wife, who was sitting rather higher up on the opposite side. She was wearing a mint-green dress, and her hair was beautifully arranged. Their eyes would occasionally meet, bashfully, as if they were not acquainted.

CHAPTER 81

After the dessert was served, an excellent lemon cheese, Ludwig Tacker delivered his traditional Christmas speech. He had a slightly muffled, gravelly voice, his face was bright red despite the fact that he never drank much, and he put a lot of force into his speech, the writing of which Tobiasson-Svartman suspected had been his principal occupation during the past year. He lived for the speeches he gave to the assembled family. Every year he laid down the truths that everyone must acknowledge. It was like a speech from the throne, read out for obedient subjects.

This year his topic was the Great War. Tobiasson-Svartman was not surprised to discover that his father-in-law was firmly pro-German. But Ludwig Tacker did not simply express his support for Germany in the war. He poured torrents of hatred on the English and French, and the Russian Empire was dismissed as 'a rotten ship that is kept afloat only by all the dead bodies in the hold'.

I have a father-in-law who really knows how to hate, he thought. What will happen if he discovers that I do not share his enmities?

During the speech he kept an eye on his wife. He realised that he had no idea about her views on the war. The speech faded out of his consciousness. I don't know my wife, he thought. I share a bed and a dinner table with an unknown woman. In the far distance he could see Sara Fredrika. She came gliding towards him, the dinner table had vanished, he was back on Halsskär.

He did not return to the dinner table until toasts were proposed at the end of the speech, and coffee was about to be served in the drawing room.

CHAPTER 82

The Christmas holidays passed. On 27 December Tobiasson-Svartman arrived for the meeting on Skeppsholmen as agreed. He waited impatiently in the cold corridor to be allowed in and receive his instructions. But no adjutant came to collect him.

The door was suddenly flung open and Vice Admiral H:son-Lydenfeldt invited him in. He was alone in the room. The vice admiral sat and gestured to his visitor to do the same.

'At short notice the naval high command has decided that no more depth soundings will be made this winter. All ships will be required to guard our coastline and to escort our merchant navy convoys. The decision was made by Admiral Lundin and confirmed by Naval Minister Boström late last night.'

The vice admiral looked hard at him.

'Have I made myself clear?'

'Yes.'

'One could argue, of course, that a very few weeks spent boring holes through the ice would hardly have a significant effect on our fleet. But a decision has been made.'

The vice admiral pointed at an envelope lying on the table.

'I am the first person to regret that depth sounding has been postponed indefinitely, even though I personally would prefer not to have to be out on the ice boring holes in early January. Am I right?'

'Of course.'

'Meanwhile you will be at the beck and call of Naval Headquarters. There seems to be no shortage of tasks needing to be carried out.'

The vice admiral placed one hand on his desk to indicate that the meeting was at an end. He stood up, Tobiasson-Svartman saluted and left the room.

CHAPTER 83

Only when he was passing the Grand Hotel did he pause and open the envelope.

The message was short. At 9 a.m. the next morning he was to present himself at the Swedish Navy's special section for navigation channels, buoyage and harbours. The order was signed by Lieutenant Kaspersson on behalf of a section head at the Naval Fortifications Centre.

He walked to the edge of the quay. Some white archipelago boats were docked there, frozen in and deserted.

He noticed that he was trembling. The counter-order, cancelling his mission, had been wholly unexpected. In connection with the task he was to perform at Gamlebyviken he had drawn up a plan that he had kept secret, even from himself. He would return to Halsskär and meet Sara Fredrika. Nothing else meant anything, only that had any real significance.

He went into the Grand Hotel and found a table in the café. It was still early, there were not many customers and the waiters had nothing to do. He ordered coffee and a cognac.

'It's cold outside,' the waiter said. 'Cognac is made for days like today.'

Tobiasson-Svartman managed to suppress an overwhelming urge to stand up and hit the waiter. He could not cope with being talked to. The decision had been a sort of declaration of war, he must resist it, make a new plan to replace the one that had just been foiled.

He stayed in the café for several hours. He was drunk by the time he left. But he knew what he was going to do.

When he left he gave the waiter a large tip.

CHAPTER 84

He said nothing to Kristina Tacker about the cancellation of his mission. She asked how long he thought he would need to stay at Gamlebyviken and when he would be leaving. He told her that it could take several weeks, but hardly longer than to the end of January, and that she should think in terms of thirty days when she did his packing for him.

That evening and night he sat hunched over his sea charts and notebooks with the new stretch of navigable channel at Sandsänkan. By five in the morning he had finished, and lay down on the sofa in his study with his naval overcoat over him.

Twice during the night Kristina Tacker had got up and peeped through his study door. He did not even notice that she was there. Her fragrances did not get through to him.

CHAPTER 85

On 9 January 1915 a violent storm raged over Stockholm. Roofs were blown off, chimneys collapsed, trees fell, people were killed. When the storm had subsided there followed a period of extreme cold. It held the city in its grip until the end of the month.

On 30 January Tobiasson-Svartman put his plan into action. He had started work on Skeppsholmen, apparently willingly and contentedly, on a check of all sea charts covering the Gulf of Bothnia. He arrived at the office as usual at eight, exchanged a few words with his colleagues about the severe cold, then asked for an interview with his boss, Captain Sturde. His section head was obese, rarely completely sober and regarded by all and sundry as a master of the art of doing nothing. He dreamed of the day when he could retire and devote all his time to his beehives in his garden near Trosa.

Tobiasson-Svartman spread his charts out on the table.

'A serious error has crept into the calculations relevant to the new section of navigable channel at Sandsänkan,' he said. 'In the notes I received from Sub-Lieutenant Welander, the depth for a section of three hundred metres has been wrongly presented as eighteen metres on average. I have reason to believe, on the basis of my own notes, that the average depth can be put at six or seven metres at most.'

Captain Sturde shook his head.

'How could that have happened?'

'No doubt you are aware that Welander suffered a breakdown.'

'Was he the one who drank himself silly? I'm told he's in a mental hospital now. Destroyed by alcoholism and the desperation caused by his having to stay sober.'

'I'm convinced my measurements are correct.'

'What do you suggest?'

'Since the measurements I am referring to can neither wait nor be carried out by anybody else, I propose that I should go down to Östergötland and make another check.'

'Isn't the sea there under ice?'

'Yes, but I can get help from local fishermen and bore holes through the ice.'

Captain Sturde thought for a moment. Tobiasson-Svartman looked out of the window and observed a flock of bullfinches squabbling over something edible in a tree made white by the hoar frost.

'Obviously something needs to be done about this,' Sturde said. 'I can't think of a better solution than the one you suggest. I just find it hard to understand how this could have happened. Indefensible, of course.'

'Sub-Lieutenant Welander was very good at concealing his alcohol abuse.'

'He must have realised that his negligence could have given rise to a catastrophe.'

'People with a severe alcohol problem are said to be interested in nothing but the next bottle.'

'Tragic. But I'm grateful to you for discovering the error. I suggest that this matter should stay between you and me. I shall give instructions to the effect that the new chart should not yet be sent out. When could you embark on this mission?'

'Within the next two weeks.'

'I'll see to it that you get the necessary orders.'

Tobiasson-Svartman left Captain Sturde and returned to his own office. He was drenched in sweat. But everything had gone according to plan. Without anybody knowing, he had taken Welander's journals home and spent several evenings altering the figures. It was a perfect forgery that would never be discovered. Even if Welander were able to leave hospital one of these days, his memories of the time spent on the *Blenda* would be twisted and muddled.

He thought about Sara Fredrika and the journey over the ice that was in store. He thought that his father would no doubt have secretly admired him.

CHAPTER 86

Somebody was practising the violin. The tone was tinny, the same phrases were repeated time after time.

It was the evening of 12 February. The severe cold lay like a carpet over the platform of Norrköping railway station when Tobiasson-Svartman stepped off the train and looked around for a porter. There were only a few passengers, black shadows hurrying through the darkness. Only when the engine hissed out steam and a shudder ran through the coaches as it began its journey further south did a man with icicles in his beard appear to take care of the luggage.

Tobiasson-Svartman had sent a telegram and ordered a room in the Göta Hotel. The river running through the town was frozen over.

The room was on the second floor and looked out on to a church squatting in the half-light. It was warm in the room – he had chosen that hotel because it had central heating. When he had closed the door behind him he stood perfectly still and tried to imagine that he was on board a ship. But the floor beneath his feet refused to shift.

That was when he heard the violin. Somebody in a room nearby was practising. It might have been Schubert.

He sat on the bed. He could still call off the journey. He thought he was mad. He was heading willy-nilly towards chaos, towards an abyss from which there was no return. Instead of continuing with it he could take a train back to Stockholm. He would be able to explain it away. He could remember at the last minute that he still had the correct figures. He could dispose of the forged chart and replace it with another one that was correct. Nothing was too late, he could put a stop to the headlong dash he had set in train, he could still save himself.

A cage, he thought. Or a trap. But is it inside me? Or am I the trap myself?

CHAPTER 87

He went down to the dining room and had dinner.

A string quartet played something he took to be highlights from Verdi operas. The dining room was almost empty, waitresses standing around with nothing to do. Outside, where it was very cold and the snow crunched underfoot, was somewhere the shadow of a war that nobody really understood, nor very much cared about, in fact.

He imagined himself with a gun, firing gas shells. A red-faced man sitting next to one of the pillars in the dining room was hunched over a newspaper. He estimated the distance as thirteen metres, then fired the gun. The man was blown to smithereens and swallowed up by flames. He killed the diners one by one, then the waitresses and the cashier, and finally the musicians in the string quartet.

He fled the dining room at midnight. He lay in bed with the cold sounding lead clutched to his body. The freezing temperatures made the hotel walls creak. The violin in the nearby room could no longer be heard.

Before he slept he tried to take his bearings. Where was he, where was he actually going to? Every movement made him feel dizzy, perhaps he was heading for his own demise. The last thing he thought about was the ice. Would it hold his weight? Had the sea frozen over as far out as Halsskär? Or would he be forced to pull a boat over the ice and row the last part of the way? Would he ever get there?

Ice floes drifted through his sleep.

CHAPTER 88

He left the hotel after a quick breakfast.

The receptionist, who spoke with a Danish accent, ordered him a cab. This was not straightforward since he wanted to be taken as far as the jetty at Gryt, where he would set out on his trek. The road was icy, and the cold could cause engine problems. After being offered ten kronor extra, a taxi driver with a Ford agreed to take him.

They left shortly after half past seven. Tobiasson-Svartman was wrapped in a thick blanket in the back seat. The driver had a scarf round his winter hat. It reminded Tobiasson-Svartman of Lieutenant Jakobsson. He shuddered at the memory of the man who had dropped dead in front of him on the deck.

The countryside was embedded in the cold.

Just before driving through Söderköping they passed the Göta Canal. Barges were frozen in beside the canal banks. They were chained by their hawsers, like animals in their stalls. He turned to look at the barges through the back window for as long as they were visible. I shall remember those barges, he thought. One of them will take me over the final border when my time comes.

At Gusum the engine began coughing and it was not possible to go any further when they reached Valdemarsvik.

He decided to stay there overnight, paid the driver and booked into a guest house on a hill beyond the big tannery on the shore of the bay. The wind was from the east and blew the smell away. The landlord, who spoke a dialect very difficult to understand, promised to arrange transport the next day.

Having installed his luggage in his room he walked down to the harbour and examined the ice. It was thick and did not give when he stood on it. He approached a man who was busy chiselling ice off a fishing boat and asked what conditions were like out in the archipelago, but he did not know.

'If it's as cold out there among the skerries, the sea will no doubt be frozen there as well. But I don't know, and I don't want to know.'

He had dinner at the guest house, avoided answering anything more than yes or no to the questions asked by the inquisitive landlord and his wife, and went early to bed.

He snuggled down deep into his pillow and tried to imagine that he did not exist.

CHAPTER 89

The Gryt jetty was deserted, a few boats frozen into the ice, a locked boathouse, a battered slipway. The driver lifted out the two rucksacks and took his payment. There was a thin layer of snow on the ice, but the only footprints were those of an occasional crow or magpie.

'Nobody's gone from here,' said the driver. 'And nobody's come neither. No boats'll be coming here until the ice melts in March or April. Are you really sure this is where you wanted to come to?'

'Yes,' Tobiasson-Svartman said. 'This is where I wanted to come to.'

The driver nodded slowly and asked no more questions. The black car disappeared up the hill from the jetty. Tobiasson-Svartman stood motionless until the sound of the engine had died away. Then he took out his sea chart. Panic was ticking deep inside him. I cannot go back, he thought. There is nothing behind me, perhaps nothing in front of me either, but I must do what I have set myself to do.

There was an easterly breeze blowing. It would take him three days to get to Halsskär, assuming the weather did not take a turn for the worse, and that there really was ice in the outer archipelago. He decided to walk as far as Armnö in the central part of the archipelago this first day. There ought to be a boathouse there where he could spend the night and be comparatively warm.

He strapped on his two rucksacks after fixing crampons to his leather boots and hanging his ice prods round his neck. It was ten minutes past ten when he took his first step out on to the ice. His route would take him round the south end of Fågelö and then he would head towards Höga Svedsholmen. He estimated the distance to Armnö to be eight kilometres, which meant that he ought to be there before dusk.

He set off. The thin layer of snow had been blown away in some places, exposing the dark ice beneath. It felt like balancing on the edge of a precipice that could give way at any moment. The archipelago was empty. He would occasionally pause and listen. Sometimes an invisible bird would call, but apart from that it was totally silent. When he had passed Fågelö he stopped, unstrapped his rucksacks and made a hole through the ice with his knife. It was fourteen centimetres thick. It would not crack under his weight.

He walked at twenty-five metres per minute. He did not want to run the risk of sweating and then freezing. He paused at Höga Svedsholmen and broke off a branch to use as a walking stick. He drank some water and ate some of the sandwiches provided by the guest house. Then he rested for twenty minutes.

When he left Höga Svedsholmen he tried pulling his

rucksacks behind him, as if they were on runners. He fastened a rope around his waist and started pulling. The rucksacks slid easily on the ice and thin snow. But before he was even halfway to Gråholmarna the small of his back started to ache. He stopped and tried to think of another way of doing it. He made a harness out of the rope, so that the weight was shared by his back and shoulders. When he began walking again he could feel that there was less of a strain.

At Gråholmarna he made a fire between some stones. Nowhere could he see any smoke rising above the tree-tops, nowhere was there any sign of human life. A whole world had disappeared from view.

While he was waiting for the coffee water to boil he stood on a rock and shouted over the ice-covered bay. The sound was tossed about, returned as a distant echo, then all was silent again. From there he could see Kråkmarö and Armnö through his telescope.

He found an unlocked boathouse by the Armnö Sound. There was a fireplace inside, and no sign of any foot-prints around the building. There were nets, decoys and a strong smell of tar in the boathouse. He opened a tin of American meat and snuggled down in his sleeping bag. He fell asleep with a feeling of being inaccessible.

CHAPTER 90

The next day he walked ten kilometres.

That took him over Bockskärsdjupet and as far as Hökbådan, where he set up camp.

He had intended to head straight for Halsskär, but a channel had opened up near Harstena and so he was forced to make a detour to the north. Hökbådan proved to be no more than a collection of bare rocks with no boathouses. Before darkness fell he managed to make a shelter of branches and moss over a crack in the rocks where he intended to spend the night. He made a fire and opened another tin of American meat. The wind was still no more than a gentle breeze when he eased himself into his sleeping bag. It had grown noticeably less cold during the day. He estimated the temperature at minus three degrees. When darkness fell and his fire died he lay listening to the sea. Was that open water he could hear lapping against the ice? Or would the thick ice stretch as far as Halsskär? He could not make up his mind what he could hear, whether it was the sea or the silence inside his head.

Several times he thought he could hear gunfire, first a distant thud and then a shock wave passing through the darkness.

Nobody knows where I am, he thought. In the middle of winter, in the cold world of the ice, I have found a hiding place that nobody could possibly imagine.

CHAPTER 91

He lit a fire as day broke. The wind was still no more than a breeze, the temperature minus one. He ate his remaining sandwiches, drank coffee, then prepared to walk the ten kilometres to Halsskär. The clouds were motionless above his head, the ice with its thin covering of snow was no longer broken by rocks and skerries. Now he was heading towards the open sea. He could see Halsskär and the Sandsänkan lighthouse through his telescope. He could still not see whether the ice stretched all the way, though.

He pulled his rucksacks behind him, the harness had chafed his left shoulder, but it was not painful enough to stop him walking for one more day.

He saw no animal tracks. He was walking eastwards and gave himself no time to rest. Every half-hour he scanned the horizon with his telescope.

He had passed Krokbåden to his right before he could be confident that there was ice all the way. There was no open water forming a barrier between him and the island. The ice extended as far as Halsskär and perhaps even to the Sandsänkan lighthouse.

He scanned Halsskär with his telescope. Eventually he was able to make out a narrow wisp of smoke rising from the skerry.

She was still there. But she was not expecting him.

CHAPTER 92

It was starting to get dark as he approached Halsskär.

His first impulse was to hurry over the ice and go straight to Sara Fredrika's cottage. But something stopped him, he hesitated. What would he say? How would he explain his return? What would happen if he changed his mind the moment she opened the door?

He squeezed the questions into a little clump: why was he out on the ice, why had he lied to set up this journey, what was he really looking for?

He reached the skerry as dusk fell without having found an answer. Sara Fredrika's boat was on land, upside down and resting on large pieces of driftwood. The nets had been taken in, an abandoned herring barrel was brimful of snow.

He made a shelter in a crevice between the inlet and the rocks where he could not be seen from the cottage. He knew the way from there, he would be able to walk it in the dark. That was the only thing he had managed to decide, he would wait for it to get properly dark and then creep up on her. He wanted to look through the window and see what she was doing, only then would he know how to take the final steps.

He crept down into his sleeping bag. Night fell, and

still he waited. The clouds dispersed, the sky was full of stars, the narrow sliver of a new moon. When he eventually got up it was nine o'clock. He made his way to the edge of the rock and looked out to sea. There was no sign of the Sandsänkan lighthouse. He screwed up his eyes, momentarily confused and wondering if he was completely disorientated. Then he realised that the light had been switched off as part of the increased security operation along the Swedish coast. The war had brought its darkness here as well.

He waited for another hour. The wind had dropped altogether, the ice continued so far out that he could not even hear the sea. He groped his way along the path. There was a faint light coming from the window. He made a start when something rubbed against his leg. It was the cat. He bent down and stroked it. The cat that did not exist.

He was careful where to tread as he approached the window. Despite the hoar frost on the pane he could see into the room, a fractured image.

He moved away from the window. The cat went with him, rubbing against his leg. He looked again through the window. Sara Fredrika was squatting in front of the fire. She was wearing a woolly cap and was wrapped in blankets.

But she was not alone. Sitting on the floor next to the hearth was a man in uniform.

He had seen a similar uniform some months earlier. Then it had been on a dead German soldier floating in the sea next to the gunboat *Blenda*.

The picture sent a shudder of pain through him.

There was a German sailor sitting in Sara Fredrika's cottage. A German sailor barring his way.

The cat was beside him, rubbing against his leg.

PART VI

The Adder Game

CHAPTER 93

Someone had taken his place, his fox pelt.

He could hear the sailor's voice through the wall. It was hard to make out all his words, he was speaking in a low voice as if he suspected or feared that there was somebody close at hand, listening.

The German Tobiasson-Svartman had learned during his hated school years was not good enough for him to understand fully what was being said. In addition, the sailor was speaking dialect, he seemed to slur words, some consonants were almost inaudible, as if he had swallowed them.

Tobiasson-Svartman pressed his cheek against the cold wall. What he really wanted to do was to smash the windowpane with his fist, kick the door open and throw the man squatting in front of the fire out into the night. But he did and said nothing, and stayed in the darkness by the cottage until the fire had almost gone out. She was lying in the bunk, and the sailor on rags and old pelts on the floor, just as he had done.

He returned to his crevice. He was very tired, his joints were aching from the cold. A wind was getting up. At dawn he obliterated all traces he had left in and around the crevice, and moved to the north-eastern cliffs which dropped steeply to the sea. There were cave-like recesses there. He found one sheltered from the wind, scrambled down to the water's edge, collected some driftwood and started a fire. With his naked eye he could see that the covering of ice extended almost as far as the Sandsänkan lighthouse. The open sea looked like a black belt, a line from the north-east to the south-west. At the very edge of the ice he could make out some black spots that moved, a little group of seals, perhaps.

He took out his telescope and scanned the horizon. Nothing but sea, no ships.

The sea was emptiness, a reminder of infinity, an absence of limits.

He warmed himself in front of the fire, and eventually dozed off. The surrounding cliffs protected him from the wind. The smoke blew out to sea, almost invisible.

He woke up when the fire started to go out. For more than an hour he crawled among the icy rocks, collecting branches, broken fish boxes, parts of a ship's rail that had been washed up in a storm. He built himself a hut, just large enough for him to huddle up inside. He made some coffee and opened the last of his tins of meat. All he had left now were a few rusks and a frozen lump of butter. He drank the coffee in a series of sips, put more wood on the fire then huddled up with his feet inside one of the rucksacks.

He assessed the situation. That evening at the latest he would have to make his presence known. He could not keep watch on the cottage for another night. There was a risk that he would freeze to death. He had all day to make up his mind, to invent a story. A man who has walked all the way here over the ice must have a convincing explanation when he reveals his presence.

He tried to think calmly. The sailor and Sara Fredrika had not been sleeping together. They hadn't touched each other, not even laughed. The man had seemed despondent. Fear, he thought. Perhaps what I could see in the sailor wearing a German uniform was simply fear?

Something moved next to him. He gave a start. It was the cat. It was hungry, sniffing after bits of food in the empty tin and on the knife he had used to open the lid.

The cat studied him with vacant eyes. It was like one of the china figurines on Kristina Tacker's shelf. One that had fallen on the floor without breaking.

He exploded in fury. He grabbed the knife, stabbed the cat in the throat and slit open its stomach. Its intestines started to ooze out, the cat only had time to hiss before it was dead. Its mouth jerked a few times, its eyes wide open. He flung the body over the cliff and down to the ice. Then he wiped the blood from his hand and the knife.

There was no cat, he thought, wild with rage. That's what she said when I asked her. There was no cat. There is no cat. There is nothing.

CHAPTER 94

His fury subsided. The cat's death a memory already.

As a child he had sometimes trapped birds, then killed them by cutting off their heads with a pair of scissors from his father's study. Afterwards he had always felt distaste and regret. When he was a naval cadet he had joined some colleagues in tying bags of gunpowder to stray dogs, which were then released with burning fuses attached to the bags. They used to make bets on which of the dogs would run furthest before being blown to pieces.

But apart from that? He had never killed, he was afraid of death. The cat had come too close. It had trespassed on forbidden territory. The cat had crossed the barrier he surrounded himself with.

He gazed up at the sky. Ten o'clock. The shape of the white sun could be seen through the thin clouds. He looked down at the cat lying on the ice. A pool of blood had formed round the body.

In fact it wasn't the cat, he thought. What I attacked was something else. My father, perhaps? Or why not Lieutenant Jakobsson with his deformed hand and swollen face?

Two shadows appeared over the ice. Two eagles were

hovering overhead. They had discovered the dead cat. He could see through his telescope that they were young sea eagles. They continued circling for a while before landing on the ice. They approached the cat cautiously, as if suspecting a trap. Then they started eating.

Life and death, he thought. My life, my death, my tins of American meat. The life and death of the cat, eagles on an endless expanse of ice.

He added more wood to the fire, stuck his feet into the rucksack and tried once again to think calmly. When he got up it had turned noon. He kicked snow over the fire, divided the contents of the rucksacks so that he could leave one and take the other with him.

The eagles were gone. All that remained of the cat was a dark patch of frozen blood.

CHAPTER 95

He approached the cottage from the inlet where the boat was, paused uneasily behind a rock and observed the scene. The cottage door was closed, thin smoke drifted up from the chimney.

He would wait for one minute. He would give himself a minute in which to have second thoughts. Even if he had run out of food he would still have enough energy to walk as far as Harstena where the biggest fishing village in the archipelago was. He could still turn back.

I'll leave, he thought. I'll walk back over the ice. Sara Fredrika has nothing to do with my life. I am risking something I do not want to lose.

He set off towards the inlet, then turned on his heel, marched up to the cottage and hammered on the door. She did not open it. But he was only going to knock that one time. He stepped back a pace, so that she would be able to see him from the window.

When she opened the door wide, not just a few centimetres, he knew she had seen him.

'You,' she said. 'Are you here?'

She did not wait for a response but let him in. The room was empty, he could sense that he had the upper hand. She had hidden the stranger in the cupboard with the nets and barrels and decoys. He could smell something unusual, old engine oil perhaps, or rifle grease. He squatted by the fire and warmed his hands.

He had prepared his story carefully. It is easier in a desolate winter landscape than in cities, he had thought. It is more difficult to check the truth in the outer archipelago.

Everything depended on the open channel.

He had once met a petty officer in Karlskrona who had been bosun on the *Svensksund*. In the summer of 1896 the Swedish hot-air balloon expedition to the North Pole led by the engineer Salomon Andrée had set off for Spetsbergen on board that ship. It had been fitted with reinforced bows so as to be able to sail through iced-over water and even force its way through pack ice. That was almost twenty years ago, nobody had ever heard a thing from the three ballooners who vanished in the fog over the Arctic Ocean.

They talked about the expedition and about the ice and its mysterious qualities. The bosun had described how ice could suddenly crack, forming enormous open channels for no apparent reason. The crack appears out of the blue. The ice seemed to carry a secret inside itself. The bosun claimed that the Eskimos call it 'the frozen soul'. As recently as 1893 seven Swedish seal-hunters had been marooned on an ice floe by a gigantic crack that had made it impossible for them to get back to land. The only one to survive, a farmer from the island of Öland, had told the bosun that the ice was thick and there was no wind when the seven of them had set off. Suddenly the hunters heard a roaring sound, the ice cracked and the sea rose up like the back of a gigantic whale and they were unable to turn back. They were doomed, the open channel grew longer and wider, and he was the only one to survive, albeit having lost both feet to frostbite; the only one who could tell the tale of that sudden crack.

The ice was alive, it was not to be trusted.

Tobiasson-Svartman now told Sara Fredrika that he had been one of a party of eight that had set out from the mainland to make holes through the ice and check some of the soundings made last autumn. Just on the other side of Kråkmarö but before coming to the outer skerries, maybe Lökskär or Tyskärsarkipelagen, he had left the others to reconnoitre. The ice had cracked and he had been cut off from his colleagues by an open channel. He had very little food, and his only chance was to walk towards the open sea, towards Halsskär where he knew she lived.

'You might not have been here, of course,' he said. 'The cottage might have been empty. But at least I would have had a roof over my head, I could have drilled holes through the ice, fished and survived.'

'I am still here,' she said.

'No doubt the open channel will freeze over again, but you never know how long it will take.'

'I'm not alone,' she said. 'You are not the first person to come walking over the ice this winter. Somebody came from the other direction.'

'From the sea?'

'In a rowing boat, like the one you had.'

'I didn't see a rowing boat in the inlet.'

'He let it drift away when he came to the edge of the ice.'

'He?'

She sat down next to him on the floor. She smelled awful.

He was usually disgusted by people who smelled bad, such as their maid Anna. While serving on board the gunship *Edda* as a cadet they were carrying out a rope-ladder manoeuvre and he had been assigned to help a simple rating with rotten teeth. The smell from the man's mouth was unimaginable. Even when he was two metres away from the rating the smell hit him in the face, it was the smell of death emerging from the sailor's mouth every time he breathed.

Sara Fredrika did not smell of death. She just smelled of dirt, a friendly, sad little whiff of muck that he could put up with.

Because I love her, he thought. That's the way it is. That's why I can put up with her.

CHAPTER 96

She sat down next to him and started speaking in a low voice.

But the man hidden in the cupboard with all the nets could not understand, he could only guess at what the voices were now saying about him.

He must be scared, Tobiasson-Svartman thought. A German sailor could not have any plausible reason for being on Swedish soil. On a rocky skerry like Halsskär, with the widow of a fisherman.

He had let his rowing boat drift away. Whoever he was, he must have burned a bridge behind him, and that was dangerous.

She said: 'I am not alone here. There's somebody in there among the nets.'

He pretended to be surprised.

'Who are you hiding? Who's hiding there?'

'You spoke about the war last autumn when you were here. Sometimes I was woken up by dull thuds that made the house shake. I went to the highest point on the skerry, and there were times when I could see fires in the distance. Once when I was taking in nets at

Jungfrugrunden, a hawser floated towards me. It was like a long snake in the water. The rope was as thick as my arm. It smelled of gunpowder, it smelled of death. I didn't touch it, it just wriggled past as if it were alive. It was clear that this bit of hawser had something to do with the war. A few days after Christmas two Finns turned up in a boat. One is called Juha, the other one is known as Arvo but is actually called something else that I can't say because round here it means something rude in Swedish. They hunt seals in these parts, but mostly they smuggle hard liquor. They've never done me any harm. They had an Ålander with them in their sloop. He was called Ville, his surname was something like Honka. He told me about the war, and he started crying and cursed us Swedes for not sending troops to Åland to defend the islands. I started to understand what the war was all about, those fires in the night and the shock waves and the thudding noises – it meant that people were dying in their thousands.'

'And then he came? The man who's been caught in your nets in there?'

'I was scared when there was a knocking at the door. I didn't open up. I grabbed a knife. He was wearing a uniform and talking in a language I couldn't understand, it sounded like somebody who used to buy eels off us when I was a child. But when he collapsed on the doorstep, he wasn't threatening any more. I dragged him inside. His ribs felt like chicken bones under his jacket, I thought he might be ill, maybe he would die. I could have invited my own death, perhaps he had an infection. I slept in the boat two nights. He came round and was rambling, he had a fever, but he wasn't injured, just hungry and dehydrated. I eventually realised that he was German. He has tried to explain to me who he is, but I can't understand what he says. His words are like slippery stones. But I'm scared, I've noticed that he listens, he listens all the time, all the time, even when he's asleep his ears are cocked and his head and eyes are concentrating on something behind him.'

'Am I a danger too?'

'I don't know.'

'I've slept here.'

'You could be dangerous even so.'

'You can believe what you like. I can't make up your mind for you.'

She hesitated. Her face was twitching, she shook her head impatiently to get her hair out of her eyes. Then she stood up, as if she were going to do a standing jump, and opened the cupboard door.

The sailor came out. He stood there, on his guard, ready to defend himself.

Sara Fredrika said, although she knew he didn't understand: 'He's not dangerous, he's a sailor like you are, he's been here before.'

Tobiasson-Svartman eyed the man. He was wearing the same uniform that Karl-Heinz Richter had on when they hauled him, sodden and semi-decayed, on board the *Blenda*. His face was pale, his hair thin, he must have been about twenty-five, maybe twenty-six.

But there was something special about the sailor's

eyes: he did not only try to see with them, but also to listen, to smell, to mind-read.

Tobiasson-Svartman held out his hand and spoke slowly in German: 'My name is Lars Tobiasson-Svartman, my job is to sound depths, I was cut off from my friends by a crack in the ice.'

He didn't know the German expression for 'an open channel', but 'crack in the ice' would do. The German seemed to understand. Cautiously, he held out his hand. His grip was limp, a bit like Kristina Tacker's.

'Dorflinger.'

'You've come here over the ice?'

The German hesitated before replying.

'I have run away.'

A German deserter, a young man who had jumped ship in a desperate attempt to get away. Tobiasson-Svartman was filled with disgust. Deserters were cowards. Deserters deserved to be executed. There was no other way to treat people who failed in their duty. People who maintained that they were being true to themselves, when they were in fact letting everybody else down. What right had this deserter to appear here and get in his way, when he was risking his marriage and his career because of an inner urge that he had to fulfil? What was the deserter risking? A man who was defending no more than his own cowardice?

They stood in the room like the tips of a triangle. He tried to decide if Sara Fredrika was closer to him than to the deserter, but there was no distance in the room, the house itself seemed to be moving, or perhaps it was Halsskär that was shifting, driven by the ice that was beating against the rocks.

The ice, he thought, the ice and the dead cat. Everything is linked. And now there is a man in my way.

He smiled.

'Perhaps we should sit down,' he said to Sara Fredrika. 'I think Herr Dorflinger the sailor is tired.'

'What does he say? I don't even know his name.'

'Dorflinger.'

'Is that his first name?'

'No.'

He asked Dorflinger what his first name was.

'Stefan. My name is Stefan Dorflinger.'

'Where do you come from?'

'A little town between Cologne and Bonn, in the heart of Germany. You can't get further away from the sea.'

'Why were you drafted into the navy?'

'I asked to be put in the navy. To see the sea. We sailed from Kiel, in one of Admiral Wettenberg's naval units.'

Dorflinger slumped down on the bed. Sara Fredrika was hovering in the shadows. Tobiasson-Svartman sat on the stool by the fire, tried to do so without making a sound, he did not know why. All too often he did certain things without knowing why, and without holding back.

'You are safe here,' he said. 'Even if you are what I think you are.'

'What's that?'

'A deserter.'

'I could not endure any more.' It came out like a scream.

When he spoke again he was calm: 'I could not suffer all that killing. I can describe what is really impossible to describe, things that even words try to escape from. Some things happen that words are even frightened of, that words do not want to be used for describing. I have dreamt about words running for their lives, like I did.'

He paused and drew a deep breath. Tobiasson-Svartman thought for a moment that someone else was going to drop dead at his feet. But Dorflinger continued, as if he had fought his way up to the surface and was able to breathe normally again.

'I was on the cruiser *Weinshorn*. On Christmas Eve in the morning, north-east of Rügen, we spotted two Russian troop carriers. The sea was calm, but it was very cold, steam was coming from the water, making it look as if cold can also reach boiling point.

'I was on a team looking after one of the heavy guns amidships. It was a 254-millimetre gun and could fire salvos at targets more than ten kilometres away pretty accurately. We were given the command "Battle stations!" and we raced to our positions. I was on the lower section of the magazine, and my job was to load powder cartridges into the hoist that took them to the loading ramp on the deck above.

'We shot nineteen shells from my gun, it was an inferno, I couldn't see if we hit the target, couldn't see what we were aiming at, every shot sent us sprawling against the walls. Some people had blood coming from their eyes and noses, and the first shot burst my eardrum.

'I didn't realise when we'd stopped firing, the lad in charge of the other hoist had to come and shake me and point. The guns were silent, we had to go back on deck. I couldn't hear a thing, it was like being behind thick panes of glass. You discover a different kind of reality when you only have your eyes to help you. When there are no sounds or voices, reality is different.

'The *Weinshorn* closed in on the troopships. They were sinking now. The water was covered in burning oil. Hundreds of men were struggling to escape drowning, the fire, the oil. But the *Weinshorn* did nothing. Not one lifeboat was launched, not a single lifebuoy was thrown into the sea, not a single rope, nothing.

'I looked at the rest of the crew. Just like me they were staring in horror at all those dying men, and nobody could understand why we did nothing to save them. We were at war with Russia, OK, but these people were already beaten. We watched them dying, I can remember how our knuckles turned white as we grasped the rail. We looked at the officers up on deck, watched them laughing and pointing.

'I couldn't hear the screams, nor the laughter. I could only watch the horrific deaths in the freezing water and the burning oil. In the end there was nobody left, they were all dead, most of them had sunk, one or two bodies were still floating, some of them so badly burned that you could see only their craniums sticking out of their tattered uniform.

'Then the *Weinshorn* moved away. That was probably the most awful part. We didn't even stay. We sailed south-west, and in the afternoon Christmas trees were raised on the afterdeck, and carols were sung. I still couldn't hear anything, I could only see my comrades jumping and dancing round the tree and I felt I had to join them.

'Two days after New Year's Eve, late at night, I cleared off. The rating on guard duty realised what I was doing. He wanted to come with me, but didn't dare. He was frightened of being shot as a deserter and upsetting his parents. I rowed away and a week later I ended up here. I clambered on to this island and let the boat drift away. I can't stay here, of course, but I don't know where to go. I have tried to explain that to the woman, but we can't understand each other.'

Tobiasson-Svartman translated for her. Not everything, only what he thought was appropriate. The storyteller owns the story. He adapted it, made no mention of the Russian ships that had been sunk, but instead made Dorflinger desert after killing one of the officers in cold blood.

'You have to understand his dilemma,' he said in conclusion. 'Military law is hard, there is no mercy, no sympathy, just a rope or an execution squad. In circumstances like that you run away. I would have done the same thing.'

'Why did he kill a man? Who was it?'

'I'll ask him.'

Dorflinger was watching him uneasily.

He still has all those images in his mind's eye,

Tobiasson-Svartman thought. Those silent images, the jerky movements of war, with no sound.

'What was the name of the rating standing guard? The one who didn't dare go with you?'

'Lothar Buchheim. He was the same age as me.'

Sara Fredrika was waiting impatiently.

'What did he say?'

'The man he killed was a bosun called Lothar Buchheim. He was a bully. In the end he went too far.'

'You don't kill people. Should I kill every Finnish bastard who comes here and tries to rape me? Or the men from the islands in the inner archipelago who think that a widow is a bloody whore who ought to be taken in hand and made to work?'

He was surprised by her language. It reminded him of that night in Copenhagen.

'I can't have a murderer in the house,' she said. 'Even if he can't cope with the war.'

'We have to protect him.'

'If he's a murderer, shouldn't he be sentenced?'

'He's already doomed. They'll hang him. We must help him.'

'How?'

'I'll take him with me when I've finished my work.'

Sara Fredrika looked at Dorflinger. Tobiasson-Svartman realised that he had misunderstood the situation.

The pair had become close. Dorflinger had been on Halsskär for a month. Sara Fredrika did not want him sentenced. She wanted to keep him. Her anger was not genuine.

He moved his stool closer to Dorflinger.

'I've told her what you said. I've also told her that I intend to help you. You're a marked man as a deserter from the German Navy, but I'll help you.'

'Why? You are also in the navy.'

'Sweden and Germany are not at war with each other. You are not my enemy.'

He could see that Dorflinger was doubtful. He smiled.

'I'm not sitting here telling you lies. I'll help you. You can't stay here. When I've finished my work you can come with me. Do you understand what I'm saying?'

Dorflinger said nothing.

Tobiasson-Svartman knew that he had understood. But he did not yet dare believe that it was true.

CHAPTER 97

During the night he slept next to the fire.

The deserter had hidden himself inside his overcoat, halfway under the bunk where Sara Fredrika was curled up with furs pulled over her head.

Tobiasson-Svartman slept deeply, then woke up with a start. He thought he could hear breathing that he recognised, his father's.

The dead, he thought. They're getting closer and closer. My father is also here, somewhere in this cottage. He is watching me without my being able to see him.

His watch told him that it would soon be dawn. He got up gingerly and went outside.

It was cold. He followed the path down to the inlet.

When dawn broke he discovered a seabird frozen into the ice. Its wings were spread, as if it had frozen to death just as it was about to take off.

He observed it for some considerable time, then walked on to the ice and broke its outstretched wings, bending them back against its body. Now the bird was resting, its attempt to escape was over.

He continued, following the route he used to row and approached the spot where the *Blenda* had been anchored. Thick cloud drifted in from the east. He had measured the precise distance to the ship and stood on the ice in the exact same place where the rope ladder had hung down. The clouds were dark, and it started snowing. He contemplated Halsskär. The grey rocks, interspersed by patches of white, looked like a shabby overcoat spread out in a field.

He had left his telescope on top of his luggage. It was a modern model, with double lenses that could be adjusted by sliding a cylindrical ring in a clockwise or anticlockwise direction. If the ring had been moved he could be certain that Sara Fredrika had taken the telescope and kept him under observation.

He was in the middle of a vast stretch of ice. Directly underneath him the distance to the bottom of the sea was forty-nine metres. He knew the precise depth at every spot on all sides.

For a fraction of a second he hoped the ice would break, that it would be all over. All this pointless searching for a place where there was no bottom, where every measuring device had to accept defeat.

Then he felt that Kristina Tacker was standing at his side. She leaned forward and whispered something in his ear, but he could not hear what it was.

He went on over the ice. The surface was rough, there were ridges that looked like seams on a garment. He went to the place where they had sunk the body of the dead sailor, and paused over the deepest part of the sea in this area.

He took his ice drill from his backpack. It had been made by the skilled craftsmen at Motala Verkstad in accordance with his own design. Unlike the ice drills used by the navy, his had a short handle. He found it made the work less strenuous because he could kneel on the ice and press down with his chest as he worked his way through the ice. He used one of his crampons to mark out a one-square-metre area. Then he started drilling.

Somewhere in the distance Sara Fredrika would be watching him through the telescope. Maybe she had Dorflinger by her side. The deserter was suspicious, of course, and for his sake if for no other reason it was necessary to put on this performance.

He made the first hole and was sure Sara Fredrika would be deceived into thinking he was sounding the depth. He drilled another hole and noted that the ice was fourteen centimetres thick.

Then he drilled two more holes in the remaining two corners of his square. He made the holes big enough for him to be able to force his fist through them. When he had finished he pressed down with his foot in the middle of his square. He took off his hat and listened.

The ice creaked loudly. He would be able to carry out his plan.

The light was dazzlingly bright. The ice reflected it into his eyes. He turned round and shielded them with his hand.

He thought he could see Sara Fredrika on a ledge just below the highest point on Halsskär. If he was right, the thing by her side was not a misshapen juniper bush, but the deserter he had promised to protect and assist.

He didn't want to mention his name, it was easier to think of him as the despicable deserter, the man who had abandoned his duty and got in the way.

CHAPTER 98

He returned over the ice.

Where the dead cat had been was only the patch of dried blood. He forced his way through the bushes growing by the shore and made his way towards the cottage.

Gunfire could be heard from out to sea. Then came the shock wave. Then another shot and another shock wave. Then all was silent again. Perhaps it was a warning signal. Perhaps the deserter was surrounded, perhaps the whole German Fleet was moving towards them at the edge of the ice? He sat down on a ledge to the north of the cottage. From there he could keep watch on it. A solitary bird flew over his head, its wings flapping madly. He imagined it to be a projectile, aimed at nobody.

Sara Fredrika came out, followed by the deserter. He had taken off his tunic and replaced it with an old jacket that must have belonged to her husband.

Jealousy.

He thought about the revolver locked away in a cupboard in Stockholm. If he had had it with him, he could easily have killed them both.

She pointed towards the inlet, they set off. The deserter suddenly stopped, took hold of her arm and pulled her towards him. She let it happen. At first the jealousy had been minor, creeping and not especially worrying. Now it had grown into something intolerable.

Then came fury.

His father had once spoken to guests at dinner about the importance of people learning to act like snakes. Cold blood, endless patience and poisonous fangs that struck at exactly the right instant. He had not been at the table, it was a dinner for grown-ups and he was only a child. But he had listened from behind the door.

Afterwards he had played snakes. He had dressed in brown, painted a stripe on his tongue so that it seemed to be forked, and tried to wriggle his way forward, wait patiently in the shade cast by a tree, stretch himself out on some rocks. He had even taught himself to spit thin squirts of saliva through his front teeth.

When he was eight he had forced himself to endure the ultimate snake test. He had caught a mouse in a trap, still alive, and bitten it and killed it. He had not been able to eat it, though.

Now here he was confronted by the unexpected. A deserter had got in his way. I shall kill him, he thought. And I'll cut off her hair that he has touched.

He lay motionless on the ledge until they were out of sight. Then he went to the cottage, found the deserter's papers in his tunic pocket and studied them. Stefan Dorflinger, born in Siegburg on 12 September 1888. Parents, Karl, regular seaman, bugler, and Elfriede Dorflinger. Signed on as a rating in the gunnery section of the cruiser *Weinshorn* in November 1912. A number of regular appraisal reports were positive. There was also a photograph of his parents. Karl Dorflinger had a prominent moustache; a friendly seeming, smiling man, but on the stout side. Elfriede Dorflinger was also large, her head seemed to rest on her shoulders with no neck. A bugler and a housewife pictured at a pavement café in a park. A shadowy, blurred waitress was walking by in the background with a tray of empty beer glasses. They were holding hands.

He studied the photograph at length. Two fat people holding hands.

He thought about the pictures that existed of him and Kristina Tacker. They used to go to the photographer's studio at least once a year. But there was not a single picture in which they made physical contact with each other, no holding hands, not even a hand on the other's shoulder.

He replaced the documents and picked up his telescope from on top of his rucksack. He opened the door and put the telescope to his eye.

The image was blurred. She had used it.

CHAPTER 99

He was standing with the telescope in his hand when he heard them approaching. He put it down on the ground, closed the door and sat down in the sun, his back resting against the house wall.

They were running. Both of them were out of breath.

'There are people on the ice,' she said.

'Did they see you?'

'Yes.'

'Who are they?'

'Presumably hunters. But you can never be sure.'

He thought for a moment.

'Did they get a good view of you, or just sufficient to see that there were two of you?'

'They are a long way away, in among the little reefs at Händelsöarna.'

The Händelsöarna islands were more than a kilometre away from Halsskär. Unless the hunters had a telescope they couldn't possibly have been able to identify the people they had seen.

'If they come here we can say that it was me and you they saw. Will they be sleeping here?'

'They can build huts on the ice. They all know that I

don't allow strange men to sleep in my cottage. Unless there's a storm or they've been in an accident.'

'He'll have to hide himself outside.'

He explained rapidly in German. The deserter seemed to trust him now and did not hesitate when they went out on to the rocks shortly afterwards. Tobiasson-Svartman led him to a crevice big enough for him to curl up in.

'Why are you doing this for me?'

'I would have done the same as you, and I would have hoped to meet somebody who was prepared to give me the same help.'

'I would never have survived if Sara Fredrika hadn't taken care of me.'

The deserter had lain down in the crevice and looked up at him. He had a scarf round his head, and the mad fox's pelt wound round his neck.

'I love her,' he said. 'I shall never forget her. One day when the war is over I shall come back here.'

'Does she know that?'

'We can't talk to each other. But I think she knows.'

Tobiasson-Svartman nodded slowly.

'Yes,' he said. 'I am sure you're right. No doubt she does know.'

He returned to the cottage and explained where the deserter was hiding. She had tied up her hair and was wearing a shawl.

She shrank back when he touched her.

'I promise to help him,' he said. 'But does he want to be helped? I'm afraid that one of these days he'll simply wander off over the ice.'

'Why would he do that?'

'He has been through something that nobody can put up with. It's important that we keep an eye on him. I'll let him come with me when I'm working on the ice. He can be of assistance.'

She stood by the window. 'I remember the first time you came here,' she said. 'I thought you were a man I could never trust. Now I'm ashamed when I recall that.'

'Why did you think you couldn't trust me?'

'I thought you were lustful and up to no good. Now I know I was wrong.'

'Yes,' he said. 'You were wrong.'

'I keep thinking about your dead wife and your dead daughter.'

'That's something we have in common,' he said quietly. 'The dead.'

CHAPTER 100

The men were from the inner archipelago. They carried shotguns and were going to hunt seabirds that were overwintering in the area. They were father and son, the father thin with sunken eyes, the son tall with a stutter. The father had a gold ring in one ear – perhaps he had been a seafarer who believed that the ring would save him from drowning, or at least pay for his funeral. Sara Fredrika had seen them before. They would call in now and then every winter, asking for nothing more than to know if she had seen any seabirds. They had decoys in baskets which they carried on their backs, and Tobiasson-Svartman noticed that the father smelled of strong drink.

They eyed him curiously and made no attempt to conceal the fact that they were wondering what on earth a naval officer was doing out here on the skerry. He told them about his depth-sounding mission in the late autumn, and that he was now checking a number of measurements.

'I remember people sounding the depths here when I was a young lad,' said the father, whose name was Helge Wallén. 'It must have been about 1869 or 1870. There were boats anchored at Barösund, measuring. My dad sold them groceries, eggs, milk, he even slaughtered a pig cos they paid him well. Us kids were half starved, but Dad knew what he was doing. He was able to buy our farm the year after, with all the dosh he raked in. They were here for ages, measuring. Can there really be so much going on down there that you have to go through it all again?'

'It's because of the boats,' Tobiasson-Svartman said. 'Bigger ships, bigger draughts, the need for wider navigable channels.'

They were standing outside the cottage. The son had stammered when he introduced himself as Olle.

'So you're still here, then?' the father said to Sara Fredrika.

'I'm still here.'

'We saw that you weren't on your own as we were passing Händelsöarna. I says to Olle, Sara Fredrika's got herself a husband.'

'I'm still here,' Sara Fredrika said, 'but my husband is still my husband, even if he's lying at the bottom of the sea out here.'

They stood a while outside the cottage. The father was chewing over Sara Fredrika's answer. Then he spat and lifted his bags.

'We'd best be off,' he said. 'Have you seen any birds?'

'At the edge of the ice. But further south, on the way to Häradskär. That's the place to put your decoys.'

The men wandered off towards the inlet. Tobiasson-Svartman and Sara Fredrika clambered up a high rock and watched them leave, saw how they turned southwards when they reached the edge of the ice.

'I'm related to them somehow or other,' she said. 'I can't quite work out how. But the link is there somewhere in the past.'

'I thought everybody in the skerries was related to everybody else?'

'We get quite a few incomers,' she said. 'The types who like to hide away, the ones that aren't tempted by the towns. I was in Norrköping once. I can't have been more than sixteen. My uncle was going to sell a couple of cows and he wanted me with him. The town has some kind of smell that made it hard for me to breathe.'

'But even so, you want me to take you away from here?'

'I reckon you can learn. Like swimming. Or rowing. You can learn how to breathe even in a town.'

'I'll take you away from here,' he said. 'But not now. First I have to help this man.'

She looked at him doubtfully.

'Do you really mean what you say?'

'I always mean what I say.'

Sara Fredrika went back to the cottage. He watched her jumping from rock to rock, as if she knew them, every one.

He waited until she had gone inside. Then he fetched the deserter, who was shivering in his crevice.

CHAPTER 101

At some point he was woken by a movement during the night.

The man lying by his side got quietly to his knees. The embers in the hearth had almost gone out, and the chill had already started to take over the room. He heard the man groping his way to the bunk, a few faint whispers, then silence, only their breathing.

He stayed awake until the man made his way quietly back to his place on the floor. His jealousy started rising from out of the depths and reached the point where he knew it was ready to burst to the surface.

CHAPTER 102

There was a change in the weather. It was warmer during the day and the snow started to melt, but the nights were still cold. Every morning for a week he took Stefan Dorflinger with him on to the ice. It developed into a peculiar sort of game, with him drawing up an imaginary line a hundred metres from where he had prepared the trapdoor in the ice. He taught the deserter how to drill, explained the principles of depth sounding and let him drop the lead down to the seabed and do the calculations. Tobiasson-Svartman played the role of magician who would occasionally predict an accurate measurement even before the lead had reached the bottom.

Nothing is as magical as exact knowledge, he thought. The man who had run away from his German naval ship had found a strange magician in the Swedish winter landscape. A man who can see through the ice, who can measure depths, not by using a sounding lead but by using his magical powers.

The deserter became calmer as the days went by. Every morning he would gaze out to sea, but when there was no sign of a ship he seemed to forget all about being tracked down.

He would occasionally talk about his life. Tobiasson-Svartman asked his questions diplomatically, always politely, never intrusive. He soon formed his opinion of the deserter's character. Dorflinger was a limited young man, with no knowledge, no interests. His greatest resource was his fear, the fear that had driven him to try to row away to freedom.

They spent the mornings out on the ice. They drilled and measured. Now and then they could see Sara Fredrika on the rocks on Halsskär.

In the afternoons he left them on their own. Every evening he told Sara Fredrika about the sailor's progress, about his increasing trust.

'I'll take him with me when I leave,' he said. 'I have colleagues who hate the German military, they will help him. I'll take him with me, look after him. Then I'll come back here and fetch you.'

Her response was always the same.

'I don't believe it. Not until I see you on the ice.'

'I'll leave you my telescope,' he said. 'That will help you to see me sooner. It will make your wait shorter.'

He spent an hour every afternoon writing up his diary. He wrote about the deserter. On 17 February he wrote:

> The day is approaching when I can do my duty and capture the German deserter who has fled to Sweden and is in hiding here. One can well ask oneself if he has made up the whole story. Perhaps he has been placed here as the furthest outpost in a network of spies preparing for a German attack

on Sweden. Since I think he could well resist, I am planning for all possible circumstances.

He hid his diary, wrapped up in a waterproof pouch, in a clump of hawthorn bushes next to the path to the inlet.

It seemed to him that he was living in many different worlds at the same time. Each one of them was equally true.

The day was approaching. He was waiting for a change in the weather. He was waiting for a chilly morning with fog.

CHAPTER 103

On 19 February, at about nine in the morning, he trained his telescope on the two hunters, father and son, who were returning to the inner archipelago over the ice. They passed to the south of Halsskär and had evidently had plenty of success. They were pulling a net behind them over the ice, full of dead birds.

Then he aimed his telescope out to sea. He sensed that a change of weather was on the way. The sun was hidden behind thick cloud and the temperature was falling. Everything suggested that they would have fog for the next few days. That day he had asked Dorflinger to drill some holes and take some measurements without supervision.

He scrutinised the man on the ice, hunched over the drill. Sara Fredrika came up to him. She had spent the morning catching cod with lines through several holes in the ice on the west side of the skerry. He suspected that she had been watching him before making her presence known.

'Why does one man watch another through a telescope?'

I once saw you naked, he thought. Without a telescope. I watched you getting washed, I saw your body. I have never forgotten that. I might forget *you* eventually, but I'll never forget your body.

'I'm just checking to make sure he's doing it right.'

She grabbed hold of his arm. 'I can't stay here.'

'What would have happened if I hadn't come?'

'I'd have asked him to take me with him.'

'Would you have gone with a man who was doomed to die?'

'I didn't know that then.'

'No,' he said. 'You couldn't have known that.'

When she went back to the cottage he followed her at a safe distance to make sure she went inside.

Dorflinger continued drilling the pointless holes in the ice.

Tobiasson-Svartman looked for a sufficiently big stone to act as a weight and kicked it on to the ice. It had a rounded bottom and slid along without him needing to put much effort into it. Then he collected some sticks and branches, broke them into pieces and left them next to the upturned boat.

The temperature went on falling. He could see the hunters again. He watched them on their way back to land until they were no longer visible.

CHAPTER 104

The next day the island was covered in fog.

Tobiasson-Svartman waited until the others were awake.

'I'm going out now,' he said. 'You can follow me in an hour. Wait to see if the fog lifts.'

'I won't get lost,' Dorflinger said.

'I'll leave a trail from the inlet. It's easy to get over-confident when it's foggy. Shout as you are walking over the ice, and I can put you right if you are off-course.'

He did not wait for a response. He strapped on his rucksack with the ice drill sticking out and set off. When he stepped on to the ice he left a trail of sticks marking the way to the holes that had been drilled. The fog was very thick. He kicked the stone a few metres ahead and took a step back, then another. The stone was lost in the fog. Visibility was four metres at most.

He thought he could hear a foghorn in the distance. He listened, but there was no second foghorn. He left his trail of sticks until he came to the place where he had bored the first holes at the corners of a square. He tried the ice with his foot. It creaked. He had kept the holes open by clearing away any ice and snow in them every other day or so. Now he bored ten more holes. He was dripping with sweat by the time he had finished. When he put his foot on the ice and pressed lightly, it cracked along all four sides. He got down on his knees and spread loose snow over the cracks, making them invisible.

It suddenly struck him that Sara Fredrika might accompany the deserter, being afraid that he could get lost. That would mean he would be forced to postpone what he planned to do. He hoped she would not appear. Changing plans would be a defeat.

He opened his rucksack and took out a piece of rope he had found in Sara Fredrika's dinghy. He tied it round the stone, which he then kicked into the fog.

He took a few deep breaths and measured his pulse. It was a little higher than normal, eighty-two beats per minute. He took off his gloves and held his hands out in front of him. His fingers were not shaking. He was a stranger, somebody who was himself, but at the same time somebody else.

Then he heard the crunch of footsteps on the ice. Dorflinger appeared out of the fog. He was alone. Tobiasson-Svartman smiled.

CHAPTER 105

It was their last conversation and it was very short.

Tobiasson-Svartman had positioned himself so that the hole in the ice was between him and Dorflinger.

'You know the fate lying in wait for a deserter,' he said. 'They'll hang you from a tree or a lamp-post. Or they'll shoot you or even behead you. They'll hang a plaque round your neck. *Deserter*. And there will be no shortage of volunteers willing to pull the rope tight or to press the trigger. A deserter is a man who stole other people's lives.'

He took a step back. Dorflinger took a pace forward. He stepped on to the square, the ice gave way and he fell into the water. Tobiasson-Svartman raised his sounding lead and hit him hard on the back of his head. To his surprise, it made a bloodstained dent in the brass. Then he saw that Dorflinger was still alive. His hands were grasping at the edge of the ice in an attempt to stay above water. He stared at Tobiasson-Svartman with gaping eyes.

Tobiasson-Svartman took one of the ice prods hanging round his neck and stabbed at Dorflinger's eyes. They must stop seeing, he must destroy what they have seen.

Dorflinger screamed just once, a sound like one coming from a little child. Then he was silent.

Tobiasson-Svartman kicked the stone to the edge of

the hole and fastened the rope round the waist of the man in the hole. The water was cold, the broken ice covered in sticky blood. He tried not to look at the man's face, the mutilated eyes. When he pushed the stone into the water the body sank immediately and vanished.

CHAPTER 106

He thought of the burial of Karl-Heinz Richter.

Now Herr Richter and Herr Dorflinger would meet in the cemetery 160 metres under water. Two men with no eyes, two men who spent five or six minutes sinking to the bottom of the sea.

He listened. Not a sound. He wiped his sounding lead clean and scraped away the blood that had spurted on to the ice.

When everything was clean around the hole, it dawned on him what he had done. For the whole of his life he had been afraid of death, of dead people. Now he had killed a man, not in a war, not obeying an order, not in self-defence. He had acted in cold blood, with malice aforethought, without hesitation or regret.

He looked at the hole in the ice, the grave opening. Down there in the depths, he thought, two people are sinking to the bottom of the sea. One is a German deserter. I killed him because he got in my way. But there is another person sinking with an invisible weight tied round his neck.

Me. The person I was. Or possibly the person I have at last discovered that I am. He felt dizzy. So as not to fall over, he sat down on the ice. His heart was pounding, he had difficulty in breathing. He stared at the hole and had a powerful feeling that Stefan Dorflinger was about to climb out of the ice-cold water.

What have I done? he thought, horrified. What is happening to me? There was no answer. The panic taking possession of him was incapable of words.

He stood up and prepared to throw himself into the water. But Kristina Tacker appeared by his side and said: 'It's not you who's going to die. It's your enemies who die. Lieutenant Jakobsson, who despised you, he dropped dead. You are alive and the others die. Never forget that I love you.'

Then she was gone.

Love is unfathomable, he thought. Unfathomable, but perhaps invincible.

He stayed for half an hour by the hole in the ice, then walked slowly back to the skerry that was still shrouded in fog. Every time he saw a piece of wood marking out the path, he bent down and threw it as far as he could, one to the left, the next to the right.

The hole would soon freeze over again. There was no longer a path behind him.

There was nothing behind him.

CHAPTER 107

It would not be difficult to explain to Sara Fredrika what had happened. The deserter quite simply could no longer cope. There were people who tried to get the better of death by taking their own lives. That was nothing special, it often happened, particularly in wartime. When living in the proximity of death, it was usual for people not only to hang on to life but also to take out an advance on death.

As he came to the skerry he threw the last bit of wood out into the fog.

She was gutting cod, and now and then a bass, up by the cottage. She knew right away that something had happened. She dropped her knife and sat down, not on the stool behind her but on the ground.

'Tell me,' she said. 'Don't beat about the bush, tell me now.'

'There's been an accident.'

'Is he dead?'

'Yes, he's dead.'

'Did the ice give way?'

'He must have drilled holes so as to create a potential trapdoor when he was alone on the ice. He stepped on the weakened patch and just disappeared.'

She shook her head.

'He took his own life,' Tobiasson-Svartman said. 'I was taken completely by surprise. He didn't say a word. He just appeared out of the fog, walked up to where he must have drilled the holes and stepped straight on to it. He didn't hesitate. He can only have wanted to die.'

'No. He didn't want to die. He wanted to live.'

She was adamant. She bit hard on her hair. He had the impression that she was in a hole in the ice, hanging on by her own hair.

'He was scared. He was surrounded by fog, but even so he was alert to pursuers. When he was asleep, he tossed and turned and looked to see if there was somebody behind him. There's a limit to what can be endured by a person who is being hunted down even in his dreams.'

'He didn't want to die.'

She put out a hand to the cottage wall and stood up. When he tried to help her she pushed him away. She flopped down on to the stool. The fog had started to lift. The sun glinted on the layer of ice covering the roof ridge.

'I don't understand this,' she said. 'He wanted to live. Didn't you see his eyes? I've never seen anything like them.'

'They were full of fear.'

'They were *self-contained*. He had eyes that made sense, that could see there was something you could reach if only you could get away from what was causing you pain.'

'You must have been mistaken. He was so scared that, in the end, he couldn't deal with it. He had evidently thought it all out, drilled the holes in the right places, filled his pockets with stones. He stepped into the water just as you would step on to the dance floor, or into a warm room out of a cold one. He did what he wanted to do. When he stepped into the water, he wasn't frightened any more.'

'I thought I heard a scream.'

'It must have been a bird crying through the fog.'

The ice on the roof had started dripping. He stood up, stretched his legs and thought that Dorflinger had never really existed: he was just a figment of the imagination.

'Why didn't he kill himself when he first drilled the holes to create the trapdoor in the ice? Why did he wait?'

'If you've decided you're going to die, there's no hurry. Perhaps he wanted to be properly prepared.'

'When he touched me he wasn't scared. There was no hint of suicide in his hands.'

He winced when she mentioned the sailor's hand. He tried not to think about it. I should tell her the truth, he thought. That I killed him, and that now she has to make up her mind: stay here or go away with me.

'He had accepted the fact that he could not go on,' he said. 'He had seen the war, he had run away from it and he was being eaten up inside by his pursuers. I might well have done the same in his situation.'

She ran away down the path to the inlet. He followed slowly after.

She was sitting on the upturned boat, crying.

He felt sorry for her, but mostly he felt sorry for himself. Did she not understand? She was the one who had forced him to kill the deserter because she had put her cottage and her bed at his disposal.

The clouds had dispersed, and the fog. He returned to the cottage and sat down to wait.

She took her time. But when she did come, it was to him, and to nobody else.

CHAPTER 108

They shared her bed that night. For the second time.

For one brief, giddy moment he thought he could smell the fragrance of Kristina Tacker's body, hear her panting breath.

Then he was back to reality. Sara Fredrika's long hair imprisoned him, as if he had been woven into a net and was being pulled towards a point where he felt like bursting. Afterwards they were calm, still. He could not tell if she was awake or asleep. But she was there. He was there. It was not like sharing a bed with Kristina Tacker, with each of them heading off in different directions all the time.

He was woken up at dawn by her looking at him. Her face was very close.

'I shall soon have to leave you,' he said. 'But I'll come back. I'll come and take you away from here.'

'I hope so,' she said. 'I have to have something to believe in. Otherwise I couldn't go on.'

Otherwise I couldn't go on. What would happen then?

CHAPTER 109

He left her early in the morning of 27 February.

He had made preparations for starting to walk back to the mainland. She went with him to the edge of the ice.

'The cat,' he said when they were saying goodbye. 'I saw a cat once, here on the island. But you said there wasn't one?'

'I don't know why I lied. Of course there is a cat. But I don't know where it's got to.'

'I thought you would want to know. Dorflinger killed it with a stone and threw it on to the ice. He killed the cat in a spasm of violent rage. I don't know why. But I thought you would like to know.'

She did not reply.

Their leave-taking was awkward, a handshake, no more.

He counted to two hundred paces. Then he turned round. She had gone. She was left behind.

PART VII

Capture

CHAPTER 110

The train came to a halt between stations. They had just passed through Åby. The station had been in darkness, but a fire was burning next to the line. It was evening, with a wind blowing from Bråviken. Tobiasson-Svartman was in the carriage next to the engine. He was sharing a compartment with a man fast asleep in a corner, his head buried in a moth-eaten fur coat. He listened to the sighing noise coming from the steam engine, and was overcome by a feeling of unreality: he would be stuck here, the train would never start moving again. There were no rails ahead of him, only an endless vacuum and sighs from the engine.

It was the second day after he had left Halsskär and started his trek to the mainland. He had spent the night in the boathouse on Armnö, but he had been unable to sleep and as soon as dawn broke he went on walking over the ice towards Gryt.

Round about Kättilö he had heard rifle shots, first one, then another. Apart from that all was silent: the ice, the islands, solitary birds.

When he came to Gryt, walking up the hill towards the church, he had a stroke of luck. A car approached and they gave him a lift as far as Valdemarsvik. The driver said not a word all the twenty-kilometre journey. There were big rust holes in the car, and Tobiasson-Svartman could see the road beneath his feet.

On the back seat was the body of a child, a little girl, wrapped in a blanket. Only when they reached Valdemarsvik did he ask what had happened.

The man replied wearily: 'She scalded herself. Knocked over a bowl of boiling water. She was soaked in it from her stomach downwards. She screamed something awful before she died. But her face wasn't burned.'

The girl was lying with her face turned towards him.

As he sat on the train he did not think about Sara Fredrika or Kristina Tacker. He thought about the girl who had scalded herself. Who had died from the stomach downwards.

CHAPTER 111

A conductor came past. Tobiasson-Svartman was standing in the corridor between the first and second coaches, and he asked the man why the train had stopped. He noticed that he had a Bible in one of his uniform pockets.

'It's the cold. A set of points has frozen. A couple of linemen are thawing it out. We're twenty-five minutes late.'

'Twenty-nine,' Tobiasson-Svartman said.

They started off again shortly after midnight. The man in the corner woke up, gave Tobiasson-Svartman a bleary look and went back to sleep.

Tobiasson-Svartman had killed a man. Was he now less scared of death than before? Or more scared? There was no answer. His instrument was dead. His sounding lead was silent in his rucksack.

They arrived in Stockholm as dawn was breaking on 2 March. Outside the Central Station he passed the conductor from his train, but the man did not recognise him.

CHAPTER 112

Stockholm greeted him with snow flurries and freezing temperatures. He stood with his luggage and a porter, wondering where he should go. At first he gave his home address, then changed his mind and named a little hotel at Norra Bantorget. The porter disappeared into the snow and Tobiasson-Svartman went back into the station. He ordered breakfast in the first-class dining room, but the food stuck in his throat and he was forced to run to the toilets and throw up. The waitress looked at him in astonishment when he returned with tears in his eyes.

She can see, he thought. She can see that I have killed a man.

He paid his bill and left. The city and the falling snow made him dizzy. He came to the hotel where the porter was waiting for him. When the receptionist told him that the hotel was full, he was furious. The receptionist turned pale and gave him a room that was in fact already booked. The porter carried up his luggage.

'That's the way to treat them buggers,' he said with a smile as he pocketed his payment.

Tobiasson-Svartman closed the door, locked it and lay down on the bed. It was like being back in the boathouse on Armnö. He closed his eyes and clutched his sounding lead to his chest. Nobody knew where he was, nobody knew where he was heading for, least of all himself.

There was a draught from the window. He wrapped a scarf round his head, moved as close as possible to the wall and waited for the strength to make a decision.

CHAPTER 113

The snow eased off at about eleven. He stood in the window and looked down at Vasagatan. He was looking for somebody among the pedestrians who might be himself.

He made his decision. He would stay in the hotel today and tonight. Then he would go home to Kristina Tacker.

The events on Halsskär began to fade. He examined his hands. No trace there of what had happened. His fingers were smooth and unmarked, his hands were unaltered.

He went out in the evening. It had stopped snowing, but it was bitterly cold and the city was deserted. Only those who had to ventured out of doors. He took a cab outside the Central Station and asked to be taken to the Grand Hotel.

As he was entering the dining room a man turned towards him. It was his father-in-law, Ludwig Tacker.

Tobiasson-Svartman could see no escape. Tacker introduced him to the man he was with, Tobiasson-Svartman understood his name to be something like Andrén. Tacker asked his companion to wait in the foyer.

'I spoke to my daughter yesterday,' Tacker said. 'She was very worried to have heard nothing from you.'

'My mission was classified as secret.'

'So damned secret that you couldn't even send a greeting to your wife? When did you get home?'

'I came to Stockholm about an hour ago,' he said. 'I haven't been home yet. I have to meet some of my superiors first and submit a report.'

Ludwig Tacker's eyes were narrow and cold.

'At the Grand Hotel? In the dining room of the Grand Hotel? Secret goings-on?'

'We shall be meeting in a special room. I just wanted to see if I was the first to arrive.'

Tacker eyed him up and down.

'And when are you intending to go back to your home and your wife?'

'I don't want to disturb her too late. I shall spend tonight in a hotel. I can't go back home like a thief in the night.'

Tacker leaned towards him.

'I don't believe you,' he said. 'I have never liked you, I could never understand why Kristina married you. You're lying. There's something fishy about you, something about you never rings true.'

He did not wait for a reply but marched out of the dining room. Tobiasson-Svartman went to the Grand Café and started drinking. His father-in-law had seen through him. Now he would have to repeat that explanation to Kristina Tacker when he got home the next day.

He would give her the details, apologise for having

spent the night in a hotel then sit down calmly by her side. She would tell him what had happened while he had been away. He would listen, and all he would say about his expedition to the frozen waters at the edge of the open sea would be that he was glad it was over.

CHAPTER 114

That night he dreamed about very deep water.

He was holding his sounding lead in his hand, using it as a sinker and gliding down through the sea, but he felt no pressure despite being several kilometres under the surface.

It was not the fissure in the Pacific Ocean where a British hydrographic vessel had claimed to lower more than ten kilometres of line into the water before the bottom was reached. This was an unknown deep spot he had himself discovered, and even as he was gliding slowly down with his sounding lead in his hand, he knew that the bottom was 15,345 metres below the surface. It was a bewildering depth, and it concealed a secret. At the very bottom was a different world and a different life corresponding to the one he led.

He carried on sinking, perfectly calm, no hurry. His only worry was that he would never reach the bottom.

He had often had this same dream, and he had always woken up before reaching the bottom. It was the same again. When he opened his eyes he remembered that there had still been quite a way to go.

He stayed in bed. His disappointment at not having reached the bottom metamorphosed into an intense desire to murder Ludwig Tacker.

Somewhere there must be a hole in the ice for him as well, he thought. One of these days Ludwig Tacker too will descend to the bottom of the sea with iron sinkers strapped to his body.

CHAPTER 115

A porter wheeled his luggage through the streets of Stockholm.

Horses ploughed their way through the snowdrifts. It was still cold. He held a hand over his mouth as he followed on the heels of the porter.

I am frightened, he thought. Not because of what I have done, but because she will see straight through me, just like my father used to do with his scary eyes.

He longed to be back among the silence and the ice. It was as if the city had turned its back on him.

CHAPTER 116

His father-in-law had got there first. Kristina Tacker's surprise at seeing him was pure artifice. The maid took his coat and left them alone.

'I arrived in Stockholm late last night. I didn't want to frighten you.'

'You wouldn't have frightened me.'

She took his hand and led him into the room in the middle of their flat, the warmest room in winter and the coolest in summer. There were flowers on a table. He was on his guard immediately. She never used to buy flowers.

She sat down on the edge of one of the red plush chairs and said something in such a low voice that he couldn't make out what it was.

'I couldn't hear.'

'I'm pregnant.'

He did not move. Even so, it felt as if he had started running.

'I've been waiting for a chance to tell you.'

He sat on a chair next to her.

'Are you pleased?'

'Of course I am.'

'The baby is due in September.'

He worked it out in his head and realised right away

when it must have been conceived: the night after he had come home in December.

'I've been frightened. I didn't know how you would react.'

'I have always wanted to have a child.'

She stretched out her hand. It was cold. Sara Fredrika's hands had been warm. He held her hand and longed to be back on Halsskär. As he was walking over the ice he had thought that he would never return. Sara Fredrika would stay there, waiting for him. But the ice would melt away without his going back, the sea would open up but he would never go back to her island.

Kristina Tacker said something he did not catch. He was thinking about Sara Fredrika and could feel his lust rising. What he longed for was somewhere else. Not in the warmest of the rooms in Wallingatan.

'Life will be different,' she said.

'Life will be as we imagined it would be,' he replied.

He stood up and walked to the window since he couldn't bear to look her in the eye.

He heard her leaving the room. Her steps were sprightly. There was a clinking noise as she started moving her china figurines about. He closed his eyes, and it seemed to him that he was now sinking down to the point where there was no bottom.

CHAPTER 117

The next morning he left the flat at about nine.

He forced himself to walk quickly, so as to shake off his tiredness.

He had not slept a wink all night. When Kristina Tacker had fallen asleep he breathed in the smell of her skin, then carefully got out of bed. He wandered around the flat, trying to understand what was happening. He was losing his grip on his surroundings. This had never happened to him before. His instrument no longer worked.

He stood with one of her china figurines in his hand, just before dawn, when time seems to stand still. He thought aloud and whispered to the china figurine with its naively painted face that in fact he was the one who no longer worked. He had no right to blame his instrument.

He was out of breath by the time he came to Skeppsholmen. He waited until his pulse rate was normal before going in through the high doors.

CHAPTER 118

Tobiasson-Svartman walked down the echoing corridors and reported to a lieutenant by the name of Berg.

Lieutenant Berg looked at him in surprise.

'Nobody told us you were coming.'

'I'm doing that now. I don't expect to be interviewed today, I've only come to report that I'm back in Stockholm.'

The lieutenant asked him to take a seat while he finished writing an urgent message. Tobiasson-Svartman sat down to wait. The clock on the wall was two minutes slow. He could not resist standing up, opening the glass case and adjusting the minute hand. Lieutenant Berg raised his head, saw what he was doing then continued writing. His pen made a rasping sound. When the letter was finished he put it in an envelope, sealed it and summoned an adjutant by ringing a hand bell on his desk. The adjutant looked strangely pale, almost as if he were made up. He left the room after giving a half-hearted salute.

'You know that man's brother,' said Berg, rising to his feet.

Tobiasson-Svartman did his usual assessment. The man towering up in front of him was two metres tall, give or take two centimetres, depending on what kind of shoes or boots he was wearing.

Lieutenant Berg stood behind his desk, as if remaining within a fortress.

'Or rather, you did know his brother. He is no longer with us.'

He paused to allow Tobiasson-Svartman time to consider his own mortality.

'Lieutenant Jakobsson,' he said. 'Your superior officer last autumn. The man who died at his post. Adjutant Eugene Jakobsson is his younger brother. Just between you and me, he's not going to go very far. The notion of his being in command of a ship is unthinkable. He's an excellent adjutant, but a very limited person, and frankly a bit stupid.'

'I didn't know Lieutenant Jakobsson had a brother.'

'He has another three brothers and two sisters. It's very rare for us to know anything about the private circumstances of our fellow officers. Unless they become personal friends, of course.'

Berg sat down again.

'How did your mission go?' he said. 'I know about it.'

'The errors have been corrected.'

'But you don't have your charts with you?'

'As I said, I didn't expect to be interviewed immediately.'

Berg consulted the fat ledger on the desk in front of him.

'The committee is due to have its regular meeting

on 7 March. You can be interviewed then. Bring the charts with you. Prepare your presentation scrupulously, your time will be limited. The admirals are nervous.'

Berg stood up.

'I have another request,' Tobiasson-Svartman said.

Berg didn't sit down. Time was short.

'I'd like two months' leave. Starting immediately. On the grounds of utter exhaustion.'

'Every poor devil is exhausted nowadays,' Lieutenant Berg said. 'The admirals chew their moustaches, the commodores get heart attacks, bosuns get drunk and fall into the sea, and the gunboat crews can't aim properly. Who the hell isn't exhausted?'

'I don't want to be a burden on the navy by going on sick leave. I'd rather take unpaid leave.'

'Very few get leave granted nowadays. The navy requires all its resources. Your request is hardly going to be favourably received.'

'But I shall be applying even so.'

Lieutenant Berg shrugged.

'Let me have a written application by no later than tomorrow afternoon. I'll make sure it gets looked at this week.'

Tobiasson-Svartman clicked his heels and saluted.

He left Naval Headquarters. The sun had broken through the clouds, and it did not seem quite as cold any more.

He went straight home, feeling relieved about the decision he had made.

There was obviously a risk that his application would not be granted. Even so, he was not especially unhappy, indeed his relief was greater. He increased his stride. He was in a hurry to be home.

Kristina Tacker was sitting at a table, reading a book. Women's poetry, he thought dismissively. I'm sure Sara Fredrika doesn't read poetry. She probably barely knows what it is.

Kristina Tacker put her book down.

He gave her a worried smile.

'I've been given another mission,' he said. 'It means that I'll have to be away again for considerable periods. But I won't have to rough it this time. No treks over the ice, no long weeks on ships out at sea.'

'What will you be doing?'

'As usual the mission is classified. You know that I can't tell you even if I wanted to. Everything to do with the navy is secret. War is just round the corner all the time.'

'All I have is a postal address,' she said. 'The Military Postal Service in Malmö. But I never know where you are.'

They were sitting in the warm room. The maid was not on duty, the building was silent. They had drawn their chairs up to the tiled stove. Its brass doors were half open. He raked the embers. He was calm, even though everything he said was meaningless. His professional secrecy merged with the mission that did not exist but that he would carry out even so. His expedition was moving in a vacuum.

Not even the sea was right.

'What I can tell you is that I shall be on the other side of Sweden. Part of the time I shall be at the Karlsborg fortress, by Lake Vättern. Then I shall be moved to Marstrand in total secrecy. You mustn't mention any of this to anybody.'

'I never say anything.'

'You mustn't even hint at the fact that I'm on a mission.'

'If you're not here, surely I have to say something?'

'You can say that I'm on leave, indisposed, that I'm in a convalescent home.'

She squeezed his hand. 'I want you here.'

I *don't* want to be here, he thought, and had to force himself not to push her hand away. I don't want to be here, I'm afraid of the baby, of these rooms, of all the china figurines and their dead eyes.

I love you, but I don't want to be here. I love your fragrance, but I dread the day when it's no longer there. I'm scared of waking up out of a dream without knowing what it meant.

He stroked her hand gently.

'I'll soon be back, and above all our child will have a father who used the nine months of waiting to gain promotion.'

'That is a worthy cause.'

He could sense her expectation.

'That's also a secret.'

'Surely you can tell me.'

He leaned over, put his face next to hers and whispered: 'I'm to be made a captain.'

He enjoyed the taste of the words, and smiled.

'I'm so pleased to hear that. It will make my father happy.'

'It's essential that this remains between you and me. You mustn't say a word to him.'

He carried on telling her patiently how he would soon be back. There was no danger, he would simply be doing his duty.

'Nothing is more important than the baby,' he said. 'I must do my duty, but the baby is the most important thing.'

'I want our son to be called Ludwig, after my father. If it's a daughter, I'd like her to be called Laura. After my sister. I always wanted to be called Laura when I was a child.'

He kept on smiling.

'Ludwig is an attractive name and has a touch of strength about it. Of course our son should be called Ludwig.'

'Maybe he should be called Hans Ludwig?'

'On no account should he have my father's name.'

'When will you be leaving?'

I have already left, he thought. I am not here, it's only an aura that I have left behind. A spoor that will be washed away.

'Soon,' he said. 'I don't know exactly when, but soon. I must be with you when the time comes, of course.'

He was sitting by her side, holding her hand.

It felt warmer now, not so cold as it had been.

CHAPTER 119

Three days later he collected a letter from Skeppsholmen.

The board stated their view in great detail that Commander Lars Svartman had always carried out his duties with the utmost care and competence. The board therefore considered it appropriate that Svartman should be granted the leave he had requested. The precise date of his return to duty would be established in due course.

After his visit to Skeppsholmen he went for a long walk in Djurgården. He wiped the snow off one of the benches as far out on the promontory as you could get at Blockhusudden. A tug was labouring to keep the channel free of ice.

He thought about Kristina Tacker and the child that was on its way, but most of all he thought about the woman he had decided never to see again.

He remained sitting on the bench until he started to feel cold. The tug was still carving its passage to the sea. The ice was dirty, grey. He worked out the distance to the stern of the tug. When it reached the hundred-metre mark, he stood up and started to walk back towards the city centre.

CHAPTER 120

He stopped at the entrance to Handelsbanken in Kungsträdgården. He was surprised not to feel uneasy about his plan to make inroads into his capital. Hitherto he had always regarded himself as being thrifty, on the borderline of being miserly. Now he felt the need to start squandering money.

He entered the bank. The man who looked after his financial affairs, Håkansson, was engaged. He was received by a clerk and invited to wait.

He observed the people moving around inside the bank. They seemed to be deep down under the surface of the sea, with none of the noise they made rising to the surface. He held his breath for twenty seconds and allowed himself to sink down to the bottom of the bank. I'm playing, he thought. I'm playing with other people's depths.

Håkansson had flickering eyes and sweaty hands. Tobiasson-Svartman followed him up some stairs to a room whose door closed silently behind them.

'The war is worrying, of course,' said Håkansson. 'But thus far the stock exchange has reacted favourably to all the gunfire. Nothing seems to inspire the market more than the outbreak of war. The snag, of course, is that the market can be capricious. However, your shares are stable at the present time.'

'I need to turn some of those shares into cash.'

'I see. And what figure do you have in mind, Commander Svartman?'

I do not have a double-barrelled name here either, he thought. As far as the bank is concerned I am simply Lars Svartman, without the protection that my mother's surname gives me.

Annoyed, he said: 'Might I point out that my surname is Tobiasson-Svartman? It is several years now since I changed my name.'

Håkansson looked at him in surprise. Then he started leafing through his papers.

'I apologise for the fact that both the bank and I had overlooked your change of name. I shall put that right immediately.'

'Cash,' Tobiasson-Svartman said. 'Ten thousand kronor.'

Håkansson was surprised again. 'That's a lot of money. It means that quite a lot of shares will have to be sold.'

'I realise that.'

Håkansson thought for a moment. 'I would suggest in that case that we offload some forestry shares. When do you need access to the money?'

'Within a week.'

'And how would you like the money?'

'Hundreds, fifties, tens and fives. An equal amount of each denomination.'

Håkansson made a note. 'Shall we say Wednesday next week?'

'That will suit me fine.'

Tobiasson-Svartman left the bank. It is like getting drunk, he thought. Deciding to squander money. To be not like my father, all that damned saving all the time.

He went to Kungsträdgården and watched the skaters on the outdoor rink. An elderly man in shabby clothes came up to him, begging. Tobiasson-Svartman dismissed him curtly. Then changed his mind and hurried after him. The man reacted as if he were about to be attacked. Tobiasson-Svartman gave him a one-krona coin and did not wait to be thanked.

CHAPTER 121

That evening they talked about the mission to come. The silence in the room rose and fell. He closed the brass doors in the tiled stove with the poker. The room grew darker.

'I'm always afraid when you go away,' she said.

A mission can always be dangerous, he thought. Especially this time, when there is no mission.

'There's no reason for you to be afraid,' he said. 'There might have been if we were involved in the war. But we're not.'

'The mines, all those terrible explosions. Ships sinking in only a few seconds.'

'I shall be a long way away from the war. My job is to make sure that as few ships as possible are affected by the catastrophe.'

'What exactly are you doing?'

'I'm preserving a secret. And creating new secrets. I'm guarding the door.'

'What door?'

'The invisible door between what a few people know and what others ought not to know.'

She was about to ask another question, but he raised his hand. 'I've already said too much. Now I'd like you to go to bed. By tomorrow you'll have forgotten everything I've said.'

'Is that an order?' she asked with a smile.

'Yes,' he said. 'That's an order.'

It is even an order that is secret.

CHAPTER 122

March turned into one long wait. On several occasions he went to Naval Headquarters without being able to get an explanation for why it was taking so long for written confirmation of the length of his leave to come through.

Lieutenant Berg was never in his office. Adjutant Jakobsson had also disappeared. Nobody could tell him anything. But everybody insisted that nothing had happened to change the situation. It was simply a matter of excess bureaucracy as a result of the war.

One cold, clear evening at the end of March he left his flat in Wallingatan, after saying goodbye to his wife, who was not feeling well. He walked to the top of Observatoriekullen and studied the night sky.

Once a year, usually on a clear winter's night, he would make a pilgrimage to the stars. When he was a young cadet he had studied the star charts and read several astronomical textbooks.

He stood next to the dark observatory building and gazed up at the stars.

It seemed to him that the clear night sky and the sea were similar, like diffuse and not altogether reliable reflections of each other. The Milky Way was an archipelago, like a string of islands off the coast up there in space. The stars gleamed like lanterns, and he thought he could discern both green and red lights and all the time he was searching for navigable channels, routes between the stars where the biggest of naval vessels would be able to proceed without the risk of running aground. It was a game involving charts that did not exist. There were no ships sailing through space, no shallows between the stars.

But in space there were bottomless depths. Perhaps what he was really looking for in the sea was an entrance into another world, a space hidden far down below the surface where undiscovered fishes swam along their secret routes.

He stayed there for an hour and was freezing by the time he got home. His wife was asleep. Silently he opened the door to the maid's room. She was snoring, her mouth wide open. The covers were pulled up to her chin.

He sat in the warmest room in the flat, poked away at the embers in the tiled stove, drank a glass of brandy and wondered where Captain Rake was.

It had been a hard winter, few harbours had been ice-free. The navy had concentrated its resources on the south and west coasts. Somewhere out there was Captain Rake. No doubt he was asleep. He was an early bird.

Tobiasson-Svartman was impatient. Having to wait was getting him down. It was 29 March already, he wanted to set off south as soon as possible. Would Sara Fredrika still be there, waiting for him? Or had she already left the island? He poked the embers again. The image of Sara Fredrika came and went.

CHAPTER 123

Late at night. He was sitting at his desk, the lamp with the green porcelain shade was on. He was making notes. What was he really measuring? Distances, depths, speeds. But also light, darkness, cold, heat. And weights. All the things external to himself, that made up the space he occupied, ships' decks, his night on Observatoriekullen. He was measuring something else inside himself. Perseverance, resistance. Truth and falsehood. Worry, happiness, introversion. What was meaningful, and what was meaningless.

He stopped. He had made similar lists many times before. They were never complete. What did he always forget? What didn't he see? There was something he measured without being aware of it.

He stayed at his desk for quite a while. Eventually he locked the sheet of paper away in a drawer, with all the other lists.

He went to the bedroom. Kristina Tacker was still asleep. He gently touched her stomach.

Sara Fredrika, he thought. Are you still there?

CHAPTER 124

One day Kristina Tacker found the large sum of money he had collected from Handelsbanken. He had left the notes under a diary on his desk.

'I don't let the maid touch your desk. I tidy it up myself. A note was sticking out. I saw all that money.'

'That's right. There is a large sum of money on the desk.'

'But why?'

'If we get involved in the war the banks might close. I took precautions against that.'

She asked no more questions.

'I've always expected my wife not to snoop around among my private papers.'

She was shaking with emotion when she replied. 'I do not root around among your private papers. The only things I touch are your clothes when I pack your bags for you.'

'I've noticed before now that you've been going through my papers. It's just that I've chosen not to say anything until now.'

'I have never touched your papers. Why are you falsely accusing me?'

'Then we'll say no more about it.'

She stood up and ran out of the room. He heard the bedroom door close with a bang. Of course his accusations were groundless. But he felt no regret at all.

Soon the waiting will be over, he thought. One day, in the far distant future, I might be able to explain to her that she was married to a man who was never fully visible, not even to himself.

CHAPTER 125

Not a word was spoken for two days. The maid crept round the flat, hugging the walls. Then everything returned to normal on the third day. Kristina Tacker smiled. Lars Tobiasson-Svartman smiled back.

The snow had started to melt outside.

CHAPTER 126

On 3 April he was notified that his leave without pay would last until 15 June 1915. It would only be cancelled if Sweden were drawn into the war. His suitcases were already packed.

On 5 April he said goodbye to his wife. She went with him to the station. In his hand he had a ticket to Skövde and Karlsborg. She waved. He thought about how often her hand was cold.

In Katrineholm he got off the train and bought a new ticket to Norrköping. He emptied his cases and transferred the contents to his two rucksacks. After removing the luggage labels he stood the cases at the side of a luggage van.

CHAPTER 127

The ice was softer now. But it was still there, all the way to the outer skerries. The sky was obscured by a thin mist. He walked fast.

In one of the bays near Hässelskären he came upon a shoe frozen fast in the ice. The sole was facing upwards, as if the wearer had fallen through the ice while standing on his head. It was a man's lace-up boot, big, patched, a boot for a large foot. He paused and examined the ice all around it. Nothing but the boot. No footsteps, nothing.

He continued his trek, walking so fast that he became short of breath. He would occasionally stop and scan the ice he had already traversed through his telescope. There was, of course, nobody following him.

He stopped again at Armnö: it would be the third time he had spent the night there. Somebody had been in the boathouse in the meantime. The herring drift nets had gone, and a newly tied pike net was in one corner. He ate his tinned meat and made a fire. He was impatient. The frozen-in boot puzzled him.

The next day he rose early and continued his trek over the ice. A wind was getting up, gusting from the north-east.

When he came to Uddskärsfjärden, the other side of Höga Lundsholmen, he met two people coming the other way. They suddenly appeared from behind the skerry, as if out of nowhere. He slipped out of the harness he was using to pull his rucksacks over the ice. It was like laying down his guns.

It was a man about the same age as himself and a boy, twelve or thirteen years old. The boy was deformed, with a misshapen head. His skull was far too big, and his skin was stretched tightly over his projecting cheekbones. He was also one-eyed, his left eye being no more than a shrivelled bag of skin. Their clothes were shabby, the man's face gaunt, his eyes flickering. They eyed him anxiously. The boy took hold of the man's hand.

'It's not very often you come across anybody else walking over the ice,' Tobiasson-Svartman said.

'We're on our way to Kalmar,' the man said. 'We come from t' north. It's quicker to walk over t' ice, when it's strong enough.'

The man spoke a dialect he could not place.

'From the north?' he said. 'How far north? Further than Söderköping?'

'I nivver 'eard of Söderköping. We come from Roslagen, near Öregrund.'

'Then you have come a long way.'

The boy said nothing. He made a snorting sound when he breathed. He suddenly burst out laughing and tossed his head about. His father took hold of him, gripping him tight like an animal you've just caught. The boy calmed down and sank back into silence.

'His mother's dead,' the man said. 'There was nowt for us up there. He's got an aunt in Kalmar. Mebbe it's better there. She's religious, so I reckon she ought to be willing to take in young ones and ailin' folk.'

'What do you do to earn a living?'

'We wanders frae farm to farm. Folks are poor, but they share with us. Specially when they clap eyes on my lad. I reckon it's mainly so as to get shot of us quicker.'

The father raised his shabby hat, took hold of his son's hand and started walking. Tobiasson-Svartman shouted to them to stop. He took some banknotes out of his inside pocket, at first low-value ones, but then he added a hundred-kronor note. He handed them to the father who stared at the money in amazement.

'I can afford it,' Tobiasson-Svartman said. 'It's not only poor people who go trekking over the ice.'

He set off again. He did not turn round until he was several hundred metres distant.

The father and son were as if rooted to the ice, gaping after him.

CHAPTER 128

He closed in on Halsskär in the afternoon of the following day.

The ice was soft still. The rucksacks he was pulling behind him were sucking up the surface slush and getting heavier and heavier. He avoided going too close to the shallows, round the rocks and skerries. He stopped three times to check the thickness of the ice. The sea was getting closer, pushing up from underneath.

CHAPTER 129

He was trembling when he focused the telescope.

There was smoke rising from the chimney. He had expected that to make him feel relieved. Instead he was nervous.

I will turn back, he thought. I must put a stop to this madness, I will go back.

Then he continued walking towards the skerry. The boat was beached, the sail furled tightly round the mast. The snow had melted away on the path to the cottage, he could see no footprints.

He sat down on one of the large stones used as a sinker and took a bottle of aquavit from one of the soaking rucksacks. He took two deep swigs, and could feel the heat spreading through his body.

He took another drink, then set off for the cottage.

I'll knock on the door, he thought. I'll open it and go inside. When I've closed the door behind me I'll start looking for a way of escape right away.

Before he had time to knock the door opened. Sara Fredrika flung it open. She was wearing different clothes, patched, worn, but clean. Her hair was not in a mess, she had put it up. She was shaking. He had never seen so much happiness.

'I knew you'd come,' she said. 'I have had my doubts, but I had not given up.'

'I said I would come. It took time. But now I've trekked over the ice and here I am.'

They went into the cottage. She had tidied. A lot had been taken away – bits of rag, odd pieces of worn carpet – but the skin of the mad fox was still there. He wriggled out of his rucksacks.

She grabbed hold of him. It was as if she were sticking fish hooks into him. She started pulling and tugging at his clothes. They tumbled to the floor in front of the fire. He burned his back, but the hooks were so deeply embedded that he could not get away.

Afterwards they got dressed in silence. He eyed her back furtively.

When she turned round he saw that her expression was different. He recognised it, he'd seen it before, but on somebody else's face. He knew straight away. She had the same look in her eyes as when his wife told him she was pregnant.

CHAPTER 130

Sara Fredrika told him the next day, as if it were the most straightforward thing in the world.

They were walking along the shore, collecting driftwood for the fire.

'I'm pregnant,' she said.

'I thought as much,' he said.

She eyed him expectantly.

'Will you be disappearing again now?'

'Why should I want to do that?'

'A naval officer and a slut from the sea. What sort of a future is there in that? We're on the edge of a precipice.'

'I came to fetch you.'

'You ought to know that I'd made up my mind. I'm pleased about the baby, even if you hadn't come back.'

'I'm here.'

She was still looking at him. He had the feeling that a rope was being drawn taut around them.

CHAPTER 131

The baby was surrounded by silence.

Sara Fredrika said nothing that was not necessary. Lars Tobiasson-Svartman tried to understand what was happening. Nothing was clear any more. He could feel an unusual sense of peace, but it was misleading. It was frequently broken by a pain that seemed to encroach from all sides at the same time.

He pushed aside all thoughts, put obstacles in their way. When he became too uneasy he clambered round and round the rocks, as if he were trying to erase some pursuers. He told Sara Fredrika that he needed to keep himself in good shape.

They shared her bed at night. Their bodies asked no questions that made him feel ill at ease.

CHAPTER 132

On 19 April a strong south-westerly wind blew up and dispersed the remains of the ice that was still covering the bays.

They went to the highest point on the island and saw that they were now surrounded by open sea. Further in towards the mainland they could still see traces of the broken-up, greyish-white ice.

The next day they launched the sailing dinghy. He was surprised by how strong she was. He stayed on shore while she rowed out to check that the boat was still watertight, and that the sail smacking against the mast did not have any tears.

'I'll sail around the island,' she shouted.

He stretched out his arms. He did not want to go with her, he stayed on the skerry. He followed her progress through his telescope. She suddenly turned to look at him, smiled and waved. She was saying something, but he could not read her lips. Further out to sea he could see another sail. He could see through the telescope that it was a little cargo boat coming from the east, heading for Barösund.

He was standing in the inlet waiting for her to round

the headland. She was rowing now, with the sail furled round the mast.

They beached the boat and he fastened a rope round one of the big stones.

'She's completely dry. Shipping no water at all. Did you see that I was talking to you?'

'Yes, but I couldn't understand what you were saying.'

'You will do next time.'

'What about that cargo boat?'

'It's on its way here.'

They walked up the path to the cottage. Spring flowers were starting to appear, moss campion and sand couch.

'It's a sailor from Åland,' she said. 'He always comes here in the spring. He says he knows when the sea is open. In fact, I think he hangs around in one of the pools where the ice never forms.'

'What do you mean, pools?'

'Holes in the ice. That never freeze over.'

He had never heard of any such thing before. 'Have you seen them?'

'How on earth could I have seen them? But others have. They are like big gills in the ice. The sea has to breathe when it's covered in ice. This man who's on his way here, ask him, his name's Olaus, he usually rows over to the island and asks if I need anything from civilisation. Or if I have any letters he can post for me.'

'Letters?' He looked at her in surprise.

'Olaus is a nice man. He thinks there might be somebody for me to write to. He thinks he's doing me a favour when he offers to post letters for me.'

They went into the cottage.

'I have a letter,' he said.

'I haven't seen you writing anything.'

'I haven't written it yet. Now that I know there's somebody who could post it, I can write it.'

'Who do you have to write to?'

'The hydrographic engineers, my superiors in Stockholm. I have various observations to report.'

'What have you seen that I haven't seen?'

That made him angry, but he did not show it. When she had gone outside he took writing paper and an envelope from one of the rucksacks and sat down at the table. He found it difficult to produce the words.

The letter was one long prevarication. It was about why it had been posted on the east coast and not from the part of Sweden where he was supposed to be. Complications, sudden changes of plan, tasks that had been cancelled, all of them secret. He ought not really to send this letter, but he was writing it even so. He would soon be going back to the fortress in Karlsborg; no doubt by the time she received this letter he would have left the melting ice of the Baltic Sea.

He finished by saying: '*I'll soon be home again. Nothing is fixed, but it will be before summer. I'm always thinking of you and the baby.*'

* * *

He went over to the window and looked at the woman outside.

For one brief moment the faces fused, one half was Kristina Tacker's, the eyes, the hair and the forehead were Sara Fredrika's.

She came in and sat down on the bed.

'Read it to me.'

'Why?'

'I've always dreamed of receiving a letter one day.'

'It's secret.'

'Who is there I could tell it to?'

He unfolded the paper and read aloud: '"The ice has melted away, the channels are navigable once more, meteorological forecasts suggest lower water levels and an increased risk of mines drifting into our waters. No sightings of foreign warships. Lars Tobiasson-Svartman."'

'Is that all?'

'I only write the bare minimum.'

'What's secret about that? Ice and water levels? I don't know what mines are.'

'Mines are a sort of iron driftwood that can explode. They blow ships and people to pieces.'

'Can't you write a letter to me?'

'I shall write a letter to you. If you leave the room. I have to be alone when I write.'

She left him alone. He sealed the letter to his wife and then wrote a couple of lines to Sara Fredrika.

'I'm so happy at the thought of having a child, after the tragic loss of my daughter Laura. I'm dreaming of the day when we can go away together.'

He did not sign the letter, but put it into the envelope and sealed it.

To Sara Fredrika. Halsskär.

CHAPTER 133

The man whose name was Olaus lay to anchor north of the skerry and rowed into the inlet. He was an old man with stiff joints who showed no sign of surprise when he saw Tobiasson-Svartman. It was a short visit, a sailor had gone ashore to make sure that the lady who lived on the skerry was in good health.

He did not seem to notice the signs, only slight as yet, that Sara Fredrika was pregnant. Tobiasson-Svartman gave him the letters, and money for the stamps.

'She wants a letter,' he said.

'Of course Sara would like a letter,' Olaus said. 'I'll post them in Valdemarsvik.'

He rowed back to his boat. When Tobiasson-Svartman got up the next day, it had already sailed. He had not asked any questions about the ice-free pools Sara Fredrika had spoken about.

CHAPTER 134

It was 9 May, warm weather, calm sea.

They got up early in order to bring in the nets that had been laid close to the little rocks that did not even have names. They rowed into the morning sun, she had unbuttoned her blouse and he was in his shirtsleeves. He rowed, she sat in the stern. He enjoyed the morning atmosphere, wanted for nothing, and just for now was liberated from all measurements and distances.

She reached for the cork float, stood up, braced herself and started pulling.

The net snagged immediately.

'Hang on,' she said. 'We've got snarled up in something.'

She tweaked and pulled. The net started to come in. But it was heavy.

'What is it?' he asked.

'If it's a fish, it's a big one. If it's crap from the seabed, it's pretty heavy.'

She hauled in most of the net, but it was almost empty, just the odd bullhead, an occasional cod. He leaned over the side to see better. Just then she let go of the net and screamed. She slumped down on the stern seat and buried her head in her hands. Caught up in the net were the skeletal remains of a human being and something that might have been a piece of leather from a jackboot.

He didn't need to ask what it was. He knew without asking. She had caught her dead husband in her net.

PART VIII

Measuring Lighthouse Beams

CHAPTER 135

It sounded as if she was howling. An animal in distress.

The net with the bits of skeleton had been snagged by the rail. She stood up and tugged at it as if fighting with a big fish. But she didn't want to have it on board, she wanted the net to sink back down to the bottom of the sea.

He sat motionless, holding the oars. What was happening was beyond his control. The net came loose and started to sink down to the bottom.

'Row,' she screamed. 'Let's get away from here.'

She flung herself at him and started to row herself. He could see her fear, feel the power in the strokes.

They were a long way from the spot where they had caught the bones when she slumped back on to the stern seat.

'Turn,' she said.

'Turn to where?'

'I was wrong. I must bring him up. I must bury my husband.'

Her fear had now become despair.

'There's no sign of the net,' he said. 'But I know where the place is.'

'How can you know when there's nothing to see?'

'I know,' he said. 'That's my special skill. I can read the sea, see what isn't visible.'

He turned the boat round, rowed nineteen strokes, then changed direction slightly to port and rowed twenty-two more strokes.

They had a little drag anchor in the boat. He knew that the depth here was between fifty-five and sixty metres. The anchor rope was only thirty metres long.

'It's here,' he said. 'But the rope is too short. I can't reach the bottom.'

'I must get him up.'

'I know where it is. We can come back to this very spot. You have a length of rope in the inlet and we can tie it to the anchor rope. That would give another forty metres, which would make it long enough.'

He didn't wait for her to answer but started rowing back to Halsskär. She sat quietly on the stern seat, hunched up, as if she'd just been exerting herself.

When they got to the inlet he fetched the rope and put it in the dinghy.

'Let me do it,' he said. 'Let me bring the net up. You don't need to be there.'

She said nothing. When he rowed out again she stood watching him.

CHAPTER 136

He let the anchor sink to the seabed.

He felt something at the fourth attempt. He stood up and pulled in the rope. The net reappeared, and in it the bits of bone and the piece of leather. It was part of a jack-boot, with a rusty stud still attached to it. He pulled the net on board. There were fish wriggling away in it, a sign of life amid all the death. He removed the fish and the seaweed, and threw the net back into the water.

He was reminded of the piece of drift net he'd seen that morning on board the *Blenda*. The soundless, lifeless movements, the freedom that meant always being on the move. Now another net had achieved freedom.

He examined the pieces of bone. There was part of a forearm, a broken rib and the remains of a left foot.

The foot upset him. There was something shameless about this well-preserved section of a man's skeleton, the only thing to remind an observer so vividly that this person had drowned in a state of inconceivable terror and loneliness.

He rowed back to Halsskär. At one point he stopped rowing and felt his forehead to feel if he had a temperature. His forehead was cool.

When he got back to the cottage he found it empty.

He put the bones down, walked back to the spring and drank deep. Then he went to look for her. She must be there somewhere. Even so, he suddenly felt all alone on the skerry.

CHAPTER 137

He found her at the far north end of the island. She had crawled into a crevice, pressed herself down into the heather, lay with her eyes wide open but seeing nothing. He sat down beside her.

There is nothing so easy as taking control of suffering people, he thought. People totally lacking in resistance. He remembered his mother, weeping, alone in one of the dark rooms that comprised his childhood home.

A flock of crows was cawing somewhere in the distance. The sound died away. He waited. Thirty-two minutes passed. Then she stood up and hastened away. She walked back to the cottage. He was about to follow her in when she came out and hurried down towards the inlet.

He stood quite still. Should he allow her to be on her own? There was nowhere she could disappear to, there were no hidden doors in the rocks that could open up.

Then he saw smoke and could smell tar. When he got there he found she had set fire to a tar barrel and was stuffing nets and eel traps into the flames.

'You can burn yourself!' he yelled. 'You can get burning tar all over you!'

He pulled at her, but she refused to budge. So he smacked her, hard, in the face. When she stood up he hit her again.

This time she stayed sitting on the ground. He knocked the barrel over and kicked it into the water. The barrel sizzled, the smoke stank. She was lying on the ground now, stained with tar and blood, her skirt pulled up way above her stomach. He reminded himself that there was a baby inside there, a baby that existed even if it couldn't be seen.

The burning tar slowly went out. There was a thin layer of smoking grease on the surface of the water. He helped her up.

'I must get away,' she said. 'I can't stay here.'

'We'll leave the island. Soon. But not yet.'

'Why do we have to stay here? Why not now?'

'I haven't finished my task.'

She examined her tar-stained hands.

'I salvaged the bones and cut off the floats,' he said. 'The net has gone.'

'It'll come floating up again.'

'It will be driven by the currents down deep in the water. It will never come up to the surface again. Not here at least.'

She looked around.

'The bones are in the cottage.'

'I have to bury him.'

She set off. When they got to the door he took hold of her again.

'I found something else.'

'His head! God, I can't take this.'

'Not his head. But a foot.'

'They were big and dirty. His feet were only important for him, not for me.'

She collected the remains on the ground in front of her and squatted down. She was murmuring, conducting a whispered conversation between herself and the bones. He leaned towards her to hear what she was saying, but he could not make out any words.

Then she stood up and fetched the fur from the mad fox. She rolled up the bones and the piece of leather inside it, and asked him to bring a spade.

The grave was a shallow hollow in one of the rocky ledges towards the west of the island. She did the digging, would not allow him to do it for her. When the spade struck rock she put the pelt in the hole and covered it with the soil. That evening she took the pipe and threw it into the fire. It seemed to Tobiasson-Svartman that she did that for his sake, removing the last trace of her husband. That night she clung tightly to his body. Her hands made it clear to him that she never intended to let go.

CHAPTER 138

The next day, in the evening, he told her that Halsskär was a sort of haven. A remote outpost in the sea for people with nowhere to go.

'It's like a church,' he said.

She had no idea what he meant by that.

'This skerry from Hell? A church?'

'Nobody commits a crime in a church. Nobody sticks an axe into his enemy's head in a church. It's a haven. In the old days outlaws were able to seek sanctuary in a church. Perhaps Halsskär was that kind of place for you and your husband? Without your realising it?'

She looked at him in a way he did not recognise. It was as if her eyes were turning away.

'How did you know about her?' she asked.

'Know about who?'

'The woman who sought sanctuary on this island. The goddess. I heard about her once from Helge. A storm had blown up and I let him stay overnight. That was when he told me about the winter's night in 1843. You can't always believe what Helge says, but he tells lovely stories. He has many words, just as many as you have. It was a severe winter that year, the ice was so thick that they say it roared like a wild animal when it formed pack ice. But there was an open channel from the sea way out near Gotska Sandön, and a woman came floating along in that channel, she must have been a goddess because there was a sort of halo all around her body. She had been thrown overboard by a drunken sailor. She was transparent and freezing cold and the open channel froze over once she had passed through it. But she reached here, and she hid herself on the skerry. The following year a dead sailor drifted ashore, he had cut his own throat. It was the sailor who had thrown her overboard, and now it was his turn to be washed up here. Helge had heard the story from his father. I sometimes think that she and I are the same person.'

She snuggled down under the covers. He sat down on the floor next to the bed, she stroked his hair.

Then he started to tell her about another goddess, the one who stood guard on the edge of the great city in the west, far away over the sea, and bade welcome to everyone who went there seeking sanctuary.

'I'll take you there,' he said. 'It's time for me to make a new start as well. You have your dead husband, I have my dead family.'

'I want to go to somewhere far away from the sea. I don't want to see it, or hear it, or smell it.'

'There are towns surrounded by desert. It's a long way to the sea from there.'

'What would you do there? In the middle of a desert? With your sounding leads and your sailor's book and your navigable channels?'

'There are things to measure in deserts as well. I could

explore the depth of the sand. I could keep track of how it keeps moving.'

'But what about the water?'

'If I started to long for it, I could no doubt find a sea out there to start sounding out.'

She fell asleep. He lay close to her, felt her warmth.

That night he dreamed about a ship sailing backwards across the horizon. It felt like somebody being taken to be executed.

CHAPTER 139

One night in the middle of May she woke him up and put his hand on her stomach. The baby was kicking.

The cry of a bird rang out through the night.

They said nothing, just the hand, the baby kicking, the cry of a bird.

He tried to conjure up the baby. Sara Fredrika's baby. Kristina Tacker's baby.

Kristina Tacker's had a face, it was his own.

Sara Fredrika's looked like the skeleton of a foot.

When she fell asleep again he got up and went out. It was a bright spring night, damp, with a breeze blowing over the rocks. He went to the highest point of the skerry and looked out to the sea.

He was overcome by his helplessness. All his lust and desire had gone. All he could envisage was dirt and misery.

I have to get away from here, he thought. Without her. I have to find a way of following her from a distance. Of seeing her without her seeing me.

I will have to enjoy my child from a distance. I cannot stay here.

CHAPTER 140

Although it was now May, it was still on the cold side.

A short but devastating storm demolished the cottage's chimney. He climbed on to the roof and repaired the damage. He could hear Sara Fredrika talking to herself inside the cottage.

As he was about to climb down he noticed a sailing dinghy approaching the island along the narrow Lindöfjärden channel. It was making good progress, its sail positively bulging.

He jumped down from the roof, and told Sara Fredrika about the dinghy.

'It will be Helge,' she said. 'You must remember him, and his son.'

He prepared to receive the dinghy.

'I want to talk to him in private,' she said. 'But I'm not going to say a word about my husband's foot in the net.'

He went into the cottage, lay down on the bed and went to sleep. When he woke up again it was already evening. He walked down to the inlet. Sara's dinghy was still there. But there was no sign of the visiting boat.

Nor was there any sign of Sara Fredrika.

He shouted for her all over the skerry. No response. It was only when he came to the steep north edge of the island that he found her, where the breakers were rolling in to the battered rocks.

She was asleep. Beside her among the rocks was a broken bottle.

CHAPTER 141

She woke with a start and sat up.

She started coughing, the smell of strong drink slapped him in the face. When she tried to stand up she stumbled and grazed her cheek on a rock. He stretched out a hand, but she pushed it away with a laugh.

'I'm drunk. Helge realised that I needed something to drink. He always has aquavit in the boat. It doesn't happen often. I'll be back to normal tomorrow.'

'You can't spend the night out here.'

'I shan't freeze to death. No birds are going to come and peck at me. I have to lie here in order to gather strength to stand up again.'

She stretched, pulled up her skirt and straightened her legs.

'You won't be able to get me to the cottage tonight. But you can stay here with me if you like.'

She grabbed hold of his leg and almost succeeded in pulling him over. She was strong, her hands were like monkey wrenches. When he tried to pull himself free she laughed even more and tightened her grip.

'Haven't you got it? I'm not going to let go of the man who's going to take me away from here.'

'I've gathered that.'

She let go and curled up in the hollow.

I have to get away, he thought. One of these days she'll stick an axe into my head when she finds out that I'm not the person who's going to rescue her. It had dawned on him that he was afraid of her. He could not control her, whether she was drunk or sober. She tore some moss off a rock and covered her face with it.

'Leave me alone now,' she said. 'Everything will be back to normal by tomorrow.'

There is no normality, he thought. She'll discover the abyss inside me if I do not leave the island. Her abyss is hers, mine is mine. I'm too close to her.

Later that night he returned to the hollow in the rocks.

He could smell that she had been vomiting. He left her there.

CHAPTER 142

The next day it was drizzling and blowing a gale from the east.

When he woke up she was sitting outside the door like a wet, shivering dog.

'I'm not taking a dead woman with me to America,' he said. 'Go inside, take your wet clothes off and get warm. Otherwise you'll be ill. The baby will die.'

She did as he said. He went down to the inlet and sat down on a broken corf.

Why would he not tell her the truth, that he could not come back and fetch her?

He knew the answer. He had killed his wife, and he had killed his daughter. He had been caught by the nets he had set out. He was being pulled down, just as her husband had been when he got caught in a herring net.

He went back to the cottage and stole a look through the window. She was sitting in front of the fire, wrapped up in a blanket, with her head turned away. Just like Kristina Tacker, he thought. Two women who turn their faces away from me.

Later that day he started to prepare for his departure. He talked to her, convinced her that she would not have long to wait. He would soon be leaving, but he would soon be back.

They continued fishing together, sleeping together, and he tried to look her in the eye all the time.

After a week he was convinced. She believed he would be coming back.

He could leave the island.

CHAPTER 143

It was 7 June, at the crack of dawn.

They were sailing northwards, with Harstena and the seal rocks to starboard, and were making good progress towards the skerries where they would turn westward towards the Slätbaken approach. He was sitting by the mast, in charge of the sail. They did not speak much, nor did they pass any other boats.

Late in the afternoon the wind died down. They found themselves drifting and they still had not reached the Slätbaken approach. They could see a warship passing by on the horizon, and shortly afterwards another one. He could see through the telescope that they were gunboats, but they were too far away to be identified. They steered to the nearest skerry, beached the dinghy, lit a fire and ate the potatoes and cold fish she had brought with her in a basket. She also had a jug of water.

The summer's night was light. A few stars twinkled in the sky. Despite everything he felt quite close to the woman he would soon abandon. She was by his side, despite his efforts to build a wall of inaccessibility around himself.

She had lain down, using the basket lid as a pillow.

'Is it true?' she asked suddenly. 'The stars, the winter

darkness and the light summer nights – is it true that they will never end? Or will they cease to exist? You must know, because you can measure depths and see distances that nobody else can see.'

'Nobody can know that,' he said. 'You can only believe.'

'What do you believe?'

'That you can go mad if you look too far out into space.'

She thought over his reply.

'My husband,' she said eventually. 'He used to dream about that. He would get restless when it started getting dark in the autumn. Strangely scared. He had to go outside at night, I had to go out with him and hold him tight. He could never explain it. He started to stammer as autumn set in. He never stammered at other times, but then, as it grew dark and the eels started to run, he would stare up at the stars and begin to stammer. He could not understand it, he said. It was beyond comprehension. There was a sailor on Haskö who got drunk and claimed that nothing came to an end, not the sky, not the stars, nothing. Everything just kept on going for ever.'

'Nobody can know that,' he said again. 'You are alone with the stars even if you see them together with somebody else.'

'Can you see your daughter up there? And your wife?'

'I can see them. But I don't want to talk about them.'

She said no more. Soon it will all be over, he thought.

The fire died out.

* * *

At daybreak they continued towards Slätbaken and the approach to the Göta Canal. They had a following wind, sailed through the sound at Stegeborg and had fresh winds when they came to Slätbaken itself.

Small boats were queuing up at the first set of locks at the entrance to the canal. They headed for the mouth of the river and rowed to the quays in the centre of Söderköping.

Their leave-taking was perfunctory. Her last impression had to be that he was telling the truth, that he really would complete his mission and hand the results over to his superiors in Stockholm. Then he would return to fetch her from Halsskär.

They moored at the quay next to the Brunns Hotel. It was low water. He clambered on to the quay. She stayed in the boat.

'Go home now,' he said. 'Sail carefully. I'll soon be there.'

He waved to her. She waved back and smiled.

He hoped she believed him. To be on the safe side he did not turn round.

CHAPTER 144

Two days later Tobiasson-Svartman was back in Stockholm. He went straight home from the station.

Kristina Tacker was surprised but delighted to see him. On the hall table was a message from Skeppsholmen, requesting him to report as soon as possible.

It was drizzling the following morning. As he crossed the bridge to Skeppsholmen he noticed a familiar face. Captain Rake looked thinner, and his face was very pale. Tobiasson-Svartman could see that something was troubling him, perhaps he had some crisis in his life.

'I've seen the new chart for the navigable channel at Sandsänkan,' Rake said. 'I hear that we'll be able to start using it soon.'

'It won't save as much time as I'd hoped,' said Tobiasson-Svartman. 'A ship progressing at full speed, let's say twenty knots, will save fifty minutes. I'd hoped for something better than that. But the seabed didn't behave itself as I would have liked.'

'So the seabed is a bit like people.'

'There'll be less of a risk of being hit by torpedoes and mines, of course. And the new channel ought to be able to cope with the considerable increase in draught that we can expect new naval vessels to have.'

Tobiasson-Svartman shook hands and made to continue on his way to Naval Headquarters. But Rake held on to his hand.

'I never cease to be surprised about how my memory works,' Rake said. 'I've seen an endless procession of bosuns and officers passing through my life, but even so, the most graphic memory is that of Bosun Rudin.'

'The man who died while he was being operated on for his appendix?'

'An insignificant spider in the massive web. But for some reason I can't shake him off. I wonder why.'

Rake let go of his hand and saluted.

'I talk too much,' he said. 'But at least I don't ask what you are doing now, because I take it for granted that whatever you're up to, it's secret.'

Tobiasson-Svartman watched Rake walking over the bridge. He was hunched, his long overcoat flapping around his legs.

CHAPTER 145

He was ushered in without delay.

To his surprise there were only two people waiting for him. One was Vice Admiral H:son-Lydenfeldt, the other a civil servant with a pale complexion and big bags under his eyes.

As he sat down in the chair provided for him, he felt a nagging pain in his stomach.

The vice admiral eyed him up and down.

'Are you aware of why you are here, Commander Svartman?'

'No, but I do know that I must ask for an extension of my unpaid leave.'

'Why?'

'I'm not restored to health.'

The vice admiral pointed impatiently at a file in front of him on the desk.

'Restored from what? The only reason you have given is exhaustion. Who the hell isn't exhausted? We're all exhausted. The *world* is exhausted. Our highly esteemed Naval Minister Boström sometimes nods off during our meetings. Not because he's bored, but because he's exhausted, he claims.'

Tobiasson-Svartman was about to justify his claim to be exhausted but the vice admiral held up his hand.

'You have been summoned here for a different reason. It has been reported that while you have been on leave you have undertaken journeys, and you have been seen in the Östergötland archipelago. We've received reports from people wondering if you are a spy working for Germany or Russia. And there are other relevant circumstances. Not least the fact that you claimed to have found errors in the charts you have produced yourself. It has become clear that you were lying. We haven't been able to throw full light on that one yet, but it is obvious that you have been making strange and clearly unjustified assertions and acting in highly questionable ways. What do you have to say to that?'

Tobiasson-Svartman was struck dumb. He had no idea how to answer. He felt himself blushing. The vice admiral had more to say:

'I don't think you are so damned stupid as to be a spy. But you have betrayed our confidence in you and caused a lot of trouble. You have proved to be unreliable. As nothing harmful has ensued, and as you are basically a competent hydrographic engineer, one of the best we have ever had, all we ask is that you resign your commission. If you refuse, we shall dismiss you and the reasons will be dishonourable. If you resign voluntarily, we shall give you the best possible reference that the circumstances allow. Is that clear?'

The civil servant with the big bags under his eyes leaned over the table. His teeth were yellow, his moustache dirty.

'I represent the minister with responsibility for the

navy,' he said in a voice that suggested he enjoyed torturing others. 'The minister is in full agreement with what the vice admiral has just said.'

H:son-Lydenfeldt slammed both hands down on to the desk.

'You have twenty-four hours in which to make up your mind. You might think that this is an unnecessarily dramatic reaction from His Majesty's armed forces, but in present circumstances the Swedish Navy cannot tolerate the slightest stain on its reputation. I believe you understand that.'

He took out his pocket watch.

'You will report here tomorrow at 10 a.m.'

The meeting was over.

When Tobiasson-Svartman left the room he was forced to lean against the corridor wall, so as not to fall.

CHAPTER 146

He paused on the steps outside Naval Headquarters. He watched some sparrows pecking away on one of the gravel paths. Then he continued. But stopped when he came to the bridge. He was still in shock. But he was thinking clearly now.

He was convinced. There was only one possible explanation. Sub-Lieutenant Welander had returned from the dead. Or at least from the *demi-monde* he had occupied while slowly recovering from the tribulations he had suffered as he wriggled out of the grip of strong drink.

He could see it all in his mind's eye.

Welander had not been cashiered but allowed to return to duty. Before that he had been reprimanded for the inadequate soundings he had made in the area surrounding the Sandsänkan lighthouse.

Needless to say, Welander had not understood what his accusers were talking about, and maintained that he had carried out his duties impeccably until the moment when everything fell to pieces. He had demanded to be confronted with the soundings Tobiasson-Svartman had attributed to him.

The truth had emerged. Welander had not in fact made any errors.

Tobiasson-Svartman started to walk over the bridge. Every step he took made him more certain that the bridge was like thin ice that could give way at any moment.

CHAPTER 147

That evening he sat in the warm room and told Kristina Tacker about his next mission. It put his mind at rest, describing an expedition that would never take place and which no superior officer had ordered him to undertake.

It was not the lies themselves that calmed him down. It was the impassive way his wife took in what he had to say. Thanks to her everything became real.

Her questions were always the same. Where would he be going? How long would he be away? Was there any danger involved?

'It doesn't have to be risky just because it's secret,' he said.

Without having prepared anything in advance he started to talk about lighthouse beams. The light projected from remote rocks or lightships in order to help ships stay on course. He talked about the beauty of the transit lines, the interplay between the red, green and white lights. He invented a mission he had never had and would never be given.

'I shall be measuring the distance from which the beams of various lighthouses can be seen in different weather conditions,' he said. 'I shall be investigating the possibility of creating an extra line of defence round our country by misleading the enemy with beams of differing strengths.'

Then he stopped. 'I've already said too much,' he said.

'I've already forgotten everything you said,' she replied.

He thought he detected a hint of alarm in her voice, barely noticeable, but there even so. *Measuring lighthouse beams.* Perhaps he had gone too far? Did she not believe him? Was there, for the first time, a vague suspicion in her mind?

She looked down and stroked her stomach. 'When will you be leaving?'

'Nothing is fixed yet, but a decision could be made at short notice.'

'I want you to be here when the baby comes.'

'Obviously, I hope the expedition will be over by then. Or that it hasn't even started. But I shall protest strongly if they want me to leave just when you are due to give birth.'

He stood up and went out on to the balcony.

He wondered where Sub-Lieutenant Welander lived.

CHAPTER 148

Two days later he had discovered that Welander lived on Kungsholmen.

When he called in at Skeppsholmen to submit his resignation he took the opportunity of visiting the personnel department. They informed him that at the moment Welander was not on board any navy ship.

His first new mission was to spend all his time outside the building where Welander had a flat.

It was four days before Welander appeared. He emerged from the front door with a woman and a girl aged about fourteen. Tobiasson-Svartman remembered vaguely that the family included a daughter and three sons. He followed them down Hantvarkergatan. When they came to Kungsholms Torg they went into a shop selling ladies' wear, and when they came out again both the wife and the daughter were carrying parcels.

Sooner or later Welander would be on his own. He would confront him. He observed Welander's face from a safe distance. The paleness and bloated features had gone. Welander really seemed to have overcome his addiction.

His wife was small and thin. She kept looking at her husband with a loving smile.

CHAPTER 149

Days passed. He waited, displaying the patience of a predator. The opportunity came one evening when he had been observing Welander for a week. The hydrographic engineer came out on his own. It was raining, and he set off towards the centre of town. He was walking fast, his gaze directed at the pavement ahead of him. Then he turned off on to a path running alongside the water in Riddarfjärden. The path appeared to be deserted.

Tobiasson-Svartman wrapped a scarf round the lower part of his face. In his pocket he had a hammer with an old sock round the head. He took it out and followed Welander along the path.

Yet he could not summon the courage to hit him, and he turned and ran away. He was afraid Welander would see him and follow, but there was no sound from the path behind him. He put the scarf and the hammer back into his overcoat pockets and forced himself to walk slowly.

When he came to Wallingatan he took his pulse. He did not go up to the flat until the rate had sunk to sixty-five.

CHAPTER 150

He continued leaving the flat every morning. He told Kristina Tacker that he was going to a meeting of the secret committee. He spent the days in museums and cafés. Eventually he reconciled himself to the fact that he had not dared to attack Welander. He was still furious, but unsure of where he should direct his rage.

Weeks passed. Kristina Tacker's stomach became bigger and bigger.

He tired of going to museums first, then cafés. Instead he went for very long walks. As dusk fell he would imagine the lighthouses, the ones that had not yet been switched off on account of the war. He could see in front of him a beam of light over the sea. Soon he must start measuring it. It was time to give himself the order to set out.

He thought about Sara Fredrika and the skerry on the edge of the open sea.

The sea is calm, he thought. For once the sea around me is dead calm.

CHAPTER 151

One evening it dawned on him that he was outside the building where Ludwig Tacker lived, the place where those dreadful Christmas dinners were held.

He recalled that his father-in-law went out for an evening walk every week.

Ludwig Tacker had once visited the British protectorate in southern Africa ruled autocratically by Cecil Rhodes. He never stopped telling his family about the long journey that had taken him to distant Lusaka via Gothenburg, Hull and Cape Town, and then by rail and on horseback to the copper mines at Broken Hill. He had never seen anything like it. Veins of copper were exposed on the ground in some places, so that you only needed to bend down to gather the valuable ore.

The object of his journey had been for Tacker to invest in the copper mines, but Rhodes had enough money and did not want anybody else to become involved. It had come to nothing. But Tacker was still interested in mining. That is why one evening every week he would meet a group of men roughly his own age who shared his interest in minerals. They met at the home of a mining consultant who lived at Järntorget in the Old Town.

As he walked home that evening it struck him that he might have found an outlet for his fury after all.

CHAPTER 152

The next week he followed his father-in-law through the streets to the mining consultant's home. He had no specific plan, he only wanted to find out what route Tacker took. He remained hidden in the shadows. It was a warm evening, and he waited for four hours until Tacker emerged and went back home accompanied by two other men. One of them stumbled occasionally, they were laughing a lot, kept stopping, then moving on again, all the time engrossed in talk.

That night, when his wife had gone to bed, he sat in his study and worked out a plan. On his desk were the hammer and the dark-coloured scarf. He was perfectly calm. It was like preparing for one of his expeditions. He did not notice that on two occasions his wife had appeared in the doorway, looking at him.

CHAPTER 153

It was a windy evening, with occasional showers.

He had put the scarf and the hammer with the sock round its head in his overcoat pockets. When Ludwig Tacker came out of his front door, Tobiasson-Svartman hurried to waylay him at a spot where it was especially dark and usually deserted. He hid in the shadows next to a wall. His father-in-law passed by so close that he could smell his cigar. The old man's walking stick tip-tapped on the paving stones. Tobiasson-Svartman wrapped the scarf round his face and took out the hammer. Seven paces, eight at most and he would have caught up.

Tacker spun round and raised his walking stick.

'Who are you?' he yelled. 'What do you want?'

Tobiasson-Svartman was terrified. He was sinking, hitting out was a way of coming back up to the surface. Tacker bellowed and defended himself stoutly, hitting with his walking stick and trying to pull off the scarf round Tobiasson-Svartman's face. Tacker was strong. He pulled and tugged and the scarf was half off when the hammer hit him on the nose. There was a crunching sound. Tacker fell heavily. Tobiasson-Svartman ran away. He threw the hammer into the water at Nybroviken, having first knotted the scarf tightly round its handle.

All the time he was afraid that somebody was going to grab him. But nobody came. He was alone with his fear.

He stood in Wallingatan for a long time. He had never been so terrified in all his life. Ludwig Tacker had almost exposed him. Everything would have collapsed.

In the end he opened the front door and walked up the stairs to his flat. Kristina Tacker was asleep. He listened outside her door.

The dead eyes of the china figurines glinted in the light from the street lamps. He sat down in the warm room and hoped that Ludwig Tacker was dead.

CHAPTER 154

The attack on Ludwig Tacker aroused a lot of attention. There were prominent articles in the newspapers. Everybody agreed that the assailant must be a madman.

But his father-in-law did not die. He had a broken jaw, a badly broken nose and he had bitten deeply into his tongue. The doctors treating him established that he also had concussion.

It was evening. Kristina Tacker had been to see her father. Tobiasson-Svartman was in his study, reading a meteorological journal, when she came into the room.

'I don't want to disturb you,' she said.

He put the journal down and pointed to the sofa in front of one of the two high windows. She slumped down.

'You're not disturbing me,' he said. 'How could you do that?'

'I've been thinking about what happened.'

'We must be grateful that he wasn't more badly injured.'

She shook her head. 'What kind of a person would try to kill a man he didn't know?'

'It's like in a war.'

'What do you mean?'

'You don't kill people, you kill enemies. And the enemy

is nearly always faceless. This man is conducting a secret war. Everybody is his enemy, nobody is his friend.'

She asked no more questions but left the room. He picked up a newspaper and read about himself. About the madman they were looking for.

I am completely calm, he thought. Nobody is going to arrest me, nobody knows. The man who appeared out of the darkness has vanished. He will never reappear. He will remain a riddle.

CHAPTER 155

The next day they went to visit his father-in-law; he was in bed at home, receiving only a few visitors.

He was tempted, just for an instant, to tell Ludwig Tacker who it had been, hidden behind the scarf.

'I'm very sorry to hear about what happened,' he said. 'It's the duty of the police to track down the madman. Let us hope they succeed. Thank goodness it didn't end in catastrophe, at least.'

Ludwig Tacker looked hard at him without saying a word. Then he made a dismissive gesture. He wanted to be left in peace.

Tobiasson-Svartman sat down on a bench in Humlegården.

It's not me, he told himself. For short periods I am somebody else, perhaps my father, perhaps somebody I could never imagine. I am searching for something, a bottom that does not exist, neither in the sea nor in myself.

His thoughts faded away. Children were playing in the park. His head was a complete vacuum. He started to feel extremely weary, it was like a bank of fog creeping up on him.

When he woke up it was late afternoon. He went home.

In the flat he found the maid waiting for him, red-eyed. Kristina Tacker had been rushed into hospital some hours previously. She had gone into labour, although the baby was not due for a long time yet.

The shock, he thought. Her shock and fear are now mine as well. I hoped her father would die. It might end up with me killing my own child instead.

CHAPTER 156

Kristina Tacker gave birth to a daughter that evening.

The doctors were very doubtful if the baby would live. For the next few days Tobiasson-Svartman did not leave the flat. He sent the maid back and forth, bringing news from the Serafimer Hospital.

The days were sultry. At night, when the maid had fallen asleep in exhaustion, he took to wandering about the flat naked. He frequently sat at his desk to write down his thoughts. But over and over again he discovered that he did not have any thoughts. All around him and inside him was nothing but a vast vacuum.

One night when he could not sleep he packed a suitcase. He tried to fold his clothes as if it had been his wife doing the packing for him.

The china figurines stood silently on their shelves. He waited.

CHAPTER 157

On 2 August he received a telephone message from a hospital consultant by the name of Edman.

He was asked to attend the hospital as soon as possible. His panic reaction was such that he had stomach pains. He hurried out of the flat doubled up in agony.

If the baby had died his wife would be very critical. He had stayed away for too long, had avoided his responsibilities. Or had something happened to her? Had she caught an infection? He had no idea, and sat shivering in the cab.

Then it struck him: Ludwig Tacker. Has he realised that I was the one who attacked him? Has he told her?

When he arrived at the hospital the first thing he needed to do was to go to the lavatory. Then he knocked on the consultant's door, heard a loud 'Come', and went in. Dr Edman was tall and bald. He invited his visitor to take a seat.

'You look very frightened.'

'Obviously, I was very worried when I was summoned here.'

'Everybody always fears the worst when they are bidden to come to the hospital. I've tried to drum it into my staff that they should try not to sound so damned dramatic on the telephone. But hospitals are frightening places, whether one likes it or not. However, you have no need to worry. Your daughter will survive. She is strong and has a powerful lust for life.'

His relief was beyond words. Once he had injured his arm when he fell from a companionway. The pain was intense and he had been given a morphine injection by the ship's doctor. He had never forgotten the feeling of relief when the injection started working. It was the same now, as if somebody had pumped some drug into his veins. His stomach pains ceased, Dr Edman stood before him like a beaming redeemer, dressed in white.

'They had better stay in hospital for a while yet,' the doctor said. 'We learn a lot every time we have an opportunity to study a premature baby.'

He left Dr Edman's office and walked along the corridor.

I do not deserve this, he thought. But my daughter wants to live, she has more of a will to live than I have.

He went to look at the little miracle.

CHAPTER 158

It seemed to him that she looked like a dried mushroom. But she's mine, he thought. She's mine and she's alive.

Kristina Tacker had a small private room. She was pale and tired. He sat down on the bed and took her hand.

'She's a beautiful baby,' he said. 'I want her to be called Laura.'

'As we had agreed,' she said with a faint smile.

He did not stay for long. Just before he left, he told her that he would have to set out on his mission now. He ought to have left already, but he had asked for a postponement until he could be confident that the baby would survive.

'Thank you for staying,' she said.

'Everything will be all right,' he said. 'I'll soon be back.'

He left the hospital. It was a relief, like sinking into warm water.

CHAPTER 159

That night he wandered around the flat naked.

Shortly before dawn he opened the door of the maid's room. She had thrown off the covers and was lying naked in her bed. He stood looking at her for a long time before leaving.

When she woke up he was no longer there.

PART IX

The Imprint of the German Deserter

CHAPTER 160

He was walking beside the river, a winding path between dry nettles and patches of tall ferns.

It was the third day after his flight from Stockholm, Kristina Tacker and the baby. In the market square at Söderköping he had gone round the fish stalls looking for somebody who would be sailing home through Slätbaken and then turning off in the direction of Finnö. A couple of farm labourers from Kättilö were willing to take him with them, and wanted paying in aquavit. They were due to meet at the mouth of the river two days later, by which time the labourers hoped to have sold all the fish they had caught in their spare time to boost their income.

There was an opening by the side of the path, a clearing leading down to the brown river. He sat on a large stone and closed his eyes. Although he had been moving slowly without exerting himself, he was breathing heavily, as if he had been running. It was not only when he moved, but also when he was sitting down, or sleeping. He was still running.

Even before he went aboard the train that was to take him south he had written a letter to Kristina Tacker. He explained his sudden departure by telling her that the war had entered an unexpected and very worrying phase. As usual, everything was top secret, every letter he wrote to her, especially if it contained the slightest reference to the character of his work, meant that he was exposing himself, his wife and the baby to danger.

He sat at a table in the first-class dining room at the Central Station. His hand shook as he wrote the name Laura. He lost control of himself and burst into tears. A waitress watched him nervously but said nothing. He pulled himself together and started to invent his new, urgent mission.

> The war is coming closer to our shores. The people cannot be told anything about it yet, but military men like myself are aware of the situation. The work of securing our borders must be intensified. I shall be on board several different ships. The location will vary, to both the north and the south of the Baltic Sea, or along the Halland and Bohus coast in the west. My letters will not be channelled via the military post office in Malmö. They will be sent from special Swedish Navy bases along the east coast. You must not mention anything I write to anybody. That would put me in danger, there could be repercussions, I could even be dismissed. I shall write again soon.

He posted the letter at the railway station, bought a ticket to Norrköping and left Stockholm. Before Södertälje the train passed through a local forest fire. The smoke was like fog outside the windows.

That is what I am looking for, he thought. I can row into the fog, just like when I approached a remote skerry and found Sara Fredrika.

He continued as far as Söderköping and spent the night in the hotel on the bank of the canal. Without understanding why, he checked in under an assumed name. He called himself Ludwig Tacker, gave no occupational title and stipulated Humlegårdsgatan as his home address.

It was a sultry night. He lay awake, on top of the covers.

Nobody here knows who I am, he thought. I am safe at present. When my position can be fixed, I have gone astray.

As dawn broke, he went for a walk along the canal, strolled up to the top of Ramunderberget, went back to the hotel, had coffee and wrote another letter to his wife. He described himself as exhilarated, happy about the birth of their child, but at the same time very conscious of his duty.

It was a short letter. He sealed the envelope and left the hotel.

It was a hot day. Only when he came to the path meandering along the river did he feel anything that could remotely be described as cool.

CHAPTER 161

As he sat on the stone in the clearing, he started thinking. Should he extend his mission and make it longer than he had at first intended? The path next to the river, the warm, damp smell of mud, led his mind to other continents, perhaps Africa, or Asia. A courier could take his letters and post them in Sweden. Kristina Tacker would be worried about distant dangers, diseases, insects and snakes. There again, the distance would make his secret all the bigger, she would never tell anybody, not even her father. Besides, she knew nothing about naval ships. If he told her that there was a ship that could sail at the prodigious speed of eighty knots, she would not question it.

Kristina Tacker never questioned secrets.

He sat on the stone and played with the thought of expeditions to distant countries.

He made a measurement he had never attempted before. How far from the truth could he transport a fantasy before it collapsed in ruins?

There was no answer to that, of course. He also imagined transforming his sounding lead into a diving bell and descending into the depths himself. How strong a pressure would he be able to tolerate? Would the shell hold or would it shatter so that he was sent shooting back up to the surface and the real world once more?

It was already late afternoon when he left his stone and continued walking towards the mouth of the river. He imagined himself trudging along a path somewhere inside a steaming rainforest in a tropical land without a name.

CHAPTER 162

The boat was the same type as Sara Fredrika's, but the sail was patched and the farm labourers drunk. They were asleep, tangled together among the empty herring barrels and baskets in the bottom of the boat. It was six o'clock when he woke them up. One of them, the older one called Elis, asked Tobiasson-Svartman if he had brought the aquavit with him. He showed them the bottles but said he had no intention of handing them over until they were south of Finntarmen and preferably had reached their destination.

And what was the destination? It was the younger man, Gösta, who asked.

'It's secret. A military operation,' he replied. 'I am to be dropped on a skerry and I shall be collected from there by a naval vessel.'

'Which island?' Gösta wondered.

'I'll show you when we get close to it.'

The men were hung-over and starting to moan, and wanted to wait until the next day before leaving the mouth of the river. But he cajoled them into setting out to sea right now, there was no time to waste. There was a following wind that would take them out of Slätbaken before they lay up for the night. Gösta sat at the tiller and Elis kept an eye on the sail. He cursed every time he tightened the sheet or let it go.

Tobiasson-Svartman made himself comfortable in the bows. He had his rucksack with the sounding lead between his legs. There was an acrid smell coming from the sea. He recognised it from his time aboard the *Blenda*.

They anchored for the night in a creek on the edge of the approach to Slätbaken. He had spent a night with Sara Fredrika on the other side of the narrow channel.

He suddenly felt pangs of guilt. It was as if he were no longer being taken south, but was descending the sounding line inside himself. He found it difficult to breathe.

It was not until the fire had died out and the farm labourers had fallen asleep that he could feel his panic subsiding.

He looked at the sleeping labourers. I envy them, he thought. But between their lives and mine is a distance that can never be bridged.

CHAPTER 163

They were between Rökholmen and Lilla Getskär when Gösta asked once again where he wanted to be put ashore.

The wind had freshened during the night and they were making good progress after a night's rest.

'Halsskär,' Tobiasson-Svartman told him.

The man looked at him in astonishment.

'That bare bit of rock near the open sea? Near the lighthouses and the seal rocks?'

'There is a Halsskär south of Västervik and another way up north off Härnösand. But I'm hardly going to be going all that way.'

'What the hell are you going to do on that godforsaken bloody place? A madwoman lives there. Is that who you're going to see?'

'I don't know anything about the island being inhabited. I have my orders. That's where I'm going to be collected from.'

The fisherman seemed amused.

'They say that all the bloody Finnish hunters without a licence wandering around the outer archipelago stop off there to get a bit of leg-over on the way out and again on the way back,' Elis said.

Tobiasson-Svartman was cold as ice. But even if he

could have killed them, he wanted to know about the rumours.

'You mean there's a trollop living on the skerry? How on earth did she end up there?'

'Her husband drowned,' said Gösta. 'How else could she make a living? I've seen her. A really filthy little scrubber. You'd have to be as randy as hell if you wanted to shag that.'

'Does she have a name?'

'Sara. Though some people say Fredrika.'

The men had nothing to add. The dinghy was making good headway. He was beginning to recognise the islands now, the channels were opening out, the ice that had covered the water was a distant memory.

He imagined the farm labourers dead, deep down at the bottom of the sea.

Late in the afternoon the sailing dinghy steered into the inlet where Sara Fredrika's boat was moored. He handed over two litre bottles and jumped ashore.

'If anybody asks, you had no passengers with you from Söderköping,' he said.

'Who would ask us?' Gösta said. 'Who cares if a couple of bloody farm yokels have anybody in the boat with them?'

'There's a war on, and what I'm doing is top secret. If you say a single word once you get back on shore you could end up in prison for life.'

He watched them go, heading south. They were talking eagerly, but he did not think they would say anything about him. He had frightened them.

He looked at the nets, corves, sinkers, all the other equipment. The boat was securely moored, it did not need to be beached when the water level was high. He looked towards the path and all the greenery clinging to the little crevices and along the sides of the rocks.

He tried to build a room around himself, but no walls wanted to rise up.

CHAPTER 164

The first thing he saw by the cottage was a cat, staring at him with watchful eyes. He had the impression it was the same cat as he had killed in his fury.

He despised the supernatural. Human beings worked constantly to make their gods unnecessary. He was an individual who made scientific measurements: one day time and perhaps also space would be measured and controlled by scales of measurements hitherto unknown. The supernatural was shadows dancing in the remains of a childhood fear of the dark. Normally he could always resist the supernatural. But the cat scared him.

It ran away as he approached the window.

Sara Fredrika was asleep on the bunk. He contemplated her enormous stomach.

She must have heard him, or sensed movement outside the window, turned her head to look, and squealed in delight. He opened the door and took her in his arms. She was warm and sweaty, steam was rising from her body. He immediately abandoned all thought of Kristina Tacker and Laura.

Now he was able to build the walls. There was nothing outside Halsskär, nothing that he could no longer control. He held all distances in his hands.

'How did you get here?' she asked. 'I didn't hear anything. I didn't sense anything either.'

'I sailed here with some farmhands from an island further south. From Lofthammar, they said.'

'Sailing this way? Where from?'

'Norrköping.'

'How did you find them?'

'In the harbour. They had bought a sailing dinghy, or got it in exchange, I couldn't quite work out what they did. But I was lucky. I'd have had to go to Söderköping otherwise.'

Not even the farm labourers belong to my story, he thought. I'm walking on water, leaving no tracks behind me.

'You've got a new cat,' he said.

'I got it from Helge. I hadn't asked for a similar one, and Helge said he hadn't seen the one I had before. It's good company. But it misses its mice, there aren't any on this skerry. And it's frightened of the snakes.'

They went indoors. Everything was as he remembered it. Nobody else seemed to have been in the cottage since he left. Nevertheless, he had a strange feeling of uneasiness, a suspicion that, even so, everything had changed since he was last here.

It was a while before he saw it.

Her eyes had changed. She looked at him in a different way.

Something had in fact happened.

CHAPTER 165

He asked her that evening.

A storm had blown in from the west, the thunderclaps were so strong that the cottage walls shook. She had a pain in her back and lay down on the bed.

'Nothing has happened,' she said. 'They threw the cat ashore from the boat. I've been waiting for you, nothing else.'

He listened carefully and could detect a change in her voice. Something had happened, but what? He ought not to ask any more, not just now.

During the night he had the feeling that she was keeping her distance. It was barely noticeable, but it was a fact. She was suspicious, maybe unsure. But what could have happened?

He was afraid. Somehow she knew now that he was married, that no woman and no daughter had fallen over a cliff.

He slid out of bed cautiously, but she woke up.

'Where are you going?'

'I just need to go out for a moment.'

'My back's hurting.'

'Go back to sleep. It's only just getting light.'

'How shall I be able to give birth here?'

'I'll sail for help when the time comes.'

The storm had subsided. The sparse grass was wet, water was running down the rocks. The cat emerged from a crack in the rock underneath the cottage and followed him down to the inlet, where he plucked a little flounder from the corf. He threw it to the cat.

Could she have found out something about him despite everything? He tried to go back over all the many things that had happened since they first met, but he could not hit upon anything.

It occurred to him that the deserter might have floated up to the surface or been caught in one of her nets. But that could not have been the case. The body could not have reappeared, the sinker was securely fastened. Besides, she did not have any nets that would go as deep as that.

He walked round the island with the cat the single member of his retinue. He climbed to the highest point, and was reminded of Lieutenant Jakobsson, peeing over the rail. Distant memories, he thought. Like dreams.

He wondered if it would be possible to sink his sounding lead through the darkness that exists below the surface of all dreams.

On the far horizon he caught a glimpse of a ship heading north. He did not have his telescope with him and could not make out if it was a warship.

The cat suddenly vanished.

Still he could not understand what had happened.

CHAPTER 166

The heatwave continued.

Sara Fredrika had difficulty in moving, her back ached and she complained that she could not keep cool. He went fishing and did whatever had to be done. When he was busy with the nets, cleaning fish or carrying water he was able to feel totally relaxed, the walls around him were constantly there. Occasionally he would see Kristina Tacker and the newly born baby in his mind's eye. Did she know what he had done, that he had denied her existence to another woman? Yet how could she know?

Early one morning in the middle of August when he was on the way to Jungfrugrunden to take up some nets, he stopped rowing. There was no wind, just a gentle swell.

He realised that he was near the spot where the two German sailors were lying at the bottom of the sea. He could row there, tie the rope in the stern of the boat round the sinker beside it, throw it and himself overboard, and it would all be over at last.

Perhaps that was the only bottomless depth he could hope to find? Sinking towards death, unaware of what happened to him after his lungs had filled with seawater?

He took tight hold of the oars and started rowing again.

The net he pulled aboard contained a lot of fish. Any thoughts about death vanished immediately.

Sara Fredrika came down to the shore to help him gut the catch. She moved with difficulty, and the pain in her back made her pull faces.

They did not say much to each other.

CHAPTER 167

The next day he cleaned his sounding lead and started measuring the depths around Halsskär. He would record the reading in a notebook then lower his lead once again.

It was as if he were listening to two voices, a never-ending conversation between sea and land. Every wave or swell brought with it a fragment of a story, every slab of rock made its contribution.

He put the sounding lead on the floor of the boat. Before, he had always thought there was a never-ending struggle between the sea and the rocks. Now he realised that was incorrect. It was an embrace that never lost its element of lust. A slowly increasing intimacy, he thought. The elevation of the land progresses invisibly, the rocks and the sea rely on each other.

He turned his back on Halsskär and gazed out to sea. The horizon was empty. He had the vague impression that there was something missing, something that ought to be there had vanished.

CHAPTER 168

When he reached home she was sitting outside the cottage, waiting.

Her eyes were blazing.

He stopped, not wanting to get too close to her.

She threw two wooden sticks that dropped at his feet. He did not see what they were at first. Then he saw the dried-out bit of rope fastening the two pins together. His ice prods. The ones he had stuck into the deserter's eyes.

He turned icy cold. He was sure he had pushed them inside the dead man's clothes before kicking the sinker into the ice hole and watching the corpse vanish into the depths.

He looked at her. Was there anything else? Was this only the beginning?

'What's that on them?' she asked.

'I don't understand what you mean.'

'They are yours, aren't they?'

'Of course they are mine. But they vanished into thin air. I don't know what happened to them.'

'Pick them up!'

He bent down. There was a dark colour dried into the light brown wood. It looked like dark brown rust. Blood, no doubt. The deserter's blood.

'I still don't know what you mean.'

'There's blood on them.'

'It could be anything. Why should it be blood?'

'Because I recognise it. My husband once cut himself with a knife. It was a deep wound, I thought it would never stop bleeding. I'll never forget that colour. Dried blood on light-coloured wood. The colour I saw when I thought my husband was going to die.'

She almost burst into tears, but managed to control herself.

'I found them on the shore. The last time I walked round the skerry before I became so fat that I dared not trust myself on the rocks any more. I shouldn't have risked it that time either.'

'I must have mislaid them.'

She was looking hard at him. He realised that it wasn't in fact the ice prods he could detect in her eyes and her voice, but her fear that he was telling lies, that there was something he had not told her.

'I saw that you had them with you every time you went out on to the ice. Then one day, they weren't there any more. And now I've found them soaked in blood.'

The lid over the abyss was parchment-thin. He tried to stop moving.

'What happened?' she asked. 'That day he died. I've never understood it, never been able to believe that he simply sank down through thin ice and met his death. Neither that, nor that he killed the cat.'

'Why do you think I would have said something that didn't in fact happen?'

'I'm saying that I don't know.'

'Are you suggesting that I killed him? Is that what you mean?'

She stood up, with considerable difficulty. 'I'm not saying that you are concealing something or that you're not telling me the truth. All I'm saying is that I found the ice prods and they were bloodstained.'

'I was trying to spare you from some of the truth. He used the ice prods to kill the cat. I found them on the ice.'

Silence.

'So you thought I told you something that wasn't true?' he said. 'Do you believe I would ever dare to do such a thing? Don't you understand that I'm scared to death of losing you?'

To his surprise he recognised that this was exactly what he was frightened of.

She eyed him up and down. Then she decided to believe him.

The lid over the abyss had very nearly given way.

CHAPTER 169

That evening and for the rest of the night, he was completely calm.

Distance had no meaning any more. He had control over himself and Sara Fredrika. The ice prods had been explained away. She was no longer worried.

As night approached they talked about the baby, and what would happen afterwards.

'When the time comes,' he asked, 'who's going to help you?'

'There's a midwife on Kråkmarö called Wester. She knows I'm pregnant. But you'll have to sail to Kråkmarö and fetch her.'

What she wanted to talk about most was the future, what would happen after the skerry. She could only associate the baby with Halsskär as the place where it was born, the place they left soon afterwards.

In his imagination he had worked out a plan for how they would leave for America. He talked about the danger from the naval fleets stalking the European shipping lanes leading to the west. But thanks to the contacts he had they would be able to travel on a Swedish ship along a secret route north of Iceland. Everything was planned. The only thing he could not be sure of was the date for their departure. They would have to wait and be ready to leave at short notice.

'You mean we'll have to wait here? Who will come to fetch us?'

'The same ship that I was on when I came here for the first time.'

His reply made her feel secure. I am creating time, he thought. I am increasing the distance to the point when I shall have to make a definite decision.

He put his hand on her stomach and felt the baby kicking. It was like cupping his hand over a flounder on the seabed. The baby was wriggling away under the palm of his hand, as if it were trying to escape.

Is that how it was with babies as well? That they wanted to escape the inevitable?

He cupped his hand. The flounder wriggled away under his palm.

CHAPTER 170

One night she woke him up.

'I can hear somebody screaming,' she said.

He listened. There was no wind.

'I can't hear anything.'

'There's somebody screaming, a person.'

He put his trousers on and went out. The ground felt chilly underfoot.

Then he heard it, a distant scream. It came from the sea.

She had got out of bed with considerable difficulty and was standing in the doorway. Her face was white in the night glow.

'Can you hear it?'

'Yes, I can.'

They listened. There it came again. He was still unsure if it was a person or a bird. Birds can also get into difficulties – he remembered the gull frozen into the ice last winter. Frozen wings, he thought. We always need to thaw out our wings in order to fly. But in the end that is no longer possible.

There was the scream again. He went to the highest point on the skerry and looked south-westwards, where the scream had come from. In the end he was convinced that it was a human scream. He set off for the inlet intending to take the boat out, but it stopped. He waited. The sea was silent.

He went back to the cottage. She was cold, pressed up against him, he put his arm round her shoulders. They lay awake as day broke, wondering who or what it had been, a person or a bird.

He got up early and scanned the sea with his telescope.

There was nothing to be seen. Breakers rolled slowly in towards the islands.

He had the feeling that the sea was like an old woman in a rocking chair.

CHAPTER 171

A north-easterly storm bringing low temperatures raged over the archipelago.

Then followed dead calm. Sara Fredrika was finding it increasingly difficult to move, and she was in continous pain from her back.

He went fishing and imagined himself to be the lord of Halsskär. He rarely gave a thought to Kristina Tacker and the baby. His memory was like a vast vacuum.

Sometimes he would give a sudden start. Kristina Tacker, Ludwig Tacker were just behind him.

One morning when he went down to the inlet he heard voices. He followed the sounds, leaned over the edge of the rocks and discovered a small brown mahogany yacht anchored off the narrow headland projecting furthest to the south-west. Two little rowing boats were heading for land. In the boats were women dressed in white and with large hats, and men in blue jackets who were doing the rowing. He could see the glint of bottles, the women were laughing. In the stern of one of the boats was a man wearing a cap back to front, holding some sort of instrument in front of his face – perhaps a camera.

He hurried back to the cottage and told Sara Fredrika.

'They look like summer holidaymakers,' he said. 'But are there any this far out? I thought they were only to be seen around Stockholm and on the bathing beaches along the west coast. And it's getting late in the year, it will soon be autumn.'

'I once heard about a man who used to come with a piano on the steamboat *Tjust* from Söderköping,' she said. 'It was always the beginning of May. He'd bring the piano with him from Stockholm, and it would be lashed down in the bows. The crew had trouble in getting it on to a cattle ferry. But once he'd settled he would sit on an island playing the piano and getting drunk every day until September, and then he would go back home again.'

'This party doesn't have a piano with them.'

'What are they doing here? On my island?'

'It's not your island. And I expect they'd take no notice if anybody tried to stop them landing.'

She started to protest, but he cut her short.

'They'll wonder who I am,' he said. 'I mustn't be seen, my orders are not to allow myself to be identified.'

'How would they know you were anybody other than a man who lives here on this island with me? People judge people on their appearance. Take some of my husband's clothes.'

That thought had already occurred to him. He took some clothes out of a chest. They smelled mouldy, of old sea.

'You look as if you're wearing hand-me-downs,' she said. 'You're taller than he was, but not as bulky.'

'I'm only borrowing them,' he said. 'When we leave Halsskär I shall burn them.'

'I want to see these people,' she said.

'You can't go scrambling over the rocks.'

'If they are where you say, on that headland in the west, there are some flat ledges I can walk along. I want to see those hats.'

When they came to the headland they found that the party had already landed. They were squatting behind a big rock. It took him a while to realise that they were making a film, one of these newfangled inventions with people flitting about jerkily in moving pictures, projected on to a white screen. He tried to explain to Sara Fredrika in a low whisper, but she was not listening.

The man had placed his cine camera on a stand. The ladies in white were running around on the rocks when suddenly a man with an amazingly long moustache and a white-painted face jumped out from behind a slab of rock and rushed towards the women.

Sara Fredrika dug her nails into Tobiasson-Svartman's arm.

'He's got a tail,' she hissed. 'There's a tail sticking out of his trousers.'

She was right. The man with black rings round his eyes had an artificial tail. The women looked as if they were praying and begging for mercy, their faces twitching. The man behind the camera was winding away at full speed, the women were screaming, but without making a sound. Sara Fredrika stood up. Her scream was like a foghorn. She bellowed and started throwing stones at the man with the tail. Tobiasson-Svartman tried to hold her back.

'It's not real,' he said. 'It's not real life, it's not actually happening.'

He snatched a stone from out of her hand and gave her a shake.

'They're only acting,' he said. 'Nobody's going to get hurt.'

Sara Fredrika calmed down. The man behind the camera had stopped winding and turned his cap the right way round. The ladies were staring in astonishment at the pair who had materialised from the rocks. The man had removed the tail and was holding it in his hand like a piece of rope. There was a flash of light from the yacht which was bobbing up and down in the swell. Somebody was watching them through a telescope.

Tobiasson-Svartman told Sara Fredrika to wait, and went over to the film-makers. The women were young and strikingly pretty. The man with the tail had a face he thought he recognised. When he held his hand out in greeting, he remembered having seen the man in a play at the Royal Dramatic Theatre in Stockholm. His name was Valfrid Mertsgren, the play was called *The Wedding at Ulfåsa*.

Mertsgren ignored his outstretched hand and eyed him up and down in annoyance.

'Who are you?' he asked. 'We were told this skerry was uninhabited. They said there was a ruin of an old cottage that we could use.'

'I live here with my wife.'

'For hell's sake, you can't live here. What do you live on?'

'Fishing.'

'Plundering wrecks?'

'If somebody gets into difficulties we help them. We don't plunder.'

'Everybody does,' said Mertsgren. 'People are greedy. They'd steal their neighbour's heart if they had the chance.'

The cameraman and the two women in white had gathered round him.

'Can you really live here?' asked one of the women. 'What do you do in the winter?'

'Where there's the sea, there's food.'

'Can't we include him and the fat woman in the film?' said the other woman, with a shrill laugh.

'She's not fat,' Tobiasson-Svartman said.

The woman who had made the suggestion stared at him. He hated her intensely.

'She's not fat,' he said again. 'She's pregnant.'

'In any case, you can't be in the film,' Mertsgren said. 'We can't have a woman with a bun in the oven. This is a romantic adventure, pretty tableaux alternating with scary ones. We don't want any cows with one up the spout.'

Tobiasson-Svartman was on the point of punching him. But he controlled himself, spoke slowly in an attempt to disguise his feelings.

'Why make a film on Halsskär?' he asked in a friendly tone. 'Why here of all places?'

'That's a good question,' Mertsgren said. 'I really don't know why we're filming here.'

He turned his back on the others.

'There's a bloodhound by the name of Hultman on the boat,' he snarled. 'He's a wholesale dealer, and he's put some money into this incredible mish-mash of a manuscript we're supposed to be filming. Maybe he's got nothing better to waste his money on. He's earning vast amounts from the war, churning out nails and explosives. Can you see what the boat's called?'

To his surprise Tobiasson-Svartman discovered that the yacht had the name *Goeben* on its bows. The same name as the German battleship he had a picture of on his desk, the ship he had never actually seen but had admired even so.

A yacht and a battleship with the same name! Women in white with large hats and dying sailors trapped inside their burning ships, a war and a man earning big money.

'I understand,' he said.

'Understand what?' Mertsgren asked.

'That Mr Hultman likes the war and death.'

'I don't know if he likes death. He likes watching women bathing through his telescope. He keeps far enough away not to be seen, nobody realises he's there, but then he aims his telescope at the woman or the part of her body he fancies.'

'But likes the war and death for the sake of his nails.'

'He certainly likes the Germans, at least. They're like his nails, he says. Straight, austere, all the same. He likes the German orderliness, hopes the Kaiser will win the war, curses Sweden for keeping its mouth shut and hiding behind switched-off lighthouses. While he sits in his yacht watching ladies through his telescope.'

Mertsgren leaned forward and whispered in Tobiasson-Svartman's ear.

'He's also enthusiastic about anything to do with erotic jokes. You're a fisherman, so he would have told you that he only sticks his rod into Thigh Bay.'

He contemplated the tail he had in his hand.

'In all the appalling and degrading roles I've had to play in my life, I've never had to wear a tail before. Not until now. Hamlet doesn't have a tail, nor does Lear, nor the malade imaginaire. But a man will do anything for a thousand kronor. That's what he's paying. For a week's work, plus fancy dinners and barrels of booze.'

He waved to Sara Fredrika.

'I understand why she got upset,' he said. 'Give her my compliments and tell her I apologise. We'll leave you in peace. I'll tell Hultman that the skerry was already booked.'

Mertsgren took the two ladies by the arm and returned to the rowing boats. The man with the camera was busy winding leather straps round his stand. Tobiasson-Svartman looked hard at the camera. The man nodded.

'A miracle,' he said. 'Something for the priests to envy us for.' He rested the stand on his shoulder. 'Are you wondering what on earth I'm on about?'

'Yes.'

'I have the mystery of life in my hand. I turn the handle and decide the speed of people's movements. With the camera we can expose secrets that even the eye cannot see. A galloping horse has all four hooves in the air at the same time, that's something the camera has been able to establish. We can see more than the eye does. But we also control what we allow others to see.'

He picked up the camera and looked from Sara Fredrika to Tobiasson-Svartman. He smiled.

'I don't really know how I got mixed up in all this,' he said. 'I was a photographer to start with, with my own little studio. Then Hultman happened to hear about me, and now I'm standing here on a rock with a cine camera and some crazy idea about a tableau the Nail Master has decided should be called *The Devil on Holiday by the Sea*. But it has sharpened my eyes, I have to admit that.'

'How do you mean?'

The man put his head on one side, a shadow fell over his smile.

'Well, for example, I can see that you are not a fisherman. I don't know who you are nor what you do. But a fisherman? Never.'

He set off tentatively towards the water, carrying his equipment. Tobiasson-Svartman had the impression that the stand was part of a cross the cameraman was having to bear.

The man stopped and turned round.

'Maybe you would be a good story for a film? An escaped criminal, somebody running away from his debts. How should I know?'

He did not wait for an answer. The first rowing boat

was already on its way back to the yacht. The women in white were laughing; there was a clinking of bottles.

Tobiasson-Svartman went back to Sara Fredrika.

'What kind of people were they? Those women hiding their eyes under their hats? I didn't like them. And tails are for animals, not for people.'

'It was just make-believe. A devil jumping around, that's all.'

'What were they doing here?'

They had started to walk back to the cottage. He was holding on to her, making sure she did not slip.

'Just think of them as driftwood. Something that happened to have been washed ashore here. Then the wind turned and they drifted away again. Driftwood that wasn't even fit for firewood.'

'Tails are for animals,' she said again. 'Tails are not for people.'

CHAPTER 172

In the afternoon he went to the highest point of the skerry, telescope in hand. The *Goeben* had left. He scanned the horizon but could find no sign of it.

The cameraman had seen right through him. He tried to work out if that implied danger.

He could not see any.

CHAPTER 173

One night she woke him up out of a dream.

Kristina Tacker had been standing in front of him, she had been saying something, but he had not been able to work out what it was.

He gave a start and sat up.

'I think the baby is on its way. It's moving, it's tensing its body.'

'But there's a long time to go yet.'

'I have no control over that.'

'What do you want me to do?'

'Stay awake. I've been on my own for long enough in my life.'

'I'm here, even if I'm asleep.'

'What do I know about your dreams?'

It's just like the man with the camera, he thought. She sees straight through me. But she does not know.

'I rarely dream,' he said. 'My sleep is empty, it's black, it doesn't even have any colours. I sometimes think I've been dreaming about flowers, but they are always grey. I've only ever dreamed about dead flowers, never about living ones.'

They stayed awake until dawn. The oyster-catchers were calling to one another, the gulls, the terns.

At about six they decided that he would sail to Kråkmarö and fetch the midwife. Even if the baby was not ready to pop out, they ought to make sure that everything was prepared.

He set sail in the easterly wind, three or four metres per second.

A thought struck him. Perhaps he should seize the moment and make a run for it, head north or south, or even east towards Gotland, and the Gulf of Riga beyond.

But he set sail in a westerly direction, to the midwife. The dinghy sped through the water, Halsskär faded into the horizon behind him.

The August day was like a buoy, he thought. Clean and white in the sunlight.

The sea was carrying him to his destiny.

CHAPTER 174

Angel was her name, the midwife.

She was not baptised Angel, of course: in the registers and on her midwifery certificate she was called Angela Wester. But everybody said Angel. That's what her mother had wanted to call her, she had had a dream about it the night before she gave birth. But the vicar refused. He pointed to the parish register and maintained that nobody was allowed to be called Angel, it would be little short of blasphemy. Her father, the ship's master Fredrik Wester, did not believe in gods but in compasses, and suggested with a growl that they should call the girl Angel even so. The vicar could not dictate what happened out in the archipelago. And so she became Angel. She never had any brothers or sisters, nor did she find a husband as she was cross-eyed and could hardly be called pretty. When her parents died she sold the house in the village and the little cargo boat that was half submerged in the creek, and moved into a crofter's cottage. She had trained as a midwife in Norrköping, and devoted her life to other people's children. She smiled a lot, had a beautiful voice, and was not afraid of mending the roof of her cottage herself if necessary. She could be ill-humoured and would sometimes set out on her own in her sailing dinghy, and everybody in the village would worry in case she never came back again. But she always did come back, and would sail her boat into the creek under cover of darkness when her depression had blown away.

Most of all, Angel was a good midwife. She was good at extracting babies that had got stuck. She had magic hands. There were a lot of midwives and old ladies who knew how to do the job of a midwife. They were all good, of course, but Angel was *deft*. Like a seamstress or a hunter or a gardener who could make things grow in hollows in the rock with hardly any soil. She had been so successful in many cases considered to be hopeless, that a doctor from Stockholm had once visited Kråkmarö in order to interview her, and although she was getting on for seventy and there were younger midwives to turn to, most people asked for her.

He moored the boat in the creek and walked up the hill to the village. The villagers were out in the fields and pointed the way. He knocked on Angel's door and she answered immediately. He had never set eyes on her before, but even so, it was as if he knew her. He went into her low-ceilinged kitchen and said where he had come from. She smiled.

'Sara Fredrika's baby,' she said. 'I assume it's yours as well?'

He could not bring himself to reply, and she did not worry about it.

'Children would no doubt like to choose their parents,'

she said. 'Maybe they do, did we but know it. But there's some time to go yet for Sara Fredrika. What's the matter with her?'

He tried to explain, saying what Sara Fredrika had told him to say. Spasmodic tension, difficulties in moving, pains in her pelvis.

Angel asked a few questions.

'Has she had a fall?'

'No.'

'And you haven't hit her?'

'Why on earth would I want to do that?'

'Because men hit their women when things go wrong. Does she have a fever? Has she been carrying heavy things?'

'She spends most of her time resting.'

'And when you left things had got a bit better?'

'Yes.'

'Then you must go back to her. Sara Fredrika hasn't had much happiness in this life. I'm not sure that you have brought her any either. But you must look after her well. Then you might be able to become the man she needs.'

'She wants me to take her away from there.'

'Why should she stay there on that barren rock, after all the terrible things she's had to go through? It's eating her up, that inhospitable skerry is scraping her to the bone.'

She went with him down the hill to the sailing dinghy.

'You haven't even said what you're called. Don't you have a name?'

'I'm Lars.'

'I don't care where you come from. Rumour says that you're in the navy. But there's something else that's more important than that. You are wearing Nils Persson's clothes. You are reconciled to the fact that there was somebody else before you.'

'What shall I tell her?'

'That it's not time yet. And that I shall come, as long as you fetch me.'

He got into the boat and she untied the painter. There was no wind in the creek, so he prepared the oars.

'Stay until the baby's been born. Then you should take her away. The youngster won't survive out there. So many young children have died on that barren skerry over the years, too many to keep count of.'

He started rowing.

'Tell her I'll come,' she shouted. 'We'll get the baby born and it will survive all right, as long as you all get away from there.'

He kept on rowing until he found some wind. Then he raised the sail and headed for the open sea.

He felt ashamed when he thought about how close he had come to running away. He would have stolen her boat like a pirate, and abandoned her. Now he was sailing as fast as possible so that she would not start to think that he had headed out to sea after all.

He was in a hurry. And the sea was still carrying him to his destiny.

CHAPTER 175

August was drawing to a close, it was unusually windy, persistent westerly winds. An autumnal thunderstorm passed over them, and a stroke of lightning felled a tree on Armnö.

He speculated that memory and forgetting shared the same key. Perhaps anger shared the same door? Kristina Tacker and the baby drifted away. But where was he himself?

The longest distance I have had to relate to is the distance to myself. No matter where I stand, the compass inside me pulls me in different directions. All my life I have crept around trying to avoid bumping into myself. I have no idea who I am, and I do not want to know either.

CHAPTER 176

Sara Fredrika could feel that her body was calm. She talked all the time about the journey they would make once the baby was delivered.

Sometimes the conversations became unbearable. The skerry began to be a heavy weight, a ballast in his pockets that made it more and more difficult for him to move. He thought about what Angel had said, about the inhospitable skerry scraping her to the bone.

CHAPTER 177

Every three or four days he would sit down to write a letter to Kristina Tacker. He had found a rock formation on the south side of the skerry that gave him both a bench to sit on and a rough desk to write on.

He described a voyage in a convoy of ships heading for Bornholm and the Polish coast. It had been a dangerous but necessary expedition. Now he was back in Swedish waters again, and by coincidence he had ended up in Östergötland, among the islands where he had already spent such a long time. He would soon be returning to Stockholm. His mission had been long and drawn out, but there was an end in sight, he wrote, an end, and then he would return home. He asked about Laura, how Kristina Tacker herself was, and not least her father. Had he recovered? Had they arrested whoever had carried out the attack?

But he also wrote about himself, tried to capture something of his own desperation without revealing the true facts. *When I'm alone I sometimes get so close to myself that I understand who I am. But then you are not there, nobody else can see what I see, only me, and that is not enough.*

He hesitated for a long time, wondering whether to

leave out the last few lines. But in the end he left them in, felt that he dared do so.

He buried the letters under a piece of turf, wrapped inside a waterproof pouch. Towards the end of August he decided he would have to send at least one of the many letters. He had intended to give the letters to some fisherman or hunter who passed by the skerry, but none of them landed. He could see sailing dinghies in among the skerries sometimes, but none of them came close. One day he decided that it could not wait any longer. He told Sara Fredrika that he was going to go to church in Gryt on the last Sunday in August.

'I'm not much of a believer,' he said, 'but after a while I feel very empty inside.'

'If you're lucky you'll be able to sail there. If there's no wind you'll have a long way to row.'

They got up at dawn and she went with him to the inlet. He had his uniform wrapped inside his oilskin.

'You'll have a good wind,' she said. 'Easterly veering towards north, a church wind in both directions. Sing a hymn for me, listen to the gossip outside the church. I've no idea who's dead and who's still alive. Bring me some news, even if it's old news.'

He stopped once on the way, landing on one of the islands in Bussund. He changed into his uniform and scrubbed away a stain on one of the shoulders. As he sailed into Gryt accompanied by other boats with passengers on their way to church, he was wearing his naval cap. He could see that his companions were bemused, but some of them must know about him, he could not be completely unknown.

There was a man on Sara Fredrika's island, the father of the baby that was about to be born.

Remarkably enough, he felt something approaching pride when everybody looked at him.

CHAPTER 178

There had been a time when you could sail right up to the church from both the north and the south.

But the sound had silted up, and now you had to walk. There were a lot of people gathered outside the church. People seldom came from the outlying islands in winter.

Suddenly he came face to face with the farm labourers from Kättilö. They were not entirely sober.

'We haven't said a word,' Gösta said. 'Nothing has slipped out.'

'Let's keep it that way,' Tobiasson-Svartman said. 'And we mustn't make it too obvious that we know each other.'

He turned on his heel and walked away. The sexton told him that the man who looked after the post in Gryt was smoking his pipe by the church wall.

Tobiasson-Svartman gave him two letters. He asked for one to be posted right away, the other ten days later.

During the service he half listened to the Reverend Gustafsson's sermon about the devil who takes possession of our flesh, and the mercy of the Son of God.

Afterwards he wandered around, listening to the conversations. He had always been an eavesdropper, skilled at sucking in what other people were talking about. Most of the congregation were talking about who was ill and how bad the fishing had been.

When he started walking towards his boat a man in uniform came alongside him. He shook hands and introduced himself as the parish constable, Karl Albert Lund.

'There aren't many people round here wearing uniform,' said the constable. 'That's why I thought I'd say hello.'

'Hans Jakobsson, Commander. I just happen to be passing by,' Tobiasson-Svartman said.

'Might I ask what it is that brings you here?'

'I can't tell you that. It has to do with the war.'

'I understand. I won't press you.'

Tobiasson-Svartman clicked his heels and saluted. He went back to the boat and sailed home. Why had he chosen the name Hans Jakobsson? he wondered.

Was it a greeting to the man who had died on the deck of the *Blenda*? Why had he not said what he had really wanted to say, that he was Sara Fredrika's new husband?

He changed out of his uniform. The wind was enabling him to maintain steady progress. On the way he invented news and rumours about unknown people that he passed on to Sara Fredrika that evening when he got back home.

CHAPTER 179

Sara Fredrika gave birth on Halsskär on 9 September 1915.

He'd had time to fetch Angel from Kråkmarö. The wind had been capricious on the way back, the sail had not been much use, and he had rowed so hard that the palms of his hands were covered in burst blisters. There were three of them in the boat, Angel had taken with her another woman to help, a maid to one of the cargo boat skippers. Once they arrived on the island Angel told Tobiasson-Svartman to keep out of the way, and to find somewhere among the rocks where there was a wind to carry the screams in a different direction if Sara Fredrika got into difficulties.

It was a chilly day. He found a crevice on the south side where he could half lie, well protected. He tried to imagine Sara Fredrika, her struggle to force the baby out. But he saw nothing, only the sea.

My innermost longing is a dream about horizons, he thought, horizons and depths. That's what I am searching for.

It was as if he had some kind of invisible seal that made him inaccessible to everybody apart from himself.

The surface was calm, like a sea when there is no wind blowing, but underneath it lurked all the duplicitous forces he was forced to fight against. Ambition, insecurity, the memory of his furious father and the silent weeping of his mother. He lived through a constant battle between control, calculation and outrageous risk-taking. He did not do what other people do and adapt to different situations, but he changed his personality, became somebody else, often without being aware of the fact.

Without warning, he started crying, forlornly, uncontrollably. Then he stopped, just as suddenly as he had started.

Late in the afternoon he heard them shouting for him. He went back to the cottage, convinced that he had a son. But Angel Wester held out a daughter to him. This time he did not think the baby looked like a shrivelled mushroom, more like heather in the spring before it acquires its full colour.

'She's healthy and strong. She will survive if God wishes her to and you look after her properly. I reckon she weighs three kilos, and a bit more.'

'How is Sara Fredrika?'

'Like all women are after they've given birth. Relief, happiness at the fact that all has gone well, a great desire to sleep. But first she should greet her husband.'

He went inside. Angel and the maid left them alone. Her face was pale and sweaty.

‘What shall we call her?’

Without hesitation, he replied ‘Laura. That’s a pretty name. Laura.’

‘She’s born now. And now we can leave this hellish island and never return.’

‘We shall leave as soon as I’ve finished my last reports.’

‘Are you happy about your child?’

‘I’m indescribably happy about my child,’ he said.

‘You got a new daughter to replace the one that fell over the cliff.’

He did not say anything, just nodded. Then he went outside and invited Angel and the maid to a celebratory drink. As it was already late, they stayed overnight.

He spent the night in a hollow covered by his oilskin coat.

He thought about his two daughters, both called Laura.

Laura Tobiasson-Svartman.

The younger sister of Laura Tobiasson-Svartman.

They’ll live their lives in ignorance of each other. Just as their mothers will never meet.

CHAPTER 180

A few days after Sara Fredrika had given birth, Tobiasson-Svartman found something extraordinary next to the rocks on a headland at the extreme eastern edge of Halsskär.

He could see something bobbing up and down close to the edge of the rocks. When he clambered down to the water he saw that it was a collection of military-issue boots, tied together to form a chain. He tried to find some marking or other that would reveal if they were German or Russian boots, but there was nothing.

There were nine boots in all, four left ones and five right. They had been in the water for a long time. Somebody had tied them together and sent them drifting over the sea.

He threw them up on to the rocks.

He had the feeling that once again he had been surprised and challenged by the dead.

CHAPTER 181

Their daughter cried a lot and kept them awake at night.

For Tobiasson-Svartman it was like being exposed to an agonising pain. He cut pieces of cork and stuck them in his ears when Laura was crying at her loudest, but nothing seemed to help. Sara Fredrika was immune to all noise, and he observed her love with envy. As for him, he had difficulty in feeling any connection with the child.

But with Sara Fredrika, it was as if he had finally understood what love was. For the first time in his life he felt terrified of being abandoned. He was scared by the thought of what would happen if one of these days it dawned on Sara Fredrika that there was no plan to leave the skerry. That the only things in existence were the barren island and all the new reports that had to be written for a secret committee.

CHAPTER 182

Sara Fredrika took every opportunity to talk about leaving.

Her questions now made him feel profoundly desperate. He wanted to be left in peace, he did not want to talk about the future.

'I'm scared,' she said. 'I dream about water, about the depths that you measure. But I don't want to see that. I want to see Laura growing up, I want to get away from this hellish skerry.'

'We shall. Soon. Not just yet.'

It was early one morning. Their daughter was asleep. It was raining. She looked long and hard at him.

'I never see you touching your child,' she said. 'Not even with your fingertips.'

'I daren't,' he said simply. 'I'm afraid that my fingers will leave a mark.'

She said no more. He continued to balance on the invisible borderline between her worry and her trust.

CHAPTER 183

At the beginning of October Tobiasson-Svartman could see that Sara Fredrika's patience was close to breaking point. She did not believe him when he said that soon, not just yet, but soon he would have finished writing his reports.

One night she started hitting him while he was asleep. He defended himself, but she kept on hitting.

'Why can't we go away? Why do you never finish?'

'I'm nearly finished. There's not much left. Then we can go.'

He got out of bed and went outside.

CHAPTER 184

A few days later. Drizzle, no wind.

He walked round the skerry. He suddenly had a flash of insight. All these rocks formed a sort of archive. Like books in a library with infinite holdings. Or faces that will eventually be picked out and examined by future generations.

An archive or a museum, he could not be quite specific about his insight. But autumn was creeping in. Soon this archive or museum would close down for the winter.

CHAPTER 185

Nights now brought frost with them. As day broke on 9 October, the baby started to cry.

That same day Angel Wester sailed out to the skerry to check up on Sara Fredrika and the baby. She was satisfied, the baby was growing and developing as it should.

He accompanied her down to the inlet when her visit was over.

'Sara Fredrika is a good mother,' she said. 'She is strong, and she has plenty of milk. And she seems to be happy as well. I can see that you are looking after her properly. I think she has forgotten her husband, the one that drowned.'

'She will never forget him.'

'There comes a day when the dead turn their backs on us,' she said. 'It happens when a new being enters our lives. Make the most of the opportunity. Don't let there be a distance between you and the baby.'

He pushed the boat out as she raised the sail.

'Will you be staying here over the winter?' she asked.

'Yes,' he said. 'Maybe not.'

'What kind of an answer is that? Yes and no, and maybe something in between?'

'We haven't decided yet.'

'Autumn has hit us early this year, as the old men say when they see the clouds and feel the winds. Early autumn, long winter, rainy spring. Don't wait too long before leaving.'

He watched the dinghy disappearing round the headland. He could hear his daughter crying in the distance.

Angel's words had hit him with full force. All his life he had been keeping things at a distance. But distance did not matter, it was closeness that was significant.

He realised that he would have to tell Sara Fredrika the truth, that he had belonged to somebody else, that he had been kicked out of the Swedish Navy and one of these days would be penniless. Only then could they start again from the beginning, only then could they really make plans to leave.

With great effort he had built walls around Halsskär. Now he would have to demolish them, in order to get out.

He was overcome by a strong sensation. Surprised and confused, he said to himself: I think my sounding lead has reached the bottom.

He was in the habit of rounding off the day by taking his telescope and climbing up to the highest point on the skerry. There was a north-easterly wind, fresh and squally. He pulled his jacket more tightly round him and gazed out towards the mainland.

A sailing dinghy was approaching. The sail was straining hard, but the boat was sitting well in the water.

He did not recognise it, he did not need the telescope to tell him that. It was longer than the boats used by the fishermen in the archipelago.

He aimed his telescope and focused it.

There was a woman at the helm and she was steering straight for Halsskär.

The woman was Kristina Tacker, his wife.

PART X

Angel's Message

CHAPTER 186

He thought it was an optical illusion.

But the boat was real. Kristina Tacker was sailing resolutely, the sail straining in the wind. She was heading for Halsskär because she knew that was where he was hiding.

He searched for a way of escape. But there was none. He had nowhere to escape to.

He set off in a hurry for the inlet when he saw her turning the boat into the wind. All the time he was trying to find an explanation. Could he have left a trail by way of his sea charts? He had never imagined that she would start to interpret them. Or had somebody given him away, somebody who knew where he was?

He could not find an answer. There wasn't one.

By the time he reached the shore the boat was inside the inlet. Kristina Tacker had already dropped anchor when she noticed him, stood up and started yelling. In order to shut her up he waded out into the cold water until it was chest-deep.

'Stop shouting,' he said. 'Everything can be explained.'

'Nothing can be explained!' she screamed. 'Why do you keep lying to me? Why are you hiding here? How can you explain that away?'

She had moved into the bows and started hitting him over the head with a piece of rope. He tried to defend himself, but she went on hitting him, he would never have imagined her capable of such fury. This was not the wife he knew, this was somebody else, somebody who smashed china figurines every time she moved them around on their shelves.

The only way he could shut her up was to pull her out of the boat. He took hold of her and dragged her into the water. She resisted, but he kept hold of her, pushed her down under the surface. Every time she came back up again she continued shouting at him. He smacked her face, once, twice, harder. She went quiet in the end. Her wet hair was sticking to her cheeks. He could no longer smell her fragrance, nothing of the wine nor the subtle perfume.

'I can explain everything,' he said. 'Provided you stop shouting.'

He had never felt as scared as he felt at this moment. If Sara Fredrika were to turn up now all the walls would crumble around him. Nothing would survive.

Kristina Tacker looked at him in disgust.

'Behind a secret there can be another secret,' he said.

She lurched at him and scratched his face. She did it perfectly calmly, without taking her eyes off him.

Blood ran down his cheek.

'I don't want to hear any lies about what you are doing and why you are here,' she said. 'I just want you to explain the only thing that is important. Why did Laura have to die? That's all I want to know.'

He took a step backwards, stumbled over a piece of rock and fell. She grabbed hold of his arm.

'Don't you try and run away again. You're never going to do that again. I'll find you no matter where you hide. All your lies leave a clear trail that I can follow, wherever you go.'

He was punch-drunk. It felt as if the cold water was penetrating his skin and making his body swell up.

'We can't stand in the water like this,' he said. 'It's too cold.'

'This is only water. Death is cold. Laura is cold, not this water.'

'What happened?'

She took hold of his head and pulled it towards her. She had tears in her eyes, he recognised her now. There were glimpses of the woman he was married to behind all the wet hair.

'After you went off I stayed in hospital for a few weeks. Laura grew as she ought to do. She grew bigger and stronger. But then one night I was woken up by her screaming. It wasn't the usual sort of scream, it was something different. Dr Edman came. He thought it was colic and would die down of its own accord. But it didn't die down, it wasn't colic, it was ileus, an obstruction of the intestine. Laura died in terrible agony. There was nothing I could do, and where were you? I thought you were on an important mission, I thought that you were with me in spirit, I thought about all the sorrow we would have to bear together. But the baby's death exposed all your lies, that was the terrible price I had to pay in order to discover who you really are.'

She leaned even further forward into his face.

'Was it you who attacked my father?'

'Of course it wasn't. But will you stop shouting, I can't bear such loud noises.'

She slapped the water with her hand so that it splashed into his face.

'What do you know about noises? You have no idea what a dying baby sounds like. Do you want to hear? I can imitate exactly what she sounded like just before she died.'

He shook his head.

'I'm devastated,' he said. 'I don't understand what you're saying. Is Laura dead?'

'On 22 August at 4.35 in the afternoon Dr Edman said that he could only express his sympathy. She is dead. But you are alive. What can't you understand?'

He did not answer. He tried to picture the dead child, but all he could see was a black hole.

'We can't stay in the water like this. It's too cold.'

She started to hit his face again.

'Can't you hear what I'm saying? My daughter is dead.'

'She was my daughter as well.'

'She wasn't your daughter. You were never there, you reacted to her by telling lies to get away from her and from me and from yourself and from everything I've ever believed in.'

She could not find any more words. She stood in the water screaming in despair.

He could picture the shelves with the china figurines slowly falling down one after another, each one smashing to smithereens.

CHAPTER 187

He led her carefully out of the water.

He was appalled by her bitterness, but shaken most of all by the boundless sorrow he had caused her. For the first time he felt utterly defenceless when facing her. This time he would not be able to wriggle off the hook. And Sara Fredrika would not be able to rescue him. Her presence would only compound the catastrophe.

'Do you remember our holiday in Oslo?' she asked. 'That day when we went to Bygdøy, the beach, the young boys bathing naked in the water, a bunch of balloons climbing up into the sky?'

He remembered, but decided to deny it.

'Of course you remember. Above all you must remember the cross we drew in the sand, and said that the most important thing in our lives would always be telling the truth. Good Lord, I believed it, I really did believe that I had met a man who was as good as his word.'

A quick gust of cold wind made them shiver.

'Who are you?' she said. 'I try to understand, but I can't. I simply can't pin you down, my image of you cracks and breaks up, you become an incomprehensible creature that seems to thrive on deceiving others.'

'I can explain,' he said.

Her response came with no hesitation at all.

'If there is one thing you can never do it is to explain. I have followed in your footsteps and it has been like climbing down into a well where the stench at the bottom gets more and more putrid. I have realised that I am married to a man who doesn't exist, a shadow with a circulatory system and a brain that is nothing more than an invention, a figment of the imagination. It is intolerable to think that my child had a figment of the imagination for a father. Can you make me understand? You are driving me mad.'

'I have to know how you found me.'

'I come here and tell you that Laura is dead. You don't react, you say you feel sorrow, but all you ask about is how I found you.'

'You can think whatever you like. But I mourn the death of my child.'

'You ought to mourn the fact that you are who you are. It was my father who helped me. When Laura died he contacted Naval Headquarters and told them what had happened. He forced his way through all the barriers, I can hear his voice inside my head: *A baby has died, my granddaughter. Her father is on a secret mission, but of course he has to be told about the tragedy that has befallen him.* There was silence. My father said that everybody seemed to be astonished. Jaws dropped on the faces of the entire Swedish high command. In the end a vice admiral informed my father that you no longer held a commission in the Swedish Navy. Then they became secretive, they couldn't go into details about why, they could only say that you were no longer enlisted. My father insisted that I personally should be given an explanation. The following day I went with him to Skeppsholmen. The vice admiral was there, and several other people, I can't remember who they were. They expressed their condolences. But when I asked them for an address so that I could send you a letter, they said that they didn't have one. My father was with me, he was standing behind my chair and put his hand on my shoulder when he heard that you were no longer in the navy. There was no mission, they knew as little about where you were as my father and I did. How do you think that felt? First I lost my baby, then I found out that I was married to a man who didn't exist. How do you think that felt?'

He said nothing. He was searching feverishly for a way of escape. It must have been Welander, he thought. There's no other possibility. Perhaps he suspected that I would head for here.

'I went home, and my father came with me. I was numb, but I was kept going by his fury. Especially after I gathered that he suspected it was you who had tried to kill him.'

'That's not true.'

'I would put nothing past you, Lars.'

She used his first name. It felt as if she were using it to hit him.

I can hit back, he thought. That is the ultimate escape route. I can kill her.

He asked a question to give himself a breathing space.

'Whose is the boat?'

'Does it matter? It belongs to one of my father's friends.'

'I didn't know you could sail.'

'I learned when I was a child. When I realised where you might be hiding I decided to get a boat and come here. My father protested, but I paid no attention to him.'

'Was it Welander who told you where you could find me?'

'He came a few days after I'd been to Skeppsholmen. I didn't want to let him in at first, but he said he'd heard rumours about your disappearance, and that you had lied to the admirals about him. He also said he knew where you might be, that you used to row to a skerry when you were working together.

'I didn't want to know at first, I never wanted to see you again. The first night after I realised what kind of a man you were I gathered together all your clothes, your overcoats, uniforms, shoes, and piled them up on the floor. The next day Anna fetched a rag-and-bone man who took the lot. I didn't even accept any money. I wanted you to cease to exist.

'But my father talked me round. He said that you shouldn't be allowed to die in sin. He contacted Welander, who came round again a few days later. He had been talking to a police superintendent or maybe it was a parish constable from round here who said he thought you were on a skerry at the far edge of the archipelago.

'I sailed into the archipelago then turned south. Somewhere round about Landsort I was becalmed, I had plenty of time to think. And I still ask myself: Why did you marry me if your only intention was to hurt me, to lie to me? Why do you hate me?'

He gave a start. A shadow had moved on a high rocky ledge, but it wasn't Sara Fredrika. It was a bird, a crow that soared up and flew off northwards over the island. There wasn't much time. He needed to drive her along in front of himself instead of cowering in the face of her accusations.

'The fact that I was dismissed from the navy is due entirely to a misunderstanding, which was due in turn to the fact that I was disgracefully slandered by Welander. I tried to protect him when he hit the bottle. Everything else is a pack of lies. He is getting his revenge for having shown me his weakness, because I saw his humiliation. He was lying on deck in a pool of vomit and had to be carried away. I couldn't tell you that I had been dismissed, that was too shameful, too much of a disgrace. I came here to think out a way of telling you about it. Not everything I have told you has been entirely correct, but there has always been a kernel of truth.'

'And what would that be?'

'My love for you. I came here in solitude to punish myself for not being able to tell you exactly how things were. I needed time, time to think, time to summon up courage.'

'But the letters? The inventions, the fantasies?'

'The same thing: shame, disgrace.'

'How can I possibly believe you?'

'Look me in the eye.'

She did as he asked. He could feel that he was starting to regain control, was able to regulate the distances.

'What do you see?'

'A person I don't know.'

'You know me. We have been married for nearly ten years. We have been intimate.'

'If I come too close to you I'm frightened of getting burned. You give off a corrosive acid, all those untrue –'

She broke off without completing the sentence.

'What I understand least of all is why you tried to kill my father.'

He felt an overwhelming urge to tell her the truth, that it was all those accursed Christmas dinners, his father-in-law's contempt for the naval commander who had married his daughter. But there was no place for the truth yet.

'It wasn't me who attacked your father. I would never turn to violence.'

'You hit me, not long ago.'

'That was only because I had to stop you screaming.'

'Can't you tell the truth for once? Can't you try? Your lies are wrapping themselves round my legs like heavy weights.'

'I have told you the truth. I hid myself away here in order to think things over.'

Fear was being batted back and forth between them, like the ebb and flow of never-ending waves. Occasionally he would glance up at the path. He knew his time was limited, and that sooner or later Sara Fredrika would wonder where he had got to.

'I want you to go back home,' he said. 'I've been ordered to terminate my mission.'

'But you haven't got a mission. I heard the admiral say so himself: you are no longer a member of the Swedish Navy, you have no unfinished missions. I heard that with my own ears. Are you incapable of telling the truth?'

'You must understand that secrecy doesn't only apply to me. He wasn't able to say that I am still working on a task.'

'What are you doing on this skerry? I've been sailing all round these grey, barren islands, I've hardly set eyes on a single soul, here by the open sea everything is dead.'

'I'll tell you, even though I shouldn't. I have a wireless transmitter here, one of the inspired inventions of the engineer Marconi and Admiral Henry Jackson, for communications between ships and land, or from one ship's captain to another. We are conducting top-secret tests of a Swedish system, a variation of the ones the warring parties are using.'

'I don't know what you're talking about.'

'Invisible waves that travel through the air, that can be captured and interpreted. A secret language that will transform all aspects of war as it has been known until now. Every day at certain times I have to be stationed by the wireless in order to receive and transmit.'

She considered what he had said.

'Perhaps that is true,' she said. 'Show me round this

island that you have made your home, show me these invisible waves that are dancing around in the air here. Show me something that is true. Show me where you live, in a cave or a hut.'

'You are right,' he said. 'One hut to live in, and another for my measuring equipment. I'll show you.'

He racked his brains for a way out of this desperate situation. It was becoming clearer to him where he really belonged. It was on Halsskär with Sara Fredrika and Laura, that was where he was at home. For the first time in his life there was something he did not want to lose. He was a stranger to Kristina Tacker and her china figurines, in the cold and warm rooms in Stockholm. All the years he had lived with her had ceased to exist. That was the biggest lie, he thought, I could never understand or control that. We had nothing in common, we just came together in a fantasy of love.

But not even that is true, he thought. I can only speak for myself. She must have felt something different. She has come here, not merely to expose a lie, but also to understand how she could have given me so much love.

She aimed her light at a cold cliff face. It never became warm. I tried to tame her all the years we lived together.

I failed. She stayed wild. The china figurines deceived me. She had more sides to her than I had ever suspected. Hidden behind her calm, almost apathetic exterior was something else.

He recalled the Christmas market when she had

intervened to stop a man hitting his child. He had not drawn the right conclusions from that. He ought to have realised even then that she was in fact a stronger individual than he was.

CHAPTER 188

It was starting to get dark. They were freezing cold. He heard footsteps on the path. Sara Fredrika emerged from the hawthorn bushes.

He wondered if she'd been waiting there, just as he used to hover out of sight.

Sara Fredrika gave a start and stopped dead.

'Who's she?'

He did not answer. His first reaction was to head for the water. He could hijack the sailing boat and then vanish, straight out to sea, or to the south, to one of the German ports around Kiel, where he could seek asylum.

Sara Fredrika was approaching now, and asked again who the woman at his side was.

'I don't know,' he said.

'Don't know?' Kristina Tacker said. 'Don't you even know who I am any more? Who's she? What do you get up to here? Do you ever say anything that's true?'

Sara Fredrika took hold of him.

'Who is she?'

He could not answer. He was trapped. He did not have his sounding lead with him.

Both women showered him with questions, who was this woman who had come from the sea, who was this woman clinging on to his arm? He said nothing, the trap had been sprung, it would soon be over and he had no idea how it would end.

Sara Fredrika and Kristina Tacker did all the talking. But he was the one they were staring at, as Kristina Tacker grew more and more outraged and Sara Fredrika more and more desperate. The cat appeared from out of nowhere, it seemed to sense that a trial of strength was taking place and was waiting to witness the outcome. He tried once again to find a way out, to identify a weakness in what he was faced with. But all he could feel was weariness and an urge to give up.

Somewhere in the rocks round about him was his father's face, his eyes would soon be liberated.

The stone hands were hovering over his head.

In the end, he told the truth: that was the only possibility left.

'Her name's Kristina. She's my wife. I'm married to her.'

'But you said your wife was dead? And your child?'

Kristina Tacker took a pace forward.

'He said that I was dead?'

'Who are you?'

'I am his wife.'

'But that's impossible. His wife fell over a cliff. And the child was dragged down as well.'

'Well, he lied to you, whoever you are! I'm alive and I am married to him.'

Kristina Tacker screamed and set off running along the path. She disappeared from view, but her screams bounced back and forth off the rocks.

'Who is she?' asked Sara Fredrika again.

'She's telling the truth. I am married to her, I have not yet concluded the divorce proceedings.'

'But you said she'd fallen over a cliff, and your daughter as well?'

'That was my first wife. I haven't told you everything about my life. I work on top-secret missions, and it's infectious, I end up by being top secret even to myself.'

She backed away from him, he could see that she was frightened.

'What's she doing here?'

'I don't know. She came here in the sailing dinghy.'

Kristina Tacker came back. He tried to embrace her and calm her down, but she avoided his grasp.

'I don't want you to touch me, never again.'

She turned her back on him and started talking to Sara Fredrika. 'Who are you?'

'I live here with him.'

'With him?'

'Yes, I just said so. What's it got to do with you? It's my life, not yours.'

'But I'm the one who's married to him. Can't you hear what I'm saying?'

'He's not married. He lives here with me, and he's going to take me away to a new country. I want you to leave here.'

Another voice joined in the argument, from the far distance, a baby crying. It was clearly audible in the silence. Kristina Tacker looked round wildly before she grasped the truth. She started shaking and then she collapsed.

'It's my baby,' Sara Fredrika said. 'My daughter. She's called Laura.'

Kristina Tacker started whimpering and crawled away, trying to force her way into the thorn bushes.

'Is she out of her mind? She'll cut herself to pieces on the thorns.'

'She's ill,' he said. 'She's very ill. She needs help.'

He tried to pull Sara Fredrika away, but she beat him off with enormous strength.

'Don't you dare lay your hands on me. I don't know what's going on here, I'm hearing things that I refuse to believe. Don't you dare touch me, and don't touch her either.'

Sara Fredrika squatted down by Kristina Tacker's side. Kristina Tacker was wrestling with the thorn bushes.

Tobiasson-Svartman looked at his wife. She was like a wounded animal. He was the one who had pulled the trigger, but he had not been able to give her the *coup de grâce*, he had only wounded her. Sara Fredrika pulled her away from the thorn bushes. Kristina Tacker did not resist. Despite the darkness he could see the blood running down her face from where the thorns had pierced her skin. She was hanging like a dead body in Sara Fredrika's powerful arms.

He was motionless. The cat was still observing proceedings from a distance. Four metres, he thought. The shadows make it hard to be precise about the centimetres. But the cat is sitting four metres away from me. Kristina Tacker and Sara Fredrika and the baby are a few metres further away. But in fact the distance between me and them is infinite, and it is growing all the time. The lines have been cut and the current and the wind are propelling us in different directions.

He was reminded of the ice. The open channels, people falling in and meeting their fate in the black cold of winter.

But most of all he was reminded of the drift net he had seen the previous summer, when the sun's rays were beating down on the water, the drift net with all the dead ducks and fish. At that time he had interpreted it as a symbol of freedom. But he was not the net, he was one of the dead fish. What he had seen then was his own downfall.

He started running along the path, running away. He stumbled and hit his face on a rock, cutting his lips. It seemed as if the whole skerry had made him its enemy and was attacking him.

The sailing dinghy was at anchor in the inlet. He waded into the cold water and scrambled aboard. But the sail was furled tightly round the mast and a locked chain prevented him from unfurling it. The tiller was also locked: she had prepared for all eventualities, she knew him far too well to leave anything to chance. She had cut off his escape route even before they had started shouting at each other in the freezing cold water. He tried to break the chain with a hammer he found in one of the pigeonholes in the cockpit. But it refused to yield, and he could see that he would break the tiller if he kept on trying. He threw the hammer into the sea and slumped on to the seat in the cockpit. Everything was still on all sides.

Beneath him, underneath Kristina Tacker's sailing dinghy, the depth was two and a quarter metres.

CHAPTER 189

He spent the night in the cockpit.

Loneliness was the walls that encircled him. He had exchanged his wet clothes for hers that he had found in the cabin. He was waiting for the conclusion to all this while dressed in his wife's underclothes. As the long night drew to a close and light started to creep in, the rocks looked to him like stones waiting to be used for the building of a mighty cathedral.

He had dozed off at one point during the night. He had dreamed about flotsam and jetsam. He had been walking along a beach, searching. The kelp seemed to be transparent, and the smell of mud very strong. Eventually he found what he was looking for, a splinter of wood from a stern. He was that splinter of wood, wrenched out of his context, drifting out of control.

The first thought that occurred to him when he woke up was that the seabed inside him had slowly started to transform itself into an infinite, unmeasurable depth.

I know how to set up a lie, he thought. But I cannot cope with living in the world that lies create. The impostor lives a life, but the deceit involved lives a different life.

CHAPTER 190

He heard footsteps on the path. It was Sara Fredrika.

It was still only half-light, and he felt very cold sitting there in the cockpit.

'Come ashore,' she shouted.

He neither answered nor moved.

'She's ill. If she stays here she'll die. I don't care what you've done, but she must have help.'

He waded ashore with his half-dry clothes over his head. The cold water made him gasp for breath. He started sobbing, but she merely shook her head dismissively at his tears. Her hair was tousled, like it had been the first time he had observed her in secret.

She kept him at a distance all the time.

'I know everything,' she said. 'She's told me all. I can cope with that even if I ought to tie a sinker round your neck and send you down to the deepest part of the seabed. I can cope. But she can't. The baby was too much. I have just one question before I run out of words. How could you give both your daughters the same name?'

He did not answer.

'It's hard to imagine that so much shit can come out of a little man like you. It just comes pouring out. But for the moment we are not important, she is. I think she's going out of her mind.'

'What do you want me to do?'

'Help me to get her to the boat. I can't take her in the dinghy, if she starts getting violent she could throw herself overboard. I can't tie her up either. I can't take a tied-up person ashore.'

'Can she cope with seeing me?'

'I don't think you exist any more as far as she is concerned. When she saw our baby, when she heard its name, something snapped. I could hear it inside me, the sound of a branch snapping. That branch was her life.'

She looked at the sailing boat.

'I've never sailed a boat as big as this, but I dare say I'll manage. How many sails does it have?'

'Two.'

'I'll be able to sail it, even if it is big.'

'Where do you intend to take her?'

'I'll make sure she gets back home.'

'You can't sail her to Stockholm. It's a long way, you'll never find your way.'

'If I could find you I'll no doubt be able to find the way to Stockholm as well. I'll take the baby with me, of course. But you will stay here. When I come back we'll leave. I don't forgive you for all your deceit, all the falsehoods you have surrounded yourself with. But there must be something genuine somewhere inside you.'

He touched against her arm. She gave a start.

'Don't come too close. If I weren't so hardened I'd be as mad as she is. All you really deserve is a sinker attached to you. But I can't bear the thought of losing another husband. Even if he does act as if he has no guts and had evil intentions when he first came to this skerry with all his kind words and smiles.'

They walked up to the cottage. He shrank back when he saw Kristina Tacker. Her face was covered in scratches from thorns and branches, her clothes were torn and covered in vomit. She was sitting on the stool, swaying backwards and forwards. Sara Fredrika squatted down in front of her.

'Let's go now. There's not much wind, but enough to get us away from here.'

Kristina Tacker did not react. Sara Fredrika had prepared a basket of food, and another one with clothes. The baby was lying on the bed, wrapped up in a fur.

'You carry the baskets,' she said. 'She and the baby are mine.'

Sara Fredrika led the way, carrying the baby and supporting Kristina Tacker.

Behind them walked Tobiasson-Svartman, carrying the heavy baskets.

Once again he had the feeling he was in a procession. Behind him were other marchers that he could not see.

CHAPTER 191

They waded out to the boat.

It was a cold, clear autumn morning. There was a south-easterly breeze. Kristina Tacker said nothing, allowed herself to be led out into the water as if she were to be baptised. Sara Fredrika laid her down in the cockpit together with the baby. He stood by, up to his waist in water. Using a key she had found in one of Kristina Tacker's pockets, Sara Fredrika first unlocked the chain round the sails, then the one securing the tiller.

'I'll come back,' she said. 'I ought to make myself scarce, but I won't. You could take the dinghy and sail away, of course, but where would you go? You'll wait for me to come back because you have no choice.'

She struck anchor and told him to give the boat a push. He stayed in the water until she had raised the mainsail and set off in a north-easterly direction.

The sailing boat disappeared behind the headlands. He waded ashore.

His only thought was to get some sleep.

CHAPTER 192

The time that followed was like a conversation with shadows.

He wandered around the island, climbed among rocks, wriggled his way into crevices where there was some protection from the autumn winds that were becoming colder and colder.

One night he was woken up by the sound of a heavy gun, and he could see the glow on the horizon. Otherwise he slept soundly, without dreaming. The cat was curled up at the foot end of the bed.

He fished only when he needed food. He started to hear voices coming from the rocks, from all the people who had lived on the skerry before it was abandoned. People used to live here once upon a time. Sara Fredrika said they had rowed here using their ribs as oars. I did not understand what she meant then, but now her words are crystal clear. They came here in rowing boats, the skerry received them in admiration. They sailed, rowed, fished and died.

People used to live here once upon a time. Nobody saw them come, nobody saw them leave, only the rock lifted its hand of stone as a farewell salute.

When he was curled up in the crevices, sheltering

from the bitter autumn winds, he tried to imagine what would have happened when Kristina Tacker had got to Stockholm. But he could not picture her. Her face, even her fragrance, had disappeared for ever.

He also tried to imagine what would happen when Sara Fredrika returned.

America, her great dream? He could certainly imagine going there, but he would want to be on his own: a Swedish naval officer could make a new life for himself in the US Navy. But he would never be able to go there with Sara Fredrika.

It was really the child he was thinking about. Laura Tobiasson-Svartman. He could see her even in pitch darkness. If he abandoned her, he would have finally abandoned himself.

CHAPTER 193

November came, frosty nights were more frequent. He was waiting for Sara Fredrika to return.

Autumn, waiting, winds from the north.

CHAPTER 194

One night he was woken up by dreaming that she had come back. He went out into the darkness and listened. Nothing but the sound of the sea.

Then he heard the beating of wings. The swishing of migrating birds, the last flocks of the autumn leaving Sweden in the night.

Over his head, this vast armada, that allowed him to stay behind.

CHAPTER 195

The first snow fell over the sea on 4 November.

He took in the nets that morning, felt the damp snow seeping into him. There was only a light breeze, he had not raised the sail but rowed slowly. Off Jungfrugrunden he noticed something bobbing up and down in the water. When he came closer he saw that it was a big mine with horns sticking out from its globular casing, most of which was submerged. It was a Russian mine, and had no doubt drifted away from a minefield set elsewhere.

He tied a rope round the damaged anchor loop and towed the mine back to the skerry. He secured it using a sinker.

It was as if he had started to fortify Halsskär.

CHAPTER 196

The next day, when he was making one of his leisurely tours of the skerry, he had the feeling that Sara Fredrika had tricked him.

She had no intention of returning, she had gone away, abandoning both him and Halsskär.

The thought filled him with panic. He scanned the horizon with his telescope, but there was no sign of any boats.

It was evening before he had managed to regain control of himself. Sara Fredrika would come back, he had seen it in her eyes. Something was forcing her to stay with Kristina Tacker, but sooner or later she would come ashore again on Halsskär.

All he could do was to wait. That was his only task.

CHAPTER 197

One day in the middle of November he saw a little yacht sailing fast towards Halsskär. He had difficulty in holding the telescope steady. He recognised the yacht, it was Angel's boat. That convinced him. Sara Fredrika was on her way. The waiting would be over at last.

He went down to the inlet. It was a cold morning, he pulled his overcoat more tightly round him, and noticed that his long hair was hanging over the collar.

When the yacht rounded the last of the headlands, he saw that Angel was alone. Sara Fredrika had not come back.

CHAPTER 198

Angel anchored the yacht and waded ashore, holding her skirt up above her knees. She was coughing badly and her eyes were bloodshot. She shook hands and gave him a letter she had stuck inside her neckband.

'It came to me,' she said. 'From Sara Fredrika. I didn't even know she was away.'

He could see that she was curious, but he paid no attention.

'Go back home,' he said. 'You're coughing and you're running a temperature. Thank you for bringing the letter.'

'I'll stay and wait in case you need to answer it.'

'That's not necessary.'

'The letter was inside another one, addressed to me. She asked me to wait for your reply.'

He tried to read the expression on her face. What had Sara Fredrika written to her?

'That's all she wrote,' she said. 'She said the baby was doing fine, and I was to wait for your reply. If there was one.'

CHAPTER 199

They walked up to the cottage. She drank a ladle of water from the bucket and sat down in front of the fire. He went outside to read the letter in private.

He examined the envelope. It was not Kristina Tacker's handwriting. Somebody else had written what Sara Fredrika had dictated.

He hesitated before plucking up enough courage to open the envelope. It was like taking a deep breath before diving into the water where it was very deep.

CHAPTER 200

The letter in the unknown handwriting:

> I am not coming back. You are still there, but you are not for me. I now realise what I didn't want to believe before, that the German soldier didn't commit suicide, but you killed him. I don't know why, just as you cannot understand how I have realised what happened. When you read this letter I will already be on my way to somewhere else with Laura. You will never see her or me again, I'm putting as much distance between us as is possible. You can do what you like with all the things on the skerry. I will never understand who you were, you hardly understand yourself who you are or want to be. Kristina hasn't been able to help me with this letter, she is ill. I'm worried about her state of mind, she might not be able to live in the real world any more. If she doesn't get any better she will be sent to a hospital for neurotics. I have been helped to write this letter by Anna, who works in your house. I'm sending it to the midwife in Kråkmarö and I'm asking her to stay until she is sure that you have read and understood it. Then she will write to me

and confirm the fact. She doesn't have an address for me, but will receive an address one day. My journey has begun, and you are no longer with me.

Sara Fredrika, November 1915.

He read the letter again. Then he lay down on the bare rock and stared up at the clouds.

They were scudding, flying, towards the south-west.

CHAPTER 201

He stood up when he heard Angel coming out of the cottage.

He had no idea how much time had passed.

'I've read the letter,' he said.

'She asked me to stay until you said that. I don't know what's in it, of course.'

They walked down to the inlet.

'The clouds are restless,' she said. 'The November weather is as restless as an animal kicking in its stall. I think it's going to be a long winter with lots of ice.'

He did not answer. Angel looked at him.

'I never got to know you,' she said, 'but I delivered your child. Now Sara Fredrika and the baby have left. I have a strong feeling that they will never come back. I can't know that for sure and it's none of my business. But I have to ask you even so: What are you going to do? Are you going to stay here on the skerry? Will you survive here? It's not that you can't feed yourself from the sea, you can no doubt manage that. But the isolation? You come from a big city, will you be able to survive the isolation when the storms really set in?'

'I don't know.'

'You ought to go away.'

He nodded. She waited for him to say something more, but he just stared ahead in silence.

'Well, I'll be off,' she said. 'You ought to go away. I don't think you could cope with life out here. The stones will eat you up.'

He watched her strike anchor and shake off the mud clinging to it. When she set sail, he turned and walked away.

CHAPTER 202

One day the two farm labourers from Kättilö sailed into the inlet.

The rumour that Sara Fredrika had left and taken the baby with her, leaving him behind, had gone round the islands. Somebody had seen an unfamiliar sailing boat approaching Halsskär with a woman on board. But nobody knew what had happened on the skerry. All they knew was that the hydrographic engineer was wandering about the skerry like a moth-eaten animal.

Somebody maintained that he had even started to walk on all fours.

The farmhands sailed out one Sunday, taking a bottle of aquavit with them. It was pure curiosity. But he merely shook his head when they offered him a drink. He did not answer their questions.

When they got back home they reported that he had definitely started walking on all fours the moment they turned their backs.

CHAPTER 203

A few days before Christmas he scratched his name into one of the rocks on the north side of the skerry, a rock that was submerged at high tide. There was a thin layer of snow over the archipelago, the temperature was now more or less constantly below zero. He had wrapped himself up in a shaggy blanket held in place by a rope round his body. He lived on with one question, the only one he still had the strength to worry about. How could she have known what happened out on the ice the day the German deserter died? He sought in vain for an answer.

He kept walking round the skerry, and feeding the cat, which was growing more and more shy, with small fish. Once every day he went to check that the mine was still at its mooring.

After Angel's visit he had stopped measuring distances altogether. He had fallen headlong into the abyss inside himself. Down there in the darkness Kristina Tacker was by his side. He tried to climb up out of the depths, but the walls were slippery, he kept sliding back down, his strength faded and eventually vanished altogether.

In the end there was nothing left.

CHAPTER 204

There were moments when his thoughts were crystal clear. Then he realised that he could never have grown close to another human being because he had an irrational fear of losing himself. There were also other moments when he wanted to tear off all his clothes, wash himself, and drag himself out of his degradation.

One day he sailed through a bitter winter wind to Valdemarsvik and bought some newspapers. He read about the war, how the sea battles had been replaced by long-drawn-out fighting in the muddy fields of Flanders. He had the strong impression that life was the same for everybody, and he sank back down into his abyss, unable to raise the strength to resist.

It was clear to him that most things in his life had been based on a lunatic idea. He had built his existence on distances instead of seeking closeness.

It was then, a few days before Christmas, that he carved his name into the rock.

Afterwards he realised that he had prepared his own headstone.

CHAPTER 205

On Christmas Day a northerly gale blew in over the archipelago.

He recalled that it was this very morning some years previously that Sara Fredrika had lost her husband.

When he clambered on to the rocks he discovered that the mine had broken loose from its mooring. He scanned the choppy water, but he could see no sign of it. It was drifting out to sea, into the shipping lanes.

I am taking part in the war, he thought. But I do not know on which side.

CHAPTER 206

Death came at New Year, 1916.

One night there was a strong, persistent, northerly gale. The cottage caught fire. He had neglected the chimney, which had cracked, and red-hot soot had forced its way through. The walls went up as if they had been soaked in petrol.

He was woken by the dazzling light. By then it was too late to control the fire. He hurried out of the burning cottage with his sounding lead, his notebooks and his clothes.

The cottage burned quickly, and was a complete ruin before dawn broke.

He felt very cold, there was a fierce wind.

During the night he thought he could see Sara Fredrika and Laura in the glow from the fire.

Kristina Tacker had not been in the flames. She was gone, silent, he could not even remember her face now.

The gale blew over by afternoon. The sea was calm once more. The ice would soon begin to form, if the cold weather continued.

He felt cold all the time, then the feeling developed into a pain approaching the intolerable.

The vital decision was creeping quietly up on him. Soon it became an obvious inevitability. There may have been a trace of fear inside him, but it was mostly exhaustion and the intense cold that he could not cope with.

He started to look for the cat so as to kill it, but he did not have the strength. It would survive the cold, it did not know what death was, it would only die if it could not find anything to eat.

He carried his sounding lead and his notebooks to the inlet, packed everything into a net and tied it to a sinker before throwing them on board.

He suddenly felt that he was in a hurry. He looked anxiously up at the sky, worried that a wind might get up again.

He wanted to set out when the sea was calm.

The boat glided out of the inlet.

He rowed to the spot where the two German sailors had sunk to the bottom of the sea. When he reached it he took in the oars, sat on the stern seat and let the boat drift. There was still no wind, the sea was as calm as a millpond. He lifted the net with his lead and the notebooks over the rail and let it sink to the bottom.

One last time he tried to clamber up the slippery walls of the abyss, but slid down again immediately.

He had made up his mind to get it all over with quickly. The sinker was heavy, he made his last measurement and decided it weighed seven kilos. He tied the rope attached to the stone round his legs.

But first he took off all his clothes. He wanted to die naked. The cold water would deaden his senses.

Then he lifted the stone over the rail and followed it down into the depths.

Some days later the boat drifted ashore at the Häradskär lighthouse. One of the pilots identified it as Sara Fredrika's sailing dinghy.

The sea froze over in mid-January.

The ice covered all the sea graves in the winter of 1916.

Afterword

This story takes place in a borderland between reality and my own invention.

I have redrawn many sea charts, given islands new names, added new bays and eliminated others. Anybody who tries to sail along the shipping lanes I have sketched out must reckon with coming upon lots of unexpected shallows and other hazards.

In December 2001 the Swedish Navy handed over responsibility for hydrographic surveys in Swedish waters to civilian organisations. I hope both they and all earlier generations of hydrographic engineers will forgive me for creating my own routines regarding the charting of naval channels. What is beyond dispute is that the sounding lead that was dropped into the water and allowed to sink down to the seabed was the instrument originally used to decide the safest route for ships to follow.

I had the sounding lead used in this novel made in Manchester. That could well have been a fact, but need not be.

Many of the ships that feature in the novel did exist, but were long since sent to the scrapyard or have otherwise disappeared from our consciousness. Other vessels have been constructed by me, in my role as shipbuilder.

I have increased and decreased tonnages, downsized the crew or added an artillery officer when it seemed to me appropriate.

To be frank, I have been rather self-indulgent.

Some of the people I describe have also existed. But most of them have never set foot on the islands in the beautiful, barren and occasionally stormy Östergötland archipelago. Nor have they been bosuns or captains on board Swedish naval vessels.

Nevertheless, I can imagine them – in the shadowy world where history and imagination merge, on the literary shores where the flotsam and jetsam of fantasy and reality intermingle.

Some years ago, in the early 1990s, I rowed through the fog in the Gryt archipelago. Later, when the weather had cleared up and everything seemed reminiscent of a curious dream, this story was born.

H.M.

Maputo, August 2004

www.vintage-books.co.uk